CEEL REVIF
JUNE 1, 2.

Mircea Eliade was born in 1907 in Bucharest, the son of an army officer. He lived in India from 1928-1932, after which he obtained a doctorate in philosophy with a thesis on yoga, and taught at the University of Bucharest for seven years. During the war he was a cultural attaché in London and Lisbon, and from 1945 taught at the École des haut études in Paris and several other European universities. In 1957 he took up the post of Chair of History of Religion at the University of Chicago, which he held until his death in 1986. His extensive body of work includes studies of religion and the religious experience that remain influential to this day, such as *The Sacred and the Profane* and *The Myth of the Eternal Return*. He also wrote numerous works of fiction, including *Bengal Nights* and *Youth without Youth*, both of which were adapted for the screen. Noted for his vast erudition, Eliade had fluent command of five languages (Romanian, French, German, Italian, and English) and a reading knowledge of three others (Hebrew, Persian, and Sanskrit). He was elected a posthumous member of the Romanian Academy.

Christopher Bartholomew was introduced to Romanian while engaged in extended gap year mission work in Romania from 1998 – 2000. He continued Romanian studies during a B.A. in English from Brigham Young University and an MBA at Westminster College in Salt Lake City, Utah. He stumbled across the early novels of Mircea Eliade in a used bookstore in Bucharest's University metro station in 2004, during a summer researching the author's early periodical writings and alleged connections to the ultra-right Legion of the Archangel Mihail. Bartholomew felt that he had discovered a fresh voice, with the power to initiate readers into the complexities of interwar Romania. He has collaborated with Istros on translations of Eliade's first two novels – *Diary of a Short-Sigthed Adolescent* and *Gaudeaumus*.

MIRCEA ELIADE
GAUDEAMUS

Translated from the Romanian by
Christopher Bartholomew

istrosbooks

First published in 2018 by
Istros Books
London, United Kingdom www.istrosbooks.com

Copyright © Estate of Mircea Eliade, 2018

The right of Mircea Eliade to be identified as the author of this work has been asserted in accordance with the Copyright, Designs and Patents Act, 1988

Translation © Christopher Bartholomew, 2018

Cover design and typesetting: Davor Pukljak, www.frontispis.hr

ISBN: 978-1-908236-34-0

Istros Books wishes to acknowledge the financial support granted by the Romanian Cultural Institute

NATIONAL BOOK CENTRE   ROMANIAN CULTURAL INSTITUTE

CONTENTS

FOREWORD BY BRYAN RENNIE

Gaudeamus igitur	Let us rejoice, then
Iuvenes dum sumus.	While we are young.
Post iucundam iuventutem	After pleasant youth
Post molestam senectutem	After distressing old age
Nos habebit humus.	The earth will have us.

Thus runs the commercium song or student anthem for which Mircea
Eliade entitled his novel, *Gaudeamus*. Originating in the Middle
Ages but given its familiar form in the late 18th century, this paean
to seizing the day is belted out to this day at university gatherings
around the world. Likewise concerned with 'seizing the day', Eliade's
Gaudeamus, written between February and March of 1928, is a com-
ing-of-age novel based on his undergraduate years at the University
of Bucharest (1925 to 1928). His earlier novel, *Romanul adolescenului
miop* (*Diary of a Short-Sighted Adolescent*, Istros Books, 2016) had
focused on the final years of his *Liceu* (Lycée) education and had been
serialized in its entirety in the Bucharest periodicals *Cuvântul, Viața
Literară*, and *Universul Literar* in the 1920s, but the manuscript of
Gaudeamus had a different trajectory. Finished before Eliade's departure for India in 1928, it remained among his papers in the family
house on Strada Melodiei in Bucharest. Only three pages, described
as an 'excerpt' from *Gaudeamus*, appeared in *Viața literară* in March
of 1928. Eliade attempted without success to place the manuscript
with the publisher, Cartea Românească, but the novel was to wait
more than fifty years to appear in print. Eliade did revisit and reread
it in 1932–33, when, according to his *Autobiography*, he found it 'both
lyrical and frenzied, too pretentious, timidly indiscreet, and quite
lacking in grandeur.' He never again tried to have it published, nor,
indeed to have any contact with it. The house was demolished in 1935
and the manuscript passed into the possession of his younger sister
Cornelia (Corina) Alexandrescu. It was not until 1981 that a high
school teacher and Eliade enthusiast, Mircea Handoca, along with the
philosopher, essayist, and poet, Constantin Noica, were given access

to Mme. Alexandrescu's attic and recovered the manuscript. Together they assembled the first 2,500 typed pages of Eliade's writings from 1921 up to 1928. Several chapters from *Gaudeamus* appeared in three issues of the journal *Manuscriptum* in 1983, three years before Eliade's death, but the entire text of the novel did not appear until 1986 when it was published in *Revista de istoire și teorie literară* and then again as a single volume with *Romanul adolescenului miop* in 1989. Curiously, the three-page passage from *Viața literară* was absent from the final version of the manuscript. Thereafter *Gaudeamus* was translated into French in 1992 and Italian in 2012, and now appears for the first time in English.

The novel is, of course, a testimony to a vanished world – the Bucharest of the late 1920s, specifically the life of the university student of the time, but it is more than just that. Eliade's principal biographer, Mac Linscott Ricketts, deems it a document of inestimable importance, 'a precious testimony to one phase of Eliade's personal spiritual itinerary'.[1] It also can be read as evidence (positive or negative?) of Eliade's literary status, of the development of his understanding of the history of religions, of his relation to anti-Semitism, and of his unfortunate sexism – and these four interdigitate intriguingly. Of course, as a novel it is difficult (but not always impossible) to know when we can recognize Eliade in the protagonist. Ricketts assesses the novel as 'being (up to a certain point in the narrative) a candid and authentic account of the author's actions and thoughts. At those points where it can be checked against other sources, it shows itself to be factual and reliable.'[2] For example, Eliade's *Autobiography* informs us that the principle female character, Nișka, is based on Eliade's real-life friend, Rica Botez, the name of the character being taken from a friend of Rica's. But, at the same time, some events were clearly fictionalized. This inseparable intertwining of fact and fiction is one of the primary characteristics of Eliade's *trăirist* style in which he seeks to invoke an inescapable authenticity.

The critic, Eugen Simion, sees *Gaudeamus* as a notable novel for two other reasons. Firstly, it introduces the 'young generation' of

---

1   Mac Linscott Ricketts, *Romanian Roots*, Vol. I, p. 229.
2   Ibid., 127

1920s Bucharest on a wide front, from sexuality to philosophy, and secondly, it attempts an innovative reinterpretation of the psychology of the couple: 'The author's thesis is that the post-war generation is destined to seek God and that the redeemed are but the insane, that is, those fleeing from sentimental and cerebral mediocrity, from the illusion of comfortable happiness.'[3] As a *Bildungsroman*, *Gaudeamus* shows the influence of authors whom we know Eliade to have read: André Gide, Giovanni Papini, Henrik Ibsen, and Jack London, but it does not follow them slavishly. Commenting on the Italian translation, the Historian of Religions, Giovanni Casadio, pointed out that *Gaudeamus* plays on three themes in three different registers. The first is the author's relation to the bohemian world of students and professors, and it sounds a comic/realistic tone with tinges of farce. The second concerns Eliade's relations with women and his intimate 'romantic education'. This uses a romantic/idyllic mode with spikes of harsh realism. The third theme is Eliade's dialogue with his own will and ego, couched in melodramatic mode; sometimes restrained, as in the novel's almost elegiac opening: 'The chestnut trees were wet after the rain, the boulevards were cold. Above me, only autumnal sky. ... I felt hopes and desires swelling and anxiously stirring ...', sometimes emerging with astonishing arrogance, as in the final – 'My soul is harsh, vast, serene. I sense the others left behind me, and before me, the glimmers of destiny' – echoing the titanic pride of Hyperion in the closing of Eminescu's *Luceafărul*.[4]

Eliade wrote *Gaudeamus* in two week-long bursts in February and March of 1928 while staying at a friend's house in Clinceni about twenty-five kilometres outside of Bucharest. That same year he was working on the *tezei de licență* (the thesis required for his Bachelor's degree), which he defended in October. His thesis was on 'Renaissance Contributions to Philosophy', to which he also referred to as 'Italian Philosophy from Marsilio Ficino to Giordano Bruno'.[5] Thus we can be comfortable that he was already aware of, and undoubtedly influenced by, both the Italian Renaissance humanists and their precursors

3 Eugen Simion, *Mircea Eliade. Nodurile și semnele prozei*, Bucharest 2011, p. 37.
4 Giovanni Casadio, Unpublished presentation, Bozza, Sept. 9th, 2012.
5 *Mircea Eliade: Ordeal by Labyrinth, Conversations with Claude-Henri Rocquet*, 204.

juvenile analysis..?

such as Dante Alighieri and Boccaccio, whom we know from the *Autobiography* that Eliade had read in his youth. It seems beyond doubt that among the many contributions to Eliade's understanding of the history of religion was Ficino, whose translations of Plato introduced the term 'Platonic Love' to Renaissance Italy and whose translations of the *Corpus Hermeticum* supported the idea that all truth is one. Of the twelfth chapter of the book, *Storm at the Hermitage*, Ricketts is confident enough to say 'I believe that the views on religion expressed by the narrator of the book are indeed Eliade's own at that time'. Here, not only does the narrator repeatedly express his inability to believe in God, he also expresses an understanding of the development of the monotheistic God that is clearly indebted to the work of Raffaele Pettazzoni, with whom the young Eliade had corresponded since 1922.

Accusations of anti-Semitism have long dogged Eliade's path, unsurprisingly, since he gave his enthusiastic written support to the Legion of the Archangel Michael for about a year spanning 1936-1937. The Legion was a fervently Nationalist Romanian political organization which spawned the terrible Iron Guard (*Garda de fier*), guilty of heinous anti-Semitic atrocities. Eliade never disavowed his support for the Legion and some have seen this as incontrovertible evidence of his anti-Semitism. Others (including myself, to be fully open) have defended Eliade against these accusations, pointing out that he cannot be accused of any known actions against any Jewish person or persons – especially of no acts of literary defamation for which he had infinite opportunity. *Gaudeamus* provides fuel for this debate. Although there is casual reference to anti-Semitism throughout the book, not only is this an accurate representation of the Bucharest of 1928, but it is never ascribed to or embraced by the narrator. On the contrary, one of his student friends warns him that 'Before long you'll turn into an anti-Semite too …' – implying that he is known *not* to be such. In fact, the narrator explicitly denies being anti-Semitic, and those who do (proudly!) identify themselves as anti-Semitic are either very dubious characters, such as 'Melec' and 'the Boss' who gate-crash a student gathering in the narrator's attic; or profoundly confused, such as the young medical student who is engaged to, and obviously in love with, a Jewish girl, yet still claims to be an anti-Semite. Although little is overtly made of the fact in the novel, one of the narrator's best friends, 'Marcu' is known to be based on one of Eliade's real friends, Mircea Mărculescu, who was Jewish. The Romanian commentator, Liviu Bordaş, is not alone in explicitly using *Gaudeamus* to defend Eliade against accusation of anti-Semitism.[6]

Far more problematic, in my estimation, than this putative anti-Semitism is the apparently dreadful sexism of the text. Eliade was explicitly influenced by the *dolce stil novo*, with its familiar theme of *angelicata* – elevating the female to a position of inhuman adoration, as with Dante's Beatrice or Petrarch's Laura. Eliade's childhood vision of 'the little girl on the Strada Mare', familiar to readers from the first pages of his *Autobiography*, is reminiscent of Dante's first encounter with Beatrice Portinari (although Eliade was four or five years younger than Dante was when this happened). In *Gaudeamus*, the narrator transforms his love for Nişka from what could have been a simple student infatuation to an act of heroic self-denial, 'elevating' her from a flesh-and-blood woman to a sacrificial fetish. Eliade explicitly invokes Dante (and Don Quixote) in the novel, and he overtly referred to the relation of Dante and Beatrice in an article from January of 1928 on 'Beatrice and Don Quixote', where he says, 'why don't we seek a Beatrice as an occasion for heroism – rather than sentimental love and sensual satisfaction?'[7] (He sees both Dante and Don Quixote as 'mad', but heroic in their madness.) *Gaudeamus* paints a picture of the narrator's 'fathering' of Nişka as object of adoration in a Pygmalion-like process of spiritual sculpting until she becomes the woman of his dreams, with whom he can fall utterly in love – and then resist! Immediately after this incredible act of manipulation and objectification, the narrator meets another female friend, Nonora (based on Thea of the *Autobiography*), with whom he has had earlier, superficial sensual encounters. He treats her, physically, even more callously in an act which brutally inverts his relationship with Nişka.

6 Liviu Bordaş, 'Between the Devil's Waters and the Fall into History: or an Alternate Account of Mircea Eliade's Diopteries, *The International Journal on Humanistic Ideology*, 4 no. 2 (2011): 43-75.

7 Mircea Eliade, 'Beatrice şi don Chuichotte', *Gândirea*, 8 no.1 (January 1928): 31-32.

Eliade was aware of early 20th century feminism, introducing 'a snub-nosed girl who read German philosophy books and was proud of her feminist views' in the opening pages of the novel. Yet, throughout, the novel is littered with statements of shocking male supremacy: 'Waiting is a feminine attitude … The feminine soul reveals itself through the process of confiding itself in a masculine soul … the feminine soul is passive, waiting to be fecundated by masculine spirit … the feminine soul tires easily … woman alone is not capable … the furrow of her soul ached for my will as for the sower.' And here the major theme of the novel emerges: the 'masculine' will. For the narrator, the truly 'masculine' soul is equipped with an ithyphallic will to which the 'feminine' yields. We know from the *Autobiography* and elsewhere that Eliade had read – and been much impressed by – both Jules Payot's *L'éducation de la volonté* and Ibsen's *Brand*. He recommended both to Rica. It is a central theme of Renaissance humanism that humanity can ascend (or descend) the great chain of being by an act of will. Papini and Friedrich Nietzsche, both authors who praise the power of the will, were models for Eliade's writing. These are ingredients in a heady brew engendering intoxicating visions of indomitable will. The true education of the student narrator of the novel lies in disciplining his will to the point that he can seize any opportunity presented to him, simply because he wants it (which is, no doubt, why he feels more sympathy for magic than for monotheism).

However, the narrator's shameless treatment of Nonora towards the end of the novel resulted from something he felt 'more strongly than my will, more strongly than my respect for Nonora's love'. The point seems to be that such acts of brutality emerge from a *failure* of the will, contrasted to the 'success' of the steadfast will required to reject Nişka. From our perspective in the 21st century, the physical abuse of Nonora casts light on the spiritual abuse of Nişka, revealing it to be a corresponding opposite: two extreme – and extremely 'masculine' – vices between which a morally virtuous mean is yet to appear. The objectification of Nişka is thus another act of violation – but it seems improbable that, in 1928, either the 21-year old Eliade, or his fictional narrator, could see that.

Known in the English-speaking world as an historian of religions,

Eliade authored more than twenty major works, including *Patterns in Comparative Religion, Shamanism: Archaic Techniques of Ecstasy,* and *Cosmos and History: The Myth of the Eternal Return.* However, decades before this success as a scholar of religions, Eliade achieved recognition as a novelist in his native Romania with *Maitreyi* in 1933 and continuing with *Huliganii (The Hooligans,* 1935), *Şantier: Roman Indirect (Work in Progress: An Indirect Novel,* 1935), *Domnişoara Christina (Miss Christina,* 1936), *Şarpele (The Serpent,* 1937), and *Nuntă în cer (Marriage in Heaven,* 1938). After his exile from Romania at the end of the Second War he focussed more on his career as an academic and his publication of novels became sporadic. In his *Journal* for 15th December, 1960, Eliade claimed that he was "more and more convinced of the literary value of the materials available to the historian of religion. … what I've been doing for the last fifteen years is not totally foreign to literature. It could be that someday my research will be considered an attempt to relocate the forgotten sources of literary inspiration" (*Journal II: 1957-1969,* 119). If there is any truth in this observation – and I am sure that there is – the understanding of the scholarly and the literary worlds of Mircea Eliade are finally interdependent and the appearance of this novel, available for the first time to the English-speaking public, constitutes a significant contribution to both. *how so?*

Bryan Rennie is a British historian of religions and Professor of Philosophy and Religion at Westminster College, Pennsylvania, USA. Rennie is known for his works on Romanian scholar Mircea Eliade and was awarded the *Mircea Eliade Centennial Jubilee Medal* for contributions to the History of Religions by then Romanian President, Traian Băsescu, in 2006.

GAUDEAMUS

1928

PART ONE

ONE: **THE SETTING**

The chestnut trees were wet after the rain, the boulevards were cold. Above me, only autumnal sky.

I walked apprehensively; intimidated by the glances the others gave me. I set my face in a scowl, to give myself courage. Leaning against a wall, in the passage that led to the administrative offices, I felt a stir of excitement. I did not want to be discovered by anyone; and yet I wanted to discover everyone. I loved everything about them, and I thought about how henceforth they would all be my classmates. There were so many young women, all of them beautiful to me, and all of them, I decided, Hypatias. I felt hopes and desires swelling and anxiously stirring about inside me. I observed; is it not true that *these* are the best years of my life? And I was not sure whether I should take control of them or allow them to control me.

Gone were the torturous nights of Greek Grammar. One painfully-clear morning I came down from my attic. I was seduced by the chrysanthemums. And the sky, the expansive blue sky. My home seemed so perfect, and so beloved. The courtyard had become my friend. Large lilac bushes bowed humbly in the sunshine. It was then that I decided: I am going to give up Greek, at least for *now*. You might say that I was waiting for something, promised long ago. But for what, I could not say.

I would have to find new friends. But I did not dare talk to any of my classmates taking their seats at the back, who looked mistrustfully at my glasses and smiling face. Nor did I dare speak to any of the young women taking their seats on the front rows, who were not looking at me at all. I would just have to wait.

It rained, and rained. I bought piles of books after the Baccalaureate exam. Alone in my attic, I read them. My first autumn, I thought. And I smiled.

Attending my first lecture in the Maiorescu Auditorium, I sat next to the window, tormented by too blood-red a sunset and the hand of the girl sitting next to me, too pale, too warm. Below, on the boulevard, passed people who had never heard of our professors. This stupid thought hindered me from understanding the lecturer's eulogy to Philosophy as the crowning achievement of human endeavour. He spoke slowly and clearly, excruciatingly slowly and clearly. At the end of the lecture, young women took the edge off their irritation by opening and closing their handbags. There were also young women who took notes. They had big ears, and hair heaped wildly on top of their white necks. Other students struck the attitude of thinkers: high foreheads, knitted brows, chins resting on their hands.

I descended the stairs, and yellow globe lights appeared in the night. *streetlamps??*

In the corridors were couples and groups. The couples were next to windows, with autumn in their eyes. The groups stood along the walls, pointing at shy students, or students whose dresses were too long. Groups always laugh; couples always keep quiet.

My first change: I developed a liking for sentimental souls. At least they don't think that everything is just a joke, I thought. Why was I saddened by the choices of adolescence, made worse in tumultuous times?

I was embarrassed by my hat, which was too big and too black. My brother had teased me about all students being poets and bohemians. But I had my attic, and I never wrote poetry. Under my big hat, I looked more like a German house painter. I only wore it when it rained. And in autumn it rained, and rained.

The first sign that adolescence had definitively ended: I stopped writing my *Diary*. From now on, everything would be worked out in my soul, in secret. Another sign: I demanded and received money for the things I published. I had plenty of money and bought myself expensive books. *ironic*

The streets were colder now, and the walls even gloomier. The chestnut trees were yet another autumn older and around the windows the ivy was turning red.

In the mornings, my soul was serene. But at night, clouds gathered. Why could I not remember the dreams that bourgeoned and took flight in nights of restless sleep?

In the corridor, one evening, in front of a door, I bumped into a girl who looked up at me angrily. I turned pale, and then red, and then pale again. I found out later that she went by the name Bibi. From then on, I greeted her timidly. She never answered. Why did I, of all people, call her Bibi?

I did not have much luck. None of my lycée friends were in any of my classes. But I had got to know a few new faces. One was a student from Bessarabia, tall, blond, and nearly bald. He was majoring in Theology, Law, and Philosophy. He never missed a class and wrote his notes in huge lined notebooks. He had been to Athens, Sofia, and Paris. No one knew anything else about him. He was friends with a Jew who was in love with a beautiful Jewish girl. He was ugly, but he loved her. I realised this when he told the Bessarabian: 'She's so intelligent!' Sad, so sad. *fake nice guy attitude*

I had also met a snub-nosed girl who read German philosophy books and was proud of her feminist views. She discussed German Philosophy and Feminism with anyone and everyone. She had a rather odd way of beginning a sentence: 'I mean, do you or do you not agree with me?' *ha ..!*

The feminist looked down on the girls who were pretty or uncultured. I overheard the following snatch of conversation. *synonyms??*

'If they haven't read Hegel, they're good for nothing!'
'Really?'
Someone else, indiscreetly, 'Who put you in charge?'
'I, sir, am a feminist.'
Another voice, 'More power to her!'
Every once in a while she would arrive with a pale, delicate young man. The students at the back whispered that he must be one of her disciples.

I also met a brunette, whose hair was cut in a fringe. She spoke in a soft voice and crammed Latin vocabulary before lectures. Once, I caught her reading a book of verse. She blushed. After that, she would smile at me, and I would say hello to her.

If it rained at night, after seminars, we sheltered in a corridor with large windows. Little by little I shed my shyness. I met theology students with long hair, and youthful, unkempt beards.

And destitute literature students, who cursed the rain, because they would miss their meal at the cafeteria. And students from distant cities, with wide eyes and mud-specked socks. All kinds of groups set off to the student halls of residence, with their briefcases tucked under their arms.

Once the rain had passed, I made my way home along cold, laved streets. I looked at the lighted windows and imagined warm, cosy rooms, with languid female footfalls on soft rugs. But I did not allow myself to feel any sadness.

*imperfect but enjoyable, atmospheric**

Autumn, with its sadness and twilight, passed. Two years later, my memories are bitter and heavy. I write this story with peace of mind, hardened by the path that I have taken. But I write a story that is not yet finished. Life goes on, and I write only of the life that has been lived.

generalities, universalities → is the beginning chapter of a novel the right place for self-reflection (contemporary readers used to "show don't tell")

TWO: **THE CHAIRMAN**

I finished that autumn, alone. And then, all of a sudden, in early December, the attic came to life. Evening fell, but upstairs, in my attic, choirs intoned. It had all happened so fast – I am beginning to forget exactly how I came to meet the doctoral student with the broad forehead and nervous smile at the corner of his thin lips. He explained to me, walking down the boulevard, how the city did not yet have a student association, how at the university year after year passed without anyone attending or establishing one. An older gentleman wished to donate his fortune for a students' club, if only an association existed, but there was no association, because students were happy to spend their years with old friends to whom they were connected by childhood or lycée. If only a room could be found somewhere, a room in which to organise.

'I have a attic.'

The doctoral student demurred; young men and women are noisy, unruly. They would disturb and annoy whoever else might be at home.

'But the attic is mine.'

He consented, but only for the choir. Happy, we went our separate ways in the night. The next morning, he climbed the wooden stairs and knocked on my door.

'So many books, so many books.'

He told me everything he had done since we parted; he had recruited five friends to form a committee, written an appeal to the city's students, taken receipt of the first funds from the old gentleman, and ordered membership cards from the printers. Medical student that he was, he gauged the volume of air in the room.

'No more than two hours, for fifteen people. After two hours we'll have to open the windows.' He had been wanting to announce a student assembly in the newspapers, but had not found a room large enough. I quickly put on my coat, and together we set off to visit the headmaster of the lycée.

The old man attempted to be nostalgic: I had first arrived there nine years ago, a small, shy boy, but look at me now: a university student! Did I still recognise my old headmaster, the parent of my adolescent soul? The doctoral student bit his lips in impatience. But what good was any of this now? A new, fruitful and dynamic life was beginning. Could he lend us a helping hand? Would he agree to let us use the music hall for our first few meetings?

'For university students, naturally.'

The student thanked the headmaster briefly but warmly, then left, heading for the university, the newspapers, the dean's office, the cafeteria.

On my way back, alone, with bitter memories of the headmaster in my soul, I encountered the first snowflakes of the season.

'December.'

Two days later, my little windows were lit blue by the snow. In my room, it was cold and dark. I brought up loads of coal and wood, dusted white. Sitting by the stove I read, in disbelief, the announcement in the columns of *Universitare*: 'Today, at five p.m., students of the university who wish to join the city choir are invited to enrol at the provisional headquarters in the attic of.'

I ran downstairs.

'We'll be having guests at five o'clock.'

'How many?'

'I'm not sure; twenty or thirty. But we'll be holding auditions – some will be leaving almost as soon as they arrive.'

Mother did not believe that I would be having 'guests' until she met a girl asking for directions.

'Excuse me, is there a attic here, some kind of provisional headquarters?'

As luck would have it, it was Bibi. The doctoral student had not yet arrived. I was nervous and wondered if it was warm enough, if the armchairs were comfortable, if the bookshelves were tidy. Bibi had not expected to see me or, even more so, to see me there all by myself.

'Are you the only one here?'

'Yes, I am … well, you see.'

'Ah, so this is your attic.'

'That's right.'

An awkward silence.

'You were working when I arrived; let me take something to read, something from here.'

She took a copy of *Corydon*. I blushed.

'Is it any good?'

'It's interesting.'

'A novel?'

'No. Gide.'

'What do you mean?'

'Haven't you read anything by Gide?'

'Yes I have. A textbook: *The Political Economy*.'

Charmed, I explained, 'That's by Charles Gide.'

'Oh! Sorry! And this is by Andrei.' She smiled, looking through the book.

'I know somebody called Andrei, a polytechnic student. He skis.'

I nodded.

'Yes, yes.'

I invited her to sit down in an armchair between the bookcases.

'Don't you get bored up here all alone?'

I lied, presumptuously.

'I wouldn't say I'm alone, exactly.'

She took a long look at me.

'That's strange; you don't look like someone in love.'

Pale, very pale.

I was saved by the doctoral student; he entered without a word, with a bag, damp from melted snowflakes, his forehead red from the cold.

'Aren't you going to introduce me to the young lady?'

How was I supposed to introduce her by her nickname, Bibi? But she introduced herself. I made a mental note of her name.

Within half an hour, the attic was full of students. The provisional committee assembled at the table. I recognised a few of them. Two from the Polytechnic: a second-lieutenant in his final year at medical school, and a stooped, skinny young man, who smoked copiously and weighed his words carefully. The others were strangers. There were only a few girls; they sat on chairs and the bed. We listened to what the chairman had to say.

He was not a gifted orator. He struggled to find the right words, but when he did find them, he delivered them resoundingly. He reminded us of the old gentleman's donation. But the association did not yet exist. It would have to be established as soon as possible. The choir and the festival would bring in funds. We would sing carols for government ministers, for the dean of the university, at the royal palace. The association would have to be officially registered. That way, we would be able to receive donations. At the same time, we had to foster 'the student life'.

My guests were inspired. They promised help, work, with enthusiasm.

'And discipline', added the chairman.

A young man with black hair was appointed choirmaster. Flattered, he asked to hear everyone's voice. The girls protested.

'We've been singing since lycée.'

The boys teased, 'Then it's been a long while, hasn't it.'

A pale, quiet girl capitulated.

'Do, re, mi, fa, sol, la, ti!'

A tall, swarthy, thick-lipped student, who stood leaning against the door, opined: 'She's a tenor.'

Laughter. The girl turned red, and shrank back apologetically. The chairman interjected, 'Gentlemen, you promised.'

A young woman, with dark, sunken eyes, moist lips, and trembling nostrils spoke up. She had wavy, neck-length black hair and her arms were bared to the shoulder.

'Chairman, sir, *they* should go first!'

The boys protested, suddenly nervous.

'Ladies first.'

'The boldest first', replied a blond girl.

Amid this hubbub, I took a look around my attic: Cigarette smoke, the smell of women's clothing, shadows. The bookshelves paid silent witness.

Above the headboard of my bed, the dried willow garland around an icon shed its dry leaves. I felt so happy and such a stranger!

aesthetic

24

amusing enough to be worth reading

The chairman's ruling solved the dilemma: 'The girls will sing scales, and the gentlemen will go downstairs and wait in the court-yard for a few minutes. Make sure not to break any windows!'

I could hear them plotting.

'But we'll catch cold.'

The girls agreed to go first, but only if the boys promised to behave themselves. The young lady with the dark eyes gave a perfect, defiant rendition of the scale.

'Your name and faculty?'

'Nonora – Law, and the Conservatory.'

The boys 'Aha!'

Two days later, rehearsals began. The young women one after-noon, and the young men the next. This arrangement was not to the liking of the men. They arrived late, smoked, and ignored the chair-man. It was decided to hold joint practice sessions. The men arrived half an hour early. Some politely asked me to forgive the intrusion. They began to discuss the student strike. Some were for it, others were carried along with the tide, and others still were against it.

'And what do you think?'

I did not want to think anything. I listened. When the first young lady arrived, the discussion grew impassioned.

'Sexual selection', I said to myself.

The women complained to the chairman about the men 'talking politics'. The chairman banned any further talk of politics, as it was conducive to disorder. If the men in the room wished to discuss such matters elsewhere, they were perfectly free to do so.

We rehearsed *Gaudeamus igitur* – a certain feeling descended into the attic, amid the cigarette smoke and the books, a feeling of Heidelberg coming to life. It was hot between the white walls, we were happy that it was snowing outside, that it was snowing heavily. Our voices resounded through the windows and enlivened the street. The women had befriended each other. They huddled around the tiled stove, and leafed through German books in fasci-nation. I divined how, evening after evening, they were becoming more drawn to the attic. In the beginning, they had voiced concern about entering so small a room, without rugs, and with so many bookshelves and burning cigarettes. But it was so novel, so unusual. They then found themselves starting to look forward to our rehearsals. It was 'pleasant'. Perhaps they were dreaming, perhaps it reminded them of novels, or perhaps they were hoping.

Nonora was becoming more and more forward. But she was still undecided. She smiled at all the men and received never-ending compliments from admirers who cast furtive looks at her knees, breasts, shoulders. She annoyed the women because every night she positively *demanded* a gentleman walk her home. Even the chairman was charmed by her. In discussions he now began to ask her to take the floor: 'And what does Miss Nonora think?'

One afternoon, I saw her standing at the top of the stairs after being kissed by a dull but handsome student.

'You've got a cheek! You've wiped off all my lipstick.'

'Is that all?'

She and Bibi had become friends. They came to rehearsals together.

'Who will help me take off my wellingtons?' → hah!!

Maybe she was speaking to me as well. Five tenors bent down to assist her.

'Wait a second, wait a second! Just my boots.'

She liked Radu. She met him one evening at my place, maybe what she liked in him was his ungainliness, his cheerful short-sightedness, his cynicism, which was that of a man who submits to fate. Radu was the only friend who had not abandoned me in the autumn. I met the others only seldom, and when I did, we talked about insignificant things. They were furious that I had hired out the attic to a club of strangers.

'Before long you'll turn into an anti-Semite, too.'

We preserved the same closeness when we talked, but I was looking for new friends. Radu might as well have been a new friend. After we had gone our separate ways, in him I had discovered very many qualities that nights spent drinking in taverns had not managed to destroy.

And Radu came to my attic every night, once he found out that Nonora came too. He alone walked her home now. Nonora liked him best of all the students, because he was intelligent, cynical and 'witty'. The others were handsome and vulgar. Nonetheless, she continued to let herself be embraced by any who dared. She kissed with open lips, her head thrown back. And she would complain afterwards about 'the savages wiping off all my lipstick'.

Bibi introduced me to Andrei, who was tall, dark, broad-shouldered, and had a look of hard-working ambition about him. He wanted to become a chief engineer. Intelligent and voluble, he pretended to be curious about science, but found it difficult to conceal his ambition. After all, he did want to become a chief engineer. It seemed as if Bibi loved him. She asked me two days later what I thought of him. I praised him, of course. Bibi had given herself away.

'Did you see his eyebrows?' *made me smile*

At the very first meeting I met a multitude of students. They couldn't believe all the chairman's promises: the officially registered body, the student club, the holiday camp. But even so, they felt happy to be in that music room with so many beautiful girls and intelligent boys. The chairman had managed to obtain the signature of the university rector for an official charter, a grant from city hall, and a permit for a carol concert, festival and raffle. His briefcase was always stuffed full and he was always in a hurry. In less than twenty days he had formed a recognised student organisation, had registered members, had found a provisional headquarters, and had delegated the workload to committee members. At the same time, with white lab coat and furrowed brow, he was preparing his thesis on balneology.

The members were thankful to him for one thing: he had given them the opportunity to get together and enjoy themselves. The tall student, who always stood next to the door was known as 'Gaidaroff'. He was the only one to interrupt the proceedings of committee meetings without being called to order. The members were fond of him, and pelted him with snowballs after every rehearsal.

At the second meeting, dues were paid. To my surprise, no one protested. After the meeting ended, we all went to the football pitch next to the lycée for a snowball fight. We threw our snowballs with great gusto, especially in the direction of the chairman, who banned the wearing of gloves and the throwing of snowballs containing stones. We chose sides in a matter of minutes. Nonora battled to the right of me, shielding herself with a briefcase, shrieking, taunting, cursing. Bending down to make a snowball, I felt snow on my neck and hair. Nonora cackled defiantly, with her head thrown back.

'Traitor!'

'The name's Nonora.'

'What if I get my revenge by burying you in the snow?'

'Burying me alive? I was only joking. You'll forgive me.'

I shivered. It was getting colder. There was a spring in my step as I went home. I felt like breaking into a run. In the attic, I gazed into the mirror for a long, long time. I decided to let my hair grow long, groom myself, buy white collars.

I read, but my soul no longer belonged to books. With a pencil, I made notes on paper about what I had gleaned from the books, what they made me feel. I worked as if fulfilling a duty, or out of a sense of obligation. I spent less time thinking about myself. I avoided analysing myself, questioning and answering myself.

Now that I had abandoned the discipline of keeping a diary, I indulged in daily self-contradictions. I no longer pursued private thoughts. School work no longer caused me anxiety. I shut it away in my brain the moment rehearsals began. I was experiencing a new and tempting life. Day after day I discovered techniques to help girls with their clothes, how to respond modestly and politely to compliments about my library, how to smile, how to soften the severity of my looks.

The austerity of adolescence had dissolved with that autumn. With gratitude, I forgot the anxieties that had previously cut my nights short. I relinquished the ambitions whereby I had survived lycée. I felt so happy to be in my attic full of young men and women. I whiled away more and more nights with Radu. We talked about Nonora. He had kissed her; passionately; biting her lips. I pretended to be indifferent, preserving the mask of my old soul, which was crumbling without my fully understanding the circumstances.

I woke up later and later every morning. I sat down at my table like a labourer waiting for the factory whistle. I read and read. You would have thought that someone was forcing me to write summaries of certain titles. I summarised them properly, without rushing. I packed the summaries away in boxes. And I caught myself thinking thoughts impudently inapposite to my card catalogue.

After the night of carol singing at the Orthodox Patriarchate and the Royal Palace, we crammed into large motorcars. The girls were wearing traditional costume. We were flushed with the wine from the Patriarchate, drunk with success. And the King had asked each of us: '*Und* you?'

'Industrial Chemistry, your Majesty.'

There had been a feast fit for a boyar at the Patriarchate. And then there was Gaidaroff, who had asked how many of the cigarettes we could put in our pockets, and Nonora, who had choked on a noodle, and the chairman, who had laughed merrily, sipping glasses of red wine, and the choirmaster, who had congratulated us.

We were in in even higher spirits when we sang our carols to the three ministers, the philanthropist, the newspaper proprietor, and the dean. After midnight, the motorcars dropped us off in front of an unfamiliar courtyard. It was a surprise from the chairman: a banquet room, at a friend's, with preparations for a party until morning. Exclamations, disbelief. I ended up sitting between Bibi and Nonora. Bibi found a greetings card envelope and amused herself by writing questions on the back. 'Who are you thinking about?' Nonora answered: 'About someone who ought to die.' I added: 'When?' Nonora wrote: 'Now.' Bibi was perplexed: 'Why?' I quoted the line from Coşbuc: 'Question not the laws.' Nonora: 'You're hilarious.' Bibi: 'Is that all he is?' Me: 'And also tortured.' Nonora: 'Liar.' Me: 'You guessed right.' Bibi: 'Prudence is the key to happiness.' Me: 'Really?' Bibi: 'What impudence!' Nonora: 'Kiss and make up.' Me: 'There isn't enough room on the envelope.'

Towards morning, with the snow frozen under the stars, I agreed to walk the ladies home. The night had passed so quickly – couples were now well-established, and tossed pointed jokes back and forth. Gaidaroff smoked all his cigarettes sitting next to a girl, a pharmacology student, a petite girl with roguish eyes and enticing breasts. With feeling, the chairman declared from the head of the table: 'Ladies and gentlemen …'

The boys replied with enthusiasm: '*Vivat profesores.*'

Bibi, smiling, said: 'I should.'

A blond girl said: 'That made me hopelessly sad. It's time to go home.'

Nonora: 'I'm bored. Radu, go fetch my overshoes.'

Radu had suffered the whole night, stuck between two girls who spoke only to the people sitting on their other side. He was happy when Nonora called for him. He walked her home, arm in arm. I walked Bibi home and searched for phrases in which I could address her as *tu* without blushing. I succeeded. *hah!*

*

Days filled with life. Self-doubt and consternation failed to find their way into my soul. I was happy at the beginning of that white winter. *this is a journal …*

THREE: **NONORA**

I found no respite to notice my anxiety. My time was less and less my own. I divided it between my books and the club. Books piled up, and the club became more and more active. We continued to meet at night in the attic. We made preparations for a ball and festival. Girls searched for young men to take part in an auction. The chairman signed more and more papers and came up with just as many new projects. The deputy chairman, a pale, calm student of industrial chemistry, examined the proposals with a smile and glacial logic. He never showed emotion, never spoke to anyone, and never allowed himself to be carried away by the general enthusiasm. He would smile after every speech and say, 'And now, let us examine the opposing position ...'

He was irritated by the rhetoric and writings of Nicolae Iorga. And that was all. The more Bibi thought about Andrei, the friendlier she became when she was around me. She was the first to accept the invitation to celebrate Saint Basil's Night with the 'elite', at my place. Also invited were Nonora, a fellow soprano called 'Florența', two sentimental medical students, the blond girl Măriuca, Gaidaroff, the committee, a few Law students, Radu, and Andrei. The chairman decided on the sum everyone should chip in for bottles of champagne.

During the day on New Year's Eve, I received a visit from a broad-shouldered Polytechnic student, with a moist smile and hazel eyes. He told me that he was a member of our club, that he had paid his dues, and that he wanted to 'see in the New Year' with us. He spoke to me as if I were a close friend, in an uninhibited bass voice, and addressed me as 'boss'. I told him he would be welcome, naturally.

As he left, with a twinkle in his eye, he said, 'Will there be any games?'

'I'm not sure; the chairman.'

'Who cares about the chairman, boss! Party *games*, we'll get along famously.'

That evening, the man who called me 'boss' arrived with a pale, serious youth, whom he introduced to us as Gabriel.

'But he goes by "Malec". He's a student too, poor chap. Law.'

He laughed familiarly. Then, to Gabriel, who did not dare cross the threshold:

'Come on, Malec! Come on! Student-like!'

An awkward silence at once descended on the attic. The girls gathered by the stove and waited. The committee was embarrassed. I smiled and offered chairs to the newcomers. Nonora gave them a defiant look. 'Boss' forgot to take off his galoshes, and stared at her.

'Is the young lady a student?'

'No.'

'A pity. We would have been classmates.'

The girls laughed. Gaideroff interjected, 'Are you unable to pay visits without your galoshes?'

'Boss' laughed boisterously.

'You're good! What do you say, Malec?'

Malec, pale-faced and serious, stared at Nonora. He was helped out of his overcoat. He took a chair without saying thank you. Again, silence.

'My name is Gabriel.'

'Yes, we know, that's what Mr … mentioned earlier.'

'Elefterescu, Elefterescu. What do you think, Malec?'

They had forgotten my name.

'Like in Cluj, with all those Hungarians. Forgive me, I almost said a swearword, but that's just me, what with me being a patriot. My father was the terror of the Jews – are you all anti-Semites?'

Mr Elefterescu's vigour made us all uncomfortable. In the ensuing silence I looked around the room and hazarded a 'yes, yes.'

'Boss' told us stories of the battles he and his sidekicks had fought in Cluj.

'It was getting out of hand. And you're only a student once! To one I only had to shout, "Hey, you!" And the fool ran off.' He laughed. Pleased with himself.

'I'm not one to back down when patriotism is on the line!'

We nodded. 'Malec' was staring at Nonora, steadily, resignedly, pale-faced. He was beginning to annoy her. She avoided his gaze, changed chairs, and pretended to be bored. But 'Malec' calmly continued to stare.

'Why are you looking at me like that?'

The question burst out furiously. Gabriel gave a start and then looked away, with dignity, making no reply. The 'Boss' made light of it.

'He's funny, isn't he? I told him that we'd have a party, just like students! We heard there'd be champagne. But not until midnight. On no account is it allowed before then. You know, I like to have a couple of glasses myself. But then again you don't know me – what do you think, Malec?'

You might say that 'Malec' was attempting a smile. But all he managed was to squint his eyes and make his lips look thinner.

'Oh, that's just the way he is. The silent type. He's a bit more talkative than usual today – you should see him when he argues with his wife. What a commotion!'

'He's married?'

'Yes, since high school. He has a beautiful wife – *Parla d'italiano con me e con altri.*'

The attic burst into life in a single moment. The girls found it difficult to disguise the interest with which they looked at Mr Gabriel. The chairman brightened up. Gaidaroff went over to him and offered him a cigarette. Mr Gabriel turned pale, almost cadaverous. The situation was strange, grotesque, tragic, and full of comic tension.

'A wife – and it's a good thing too: he's got a house, meals, everything he needs. He works, his wife's at the university: a happy couple.'

Mr Gabriel once again attempted to smile. He did not succeed. Sitting icily, he once more stared at Nonora. An irritating, disturbing look, hinting at nightmarish horrors, depression, danger. Nonora got up from her chair.

'I'm leaving.'

Mr Gabriel reacted in a way no one ever would have predicted, given his glacial serenity. He convulsed, threw on his coat, and ran out of the door. We didn't even have time to turn on the light to the wooden flight of stairs. In fright, we heard him stumbling, stamping down the stairs.

'What's up with you, Malec? Where are you going? Why don't you stay, to party with these students? Champagne, games!'

The 'Boss' came back smiling.

'That's just the way he is – but he's a good chap.'

He started to speak. We all listened to him in bewilderment. Radu smoked heavily, Nonora was annoyed. Whispers:

'They've ruined our party!'

Then we heard soft snowballs hitting the windows. Peering out of the window, I could see 'Malec' down below. Mr Elefterescu waved to him. We all looked at each other in bafflement.

'He's crying, poor chap. I best be going.'

Right then it seemed to me that the attic had grown cold. I put some more wood in the stove. The 'Boss' shook a few hands, smiling regretfully.

'Too bad about the champagne.'

After we heard the gate close in the courtyard down below, we took a deep breath. The chairman was furious.

'Who invited them?'

'Savages!'

'Malec is in the preliminary stages of mental debility.'

The deputy chairman proffered his clear and objective opinion: 'It is, I believe, the result of inbreeding.' Funny

We were unable to forget the episode until close to midnight. The bizarre, grotesque atmosphere left by the stares and attitude of 'Malec' and the suspicious effrontery of Mr Elefterescu the polytechnic student vanished. We ate, and filled our glasses with red wine. Gaidaroff positioned himself next to Măriuca, Radu next to Nonora, and the medical student girls next to members of the committee, 'Florenţa' between the two law students, Bibi between Andrei and myself. Bibi was the most disturbed by the visit and the harsh verdict of the deputy chairman. She was sullen, and stared at Andrei and him alone.

After the champagne, we decided to play games. We were all in high spirits. I suppose that the aftermath of the odd experience, and the magnitude of the averted crisis, had generated a surplus of energy waiting to be released.

The one thing I had feared at the beginning of the game did indeed occur, that is, having to kiss Nonora. With everyone else revelling in the sight and judging me to be too timid.

Nonora was calm; her eyes seared like a branding iron, but then grew clouded and sad.

'Come on, get on with it – don't bore me.'

'Should I start with your forehead?'

'If you're perverse.'

'How many times?' I said, trying to delay.

'Why don't you start, and then I'll tell you when to stop.'

But with everyone laughing, how could I tell them I could not kiss Nonora like *that*?

'One ... two ... three ... five ... nine ... five ... four ... The boys counted. Nonora, having tired of it, stopped me. She laughed.

'You have no idea.'

I was agitated, furious. I had to defend myself, but I didn't know what to say.

'In front of an audience, obviously I don't know how.'

'There's no point; don't flatter yourself.'

The next morning, I woke up distraught. I would like to have written down everything that was going on in my soul. But I had got out of the habit of writing my *Diary*. And besides, I didn't understand what was going on. I had allowed myself to be carried away by life, the club, the chairman, Nonora, Bibi. I fell asleep again and dreamed strange dreams, in which men shouted: 'Boss, boss, Malec is calling for you!'

We saw each other nearly every day. Nonora brought over most of the items for the raffle. Radu came with her and unloaded the packages from a cart, discontentedly smoking cigarette after cigarette. Radu may have still gone to bed at dawn, but he never missed a chance to meet up with Nonora. Whenever we were alone he praised Nonora's eyes, lips, arms, shoulders, and skin. He told me about touching her knee in the cinema, only to be checked by her fist; about kisses in passageways and backstreets. None of it really affected me. It *interested* me as something new and different. Nonora, who suspected Radu's indiscretions, looked at me with defiant eyes. She tried to provoke a reaction by stopping in the middle of one of her anecdotes: 'He doesn't understand.'

I knew Nonora didn't believe what she was saying. But all the same I was humiliated by the pitying looks from the girls and the vulgar superiority of the boys. Even so, I endured the situation with a mix of amusement and forbearing that I could not quite understand. One night, I would be alone with Nonora, make my move, clasp her wildly, kiss her long and hard on the mouth. But I knew that *that* was as far as I would go. I cannot tell you how many times I heard Radu complain about how she led him on, how she laughed seductively in his face, how she kissed him, how she cuddled him, gritting her teeth, but holding his sweaty hand in her own, before pulling back, with a devilish smile: 'That's quite enough! Now go away!'

I could have done the same. But why did I avoid it, determined to be viewed as an anomalous example of purity and innocence, when I had the same mediocre sex life as everybody else, dependent on pure chance?

I did not understand my attraction to Nonora. But from the first time she spoke my name, I was happy. I wasn't brave enough to ask myself whether I liked her. But I had the feeling that something else altogether attracted me to her and delighted me in her presence. I knew how futile it was to read German after Nonora left. I think of all the pages I failed to absorb, because of the overpoweringly fresh scent of her that still lingered in my nostrils and the scenes recounted by Radu that flashed before my eyes.

I was afraid of her, and I wanted her. Catching myself desiring her, I would feel humiliated, I would scold and deride myself. A few hours would then pass, and again I would find myself wanting her.

The morning of the festival, she came to the train station, nervous about the role she had been assigned in the play. She hadn't quite memorised her lines yet. With Radu, she drank four cognacs in the station buffet. She refused to let him pay.

'You'll cater to my every whim at the ball. Maybe you'll even make me your queen.'

Radu sat enigmatically, whispering to her between puffs on his cigarette, 'You're so delicious.'

'You're insufferable!'

'Your nostrils are quivering.'

'And you assume it's because of you?'

'Naturally.'

'You're such a brute.'

'I know; but you like me.'

Nonora feigned laughter.

'You look like a convict: ugly, short-sighted, vulgar.'

'But you still like me.'

'You're annoying, and you have a stutter. Go away; you aren't fun anymore.'

Bibi was sick with longing for Andrei. Gaidaroff carried the makeup kit. The chairman, with lively eyes shining beneath a weary brow, ran back and forth with crates of items for the raffle, a crate of costumes, tickets for members, a folder of documents. The committee tried, without much success, to bring order to our expedition. Our raucous party occupied an entire train carriage. The chairman suggested we sing together, but was rejected by insurgents, who preferred to joke around in front of the windows.

We worked for three hours decorating the hall with pine boughs and paper streamers. The piano was out of tune, with three missing keys. But even so, I tried to play a bit of Grieg.

At dinner, in an empty restaurant warmed and brought to life by our energy, Nonora sat down between Radu and I.

'Give me some wine! Give me some wine!'

Her acting, in the festival, had been far better than we could have suspected. After the curtain came down, she sought refuge in a nearby room and asked for some cigarettes. I had a packet and was about to offer her one of mine, but Radu proffered his packet first. She kissed him passionately, in front of us all. Radu blushed, but without losing his cool.

'I would have kissed anyone who gave me a cigarette.'

The chairman, bewildered, had to overlook it; she had performed too well.

The girls pretended to be upset. Although saddened, only Bibi defended her.

'That's how she rewards them.'

Gaidaroff muttered to himself: 'It's my father's fault, he never allowed me to smoke.'

Then came the ball: provincial girls with bad makeup, the entrants in the beauty contest, families who drank numerous bottles of soda water, engaged couples in black clothes and shoes that were too tight, second-lieutenants who ironically remarked: '*Mademoiselle* is pensive.'

The chairman entrusted me with overseeing the most difficult task: the cloakroom. I had to keep tabs on four hundred overcoats, capes, hats and pairs of galoshes, stowing them on two tables. It was a great responsibility. Gaidaroff helped me and wielded his humour to assuage the impatience of the people queuing up with their coats. At around ten o'clock, Mr Elfterescu showed up, insisting that he was a student and should not have to pay.

'Boss, why didn't you tell me that we were having a ball tonight! I just caught the last train. I didn't even have time to drop by Malec's place. Poor lad, he'll be so disappointed.'

I sent him to our room, which was next to the ballroom and the cloakroom. I laughed with Gaidaroff in anticipation of the enthusiasm with which the 'Lion's' arrival would be greeted. Then Nonora appeared.

'Can you believe it? He addresses me as *tu*! He's revolting! Worse than Malec! I shall slap his face!'

'Don't go over the top.'

'I shall slap him, I tell you, I shall slap him – both him and Malec! Who, may I ask, told him that we were having a ball! Wherever did you find them?'

While we were enjoying Nonora's tirade, Radu left the room, followed by the deputy chairman and Măruica. They were annoyed.

'Did you know that Malec's friend is here? He won't shut up about Malec. We can't take it anymore.'

'He keeps saying, "He'll be so disappointed!"'

'And he's addressing everyone as *tu*.'

'And he's so impertinent', added Măriuca timidly. 'He called me his "little hen". Do I look like anybody's little hen?'

Gaidaroff gallantly exclaimed, 'Unbelievable.'

The deputy chairman searched for a practical and discreet way of getting rid of him.

Nonora had plucked up her courage: 'I'll hit him!'

'Be reasonable', we hastily advised her.

Just then the chairman came in, looking apprehensive.

'Guess who has turned up? It's him – Malec's friend.'

'The "Lion", we know.'

'Why did you let him in? He's going around telling everyone how he met Malec. He's laughing at his own jokes, clapping his hands. He's ruined the party.'

We were all furious, although we couldn't help but admire how comical and bizarre was the situation Mr Elefterescu had forced upon us for the second time: it was like something straight out of vaudeville. I laughed without any ill will and promised the chairman I would write a comedy with those two strange friends.

A local girl asked me, softly and in embarrassment: 'Excuse me, is it true that the student sitting at the mayor's table met Malec or is it a joke?'

Nonora hotly explained the difference between Malec the movie star and Malec the friend of Mr Elefterescu. It wasn't long before the 'Lion' himself made his entrance, flushed with wine.

'It's too hot in here, open the windows and then you'll cool off – that's how Malec's sister cools off!'

No one dared make a move. The natural affability of the 'Boss' was disarming. He went up to Nonora and gave her a roguish wink.

'Have you ever been with a Jew?'

The chairman intervened.

'No politics, please, and no innuendoes. The young lady is indisposed.'

'I'll take care of her, boss, but maybe she's already in love?'

The deputy chairman, polite and restrained, began a sentence with two premises.

'Therefore, the conclusion.'

'Joking aside, boss! We're only students once.'

Nonora hastily put on her coat, said 'Good night', and left.

Radu and I ran into the street. There was no way she was coming back.

'He torments me! He's obsessed with that Malec of his. I see him – *he's here*. They're both insane, or else he's drunk.'

Radu wanted to accompany her home, but Nonora accepted my offer. We waited in the train station for the eleven-fifteen. Nonora asked for a liqueur and coffee. I offered a packet of cigarettes. She didn't seem to remember.

'I'm bored again. Anyway, cigarettes are bad for you, and you're wasting your time if you think I'm going to kiss you, especially without an audience or any rivals.'

Then I grabbed her hand and bit it savagely. Her eyes glazed over in dark circles; she trembled. She hid the bite under a handkerchief. Silence. Several travellers stared and then looked away from us. Nonora didn't seem embarrassed; she smoked and filled her shot glass with liqueur. I admired her composure.

'Maybe you also know how to kiss?'

The question hissed forth from her lips and eyes.

'Yes.'

'What a shame. You've ceased to be interesting.'

I knew she was playing hard to get. I was closer to her now than I had ever been. I wasn't sure what to say to her. I didn't know anything; neither how to look at her, nor where to put my hands, nor whether I should bite her again.

'Nonora!'

'You're being affected.' *foreigning translation*

I spent the two-hour train journey in an agitated state, forcing myself to not kiss her, or to hold her. I kept asking myself, without knowing whether I wanted to ask, or whether the question had a mind of its own: Do I love her? I did not have an answer. But I felt very sad when my answer was: Yes, I love her. It seemed to me that a new question sprouted from this answer: It is love? And I thought to myself: No! No!

Nonora was bored, so she whistled. She told me how much I would have to change for her to like me: I would have to learn jokes, take her to the theatre, learn how to walk arm in arm with her without tripping up, speak with her chivalrously in public, without showing myself up, be self-confident, learn how to dance, have my suits tailored on Victory Avenue, give up books, end my friendship with Radu.

In the train station we barely managed to find a horse-drawn cab. Nonora was deep in thought. She spoke to me more gently than before. From the depths of my soul arose forgotten longings from adolescence, from the years when I was writing the *Diary*. Someone screamed inside: will power, will power, will power! My soul lit up, as if after a rediscovery. But the light was pale, flickering. Nonora spoke to me kindly and warmly. And then again grew silent.

Within me the longings swelled, expanded. I saw the whole year crumbling away because of Nonora. If only I liked her. But I did not like her. She merely troubled me.

As we neared her house, Nonora whispered to me, with her mouth very close: 'Tomorrow I'll come over.'

'I might not be at home.'

Smiling, Nonora looked at me, without growing annoyed, without frowning.

'You're beginning to be interesting.'

I paid the cabman, who drove away with his ears pricked up. I felt the urge to say: 'Nonora, I'm the one who's bored now. I have feelings, I'm made of flesh and blood. You irritate me without even being a *femme fatale*. And you're certainly not *La femme et le pantin*. Under no circumstances will I go to the cinema with you, and I won't even see you very often. You're pursuing me in vain. And besides, I have things to do.'

Nonora was walking beside me. I sensed something was wrong.

'You're ridiculous. You and Radu are both sick: you both think that you're irresistible. You probably think I wanted to seduce you, am I right? I only ever visited you in passing, that's all. Don't play the victim. You might have been more polite, if you had other things to do.'

I was not sure how to respond. We wished each other a cold and reserved good night. On the street, on my way back home, I felt strange but somehow happy. 'I have will power, I have will power.' I lied to myself.

After that, Nonora never knocked on the door of my attic again.

They got rid of Mr Elefterescu through questionable methods: they gave him rum and white wine to drink. He sang *Gaudeamus* all by himself in the restaurant, started crying, swore that he loved Nonora, and promised to enrol Malec's wife and sister in the club.

Gaidaroff and Radu sat next to him, to make sure he did not break any glasses. The chairman personally apologised to the families the 'Lion' had sat down next to and asked: 'Are you anti-Semites?'

After midnight, he started speaking Italian with Gaidaroff, ending every phrase with the lament: '*Il fovero, Malec.*'

He accused the association of not knowing how to party 'like students': they should have made Nonora stay, and punished her by forcing her to kiss him. What was more, they should have banned dancing in couples and forced the public to perform a traditional Romanian ring dance. He said he would have sung, if Nonora had accompanied him. He told numerous stories about Malec's father, who knew how to play the flute. He laughed so loudly during these stories, that he had to take off his collar. He wanted to enter the hall and address the public. To hold him back, Radu stepped on his foot. Mr Elefterescu began to cry and then insulted the chairman in his absence, calling him a 'Yid'.

After two bottles, he passed out.

FOUR: INTERMEZZO

It was a dark and restless winter for me. For two months, from when I first met the chairman to the night I parted with Nonora, I had been a stranger to myself. I felt, at an organic level, how I had changed under the influence of the visitors to my attic. *nice one*

I had grown incoherent, disoriented, beset by weaknesses, like all the other members of the choir. I spent too much time thinking about Nonora, and these thoughts did nothing to enrich my soul, but rather upset it, sucked it dry, coarsened it.

The walk home was excruciating. I had felt so wonderful, every evening, in a full attic. Warmth, cigarette smoke, young voices, Nonora's nearness, Radu's friendship, Gaidaroff's jokes – but now, silence. I had forgotten about the temptations that overwhelm the soul on solitary evenings. I rediscovered the austere voluptuousness of a day concluded in silence, at a wooden table, unknown and unwanted by anyone. The nostalgic serenity printed on my brow by temptations overcome, by a society life left behind once and for all, by the joys the soul had tasted, savoured, and never revealed to another soul.

Day after day I forced myself back onto my old path. I sank into difficult questions, fretted about the decisions I had to make, without having the courage to do so. Once again my nights were disturbed by insomnia-induced anxiety. I promised myself that I would not avoid the deepest self-scrutiny.

My first decision: to repair the deficiencies I had discovered in the autumn. I rediscovered the discipline of morning study in my attic, writing notes and abstracts. But such work neither drained nor soothed me. Torment came in the form of Nonora and the experiences I foresaw with the continuation of our relationship. I told myself: that was life, this is reading; that was courage, freshness, novelty, this is undemanding cowardice and vicariousness. And I was not sure whether I should congratulate myself on the step I had taken, one that provided me with a purpose and focus, but which had, perhaps, separated me from life.

I attempted a return to asceticism. Insincere, and subject to Radu's temptations, my asceticism would soon fail. I had resigned myself to submit to biology, without sentimentality and without wasting any more time. I did not want to squander myself on pointless sexual liaisons. What could Nonora have offered me in exchange for my self-denial? A few months of sexual companionship, and even then her promises were doubtful. But I would have welcomed those months, genuinely and with arms flung wide, on a purely sexual basis, as befits two creatures with different souls and minds. But the danger lay elsewhere: in the derivatives of the carnal act, in the sentimentalism and posturing. I was afraid we would lie to ourselves and waste time in cheap and idle talk. The time of my youth, dedicated to struggle or delight. Time, which I fiercely desired and fecundated with my blood and brains, would drain away to nothing with Nonora, as with any other thoughtless and mediocre youth.

The sincerity I had struggled stubbornly to maintain would have been destroyed, all the experiences of adolescence annulled. I would have become a statistic, a marionette, a frame animated by the life of other bodies.

If I only loved her.

The hours were more and more my own, and yet they brought me no solace. I waited for it; a tranquillity as cold and serene as the clarity of the sea after a storm. But my soul was murky, murky.

Difficult days followed, in a snowed-in attic. My decision to remain alone made its impression on my new friends. The chairman found another headquarters, in a room at some company. I was so sad the day they took away the files, the leftovers from the raffle, the library. Nothing remained but shadows in an empty room and memories in my soul. An autumn and a past started to coalesce. Oh Nonora, Nonora – if only her lips and her curves had never tempted me, I would have remained close to everyone else. I would have come to know mediocre happiness and the dull grey of a life lived, without any significant steps forward. I would have acquired the cynical, sentimental bitterness of those who say: I was so alive when I was young! Why do people confuse wasting youth with living it? Why do my peers not understand that a certain kind of personality, guided by a certain kind of mind, can, over the course of a few vivid and intense weeks, experience whole years' worth of their hopes and dreams? And why do they not understand that the imperative of youth is always to move on?

I waited, waited for the quiet and calm of winter thaw. But once my troubles with Nonora had departed, other troubles took hold of me. I was not trying to find out who I was. None of the people who endured the flesh and the spirit alongside me knew themselves, so I told myself. I would never succeed in knowing myself as well as I knew my library. But sometimes, I surprised myself. I had moments of clarity; I was struck by the feeling that this was me, and anything I did or said differently came not from me, but from someone else inside me. I tried to make sense of these experiences. But I found little success; they were mutually exclusive, contradictory, and cancelled each other out.

I decided to choose certain of my personal traits and declare: this is me! I correlated these features and commanded myself not to live inwardly except to nourish them and help them to grow. I wanted to create a unified whole, no matter the risk of self-denial and self-mortification. Otherwise, I would never accomplish any of the things I had postponed until full adulthood. Maturity meant oneness, I decided.

My youth had to have some meaning outside of books. I needed to start maturing, to prepare my soul for the revelations that would soon bestow life upon me. And this new life would take place only inside me, without anyone suspecting a thing. Soon, all my supervision and fostering of my inner life would release into my mind and soul a flood, whose source no one would be able to comprehend.

After a winter that had begun violently and ended in darkness, I knew and felt a single truth: that I would live two lives, one hidden, the other in full light.

The subterranean life would dominate, and when put to the test, in times of crisis, I would know which to choose.

FIVE: THE PROFESSOR

After the holidays, philosophy lectures were less well attended. I met students who did not understand a thing the professor said, whether in lectures or to them personally. They had assumed philosophy was a discipline that began, like any other, with an exposition of the fundamentals: atoms, chemical processes, basic theories. But at the university, philosophy was neither a science, nor a methodology, but a conglomerate of courses. And for every course there was a professor who lectured on whatever was of interest to him.

None of these students really understood what philosophy was. In seminars, they had learned that it covered a wide range of varied and interesting topics. In History of Philosophy, they had discovered fascinating things about the pre-Socratics. But in Logic, nothing; because the professor spoke too clearly and too convincingly, after a few lessons the audience had lost the thread of the course and the professor had found five others.

Those students who had enrolled for Philosophy without prior studies or experience found themselves disoriented and missed lectures, preferring to attend the History of Modern Romanian Literature, where the professor was witty and the class was always in high spirits. In the Literature Faculty there was a custom that no student could go into journalism without engaging in vulgar polemics with the Professor of Romanian Literature and Literary Aesthetics or fawning over him in seminars. The professor was middle-aged, plump, myopic and kind. His speech was irresistible, slightly rambling, with excusable grammatical mistakes. He lived only for literature, and as such, an institute and academic discipline had been entrusted to him, thanks to the kindness of the government and student donations. But he did not have any real followers. In reality, the plight of the professor was tragic and somewhat pitiful; he was admired and respected only by those students who had books to print but too little courage to look for their own publisher. Or students who aspired to departmental chairs, conferences, academic posts, or literary scholarships.

The professor had a strange and perverse naiveté. He understood practically nothing, he spoke and wrote in such a way that nobody might understand him, and yet he was thought of as the country's only real critic of aesthetics, and regarded as a genius, because he was mocked, was good, was kind, and smiled.

Seemingly innocuous, he nonetheless contributed year after year to lies and the suspension of literary common sense. He fanatically – perhaps regretfully – persecuted all those who opposed him or his system of aesthetics. The few who had the courage to stand up to him, suffered the consequences for years: this or that publishing house would be forever barred to them; various obscure journals insulted or ignored them; and at the University they would encounter mistrust and animosity. The Professor of Literary Aesthetics was both feared and ridiculed. He was despotic and rejected doctoral theses that failed to make reference to his system. No other man in the country was the target of such furious abuse, but he took no offense. His ripostes were pitiful, his attempts at polemic met with little success. He was the most celebrated professor at the University, with the largest and most distinguished lecture hall. Students from every year and from every college attended his lectures.

His voice was irresistible. Only the young women were incapable of understanding why the maestro was persecuted. They listened to him, and since they could not understand him, they concluded that he must be profound. The girls had read his nebulous, interminable course, which only increased their respect for him, since they were unable to learn it by heart. These young women listened in delight to the verbal attacks launched by the young men, but disagreed with them, unless the speaker happened to be dark and handsome.

Then there were the French Literature and Philology lectures. These were attended mainly by sentimental couples: girls who worked at the Academy Library, and boys with a romantic or nationalist bent. The students of French Literature were overwhelmingly female. Fragrances and rustling gowns descended on the lecture hall, the same as in a salon. The couples seated themselves at the back, by the windows.

Art History lectures were given in a cosy auditorium, where the professor used a riding crop to point at the works of art projected onto the walls. In the dark, the lecture hall was like a body breathing passionately, but warily. Fashionably modern couples attended: girls who scorned sentimentalism, and young men who knew how to take advantage of the bits the girls did not scorn. They sat next to each other, with briefcases and furs on their knees. Gritting their teeth, they all repeated the same move, which they had discovered in some novel then *en vogue*. In time, inhibition faded. Each knew that his or her neighbour was equally distracted, and many an all too genuine gasp failed to shock anyone. When the lights came back on, they would be revealed, blushing, flustered, overheated.

Rumours of the particular advantages of the Art History course spread astonishingly far and wide. Consequently, as we left the lecture hall, we would meet students from the Polytechnic and girls from Pharmacology. A law student friend always attended with a beautiful, impish girl, who had not yet finished school. The few demure girls in class sought refuge in the front rows or seated themselves on folding chairs along the walls. The boys arrived ready for action.

The professors knew what went on in the lecture hall. But the Art History course could only be taught in the dark. And thus, the vice was as inoffensive as the practice was universal.

In philosophy seminars one short, blond, articulate, well-dressed third-year student always spoke. The students at the back nicknamed him Ghiţa, while those in the front called him La Fontaine, and girls referred to him as Gigi, because he was charming and bold.

He would stand up and begin:

'To highlight from a strictly pedagogical and rigorously scholastic standpoint contingently relative to time, place and persons' – here he smiled – 'and to attempt to subsume those elements directly fecundated by the formal exercise of methods that do not rule out an interest in the gnoseological, accessible via a new structuration.'

Nobody ever understood what Ghiţa was trying to say. The professors meekly put up with him. None of his classmates dared challenge him. If challenged, he would respond promptly and obscurely:

'Kantian ideation and rationalisation though recurrence ...'

He was always in search of original ways of putting things. Even when paying a compliment he would employ dozens of epithets.

'You display accessible flair in your ethical symptoms, or rather in your neurologico-spiritual manifestations, or in the equation of your inevitable capitulations ...'

One evening a student came to class who was just as short, erudite, and well-dressed. He was known as the Galvanometer or Little Kant. He spoke with the voice of an adolescent and pounded his fists on his bench.

'You're a subversive!' he accused Ghiţa.

'You're dicotyledonous!'

'Who, me?'

'You're amphibiously metaphysical!'

'Place that definition on the plane of coherency and obvious logic.'

'I do not accept methodological advice in the form of personal dialectical rejoinders.'

'You're impertinent.'

'Peripherally corrosive.'

The professor, dumbfounded, intervened.

'Gentlemen, please!'

'Please retract your words.'

'I retract them, very well, imputing to myself only my inevitable organic predilection towards ...'

The listeners in the back moaned.

'Ghiţa!'

Astonished:

'Who, me?'

Philosophy courses were attended by serious, hard-working, half-educated students. The uninitiated had no hope of under-standing, while the half-educated matured in their awareness and understanding of the subject through self-study. The only course students attended even if they stood no chance of following the discussion was Logic and Metaphysics. The young professor had a swarthy, furrowed face, and oddly blinking deep-set eyes, with blue irises rimmed by dark circles.

The professor would enter smiling, his shoulders slightly stooped. He sat himself comfortably on his chair, without the usual academic gravitas, and began to speak naturally and clearly, surveying the class. Each sentence seemed to be conceived then and there. He took pleasure in a newly coined expression, and would repeat it, modulate it, convey it while leaning forward across his desk, he would articulate it with perfect emphasis, strip it naked. The syntagma would lead him down a line of reasoning the results of which were impossible to anticipate. The classroom ran forward with him for a few steps and then listened as he retreated, tormented by the darkness still enveloping the new formula, saddened by his listeners' mental darkness. He was tempted all the while to leave the thought unfinished and to revert to a more familiar means of expressing it, one more accessible to the students. And so the hour passed with the tormented professor at his desk, and a stunned audience in their seats, seduced by the agony conveyed by his irises, the dark circles under his eyes, his stooped posture, his gestures, and his probing questions: 'Is it not so? Is it not so?'

When his class remained inert for too long, the professor revived them with sallies against philosophy textbooks and against Kant. The professor divulged what was missing from the logic textbooks was logic.

'But that doesn't mean you don't have to read them. Read them, but don't believe them.'

The girls concealed their smiles behind their handkerchiefs. After he left, they commented on the professor's eyes and his seductive ugliness; the boys voiced their misgivings. The literature students could not understand how he had been awarded a PhD for a thesis that was on mathematics. The polytechnic college students could not understand how he could be an Orthodox mystic. The theology students could not forgive his jokes or his secular leanings.

To me, all these things seemed natural and commendable. I had long since learned not be surprised by a geometer poet, a musical philologist, or a mystical professor of anatomy. But I was troubled by his Orthodox fanaticism. I understood that his religious experience could be both authentic and outside the bounds of logic. But what about his respect for dogmas, taken to be not only nuclei of potentiated faith, but also actual truths that could be rationally proven? Was his Orthodox faith actually or implicitly the result of some need for pure spirituality? Or was it based on theological conclusions?

The life of the Logic Professor provided me with the certainty that answers to the crises originating in my adolescence would eventually become clear to me. If that life was the one he allowed to be glimpsed. And, in particular, if he did not believe in the primacy of grace. But what about his state of eternal temptation, now vanquished, now victorious, glinting in triumph within blue pupils framed by dark rings? Disquiet, which was more than mere logic clashing with metaphysics and theology, could not exist in the mind of one who had found God. What if the professor did not believe in God, as I did not believe in Him, despite the callings that trouble the soul? If he did not believe, then what hope did I have of finding peace on the path I walked, led by destiny and self-sacrifice? What other path was open to me, if the Logic Professor had not already followed it ahead of me?

And despite everything, what if he still believed? How could I tell him that I was a Christian who did not believe in God? How could I tell him that Jesus was sometime made manifest to me, *in myself and from myself*? Could I logically say that God did not exist, because ignorant and prideful sinner that I was, I had not yet had the opportunity to make his acquaintance? And this relationship with God – something I knew nothing about – how could I discuss it with him? Could I speak with him honestly, or try to test him with questions? But how could I test *him*, the university's most astute dialectician?

With every new logic lecture I grew more and more troubled. Over the last few years, I had been plunged into confusion and desperation every time I had tried to follow the problem through to its logical conclusion. I was dissatisfied with classic solution once I realised the subjectivity inherent in the divisions of concepts, judgements, and reasoning; as soon as I understood for myself that judgements were not always the product of relationships having been established between two concepts, or between a concept and an object, or between two objects, I abandoned it. I reached the point where I could not distinguish a concept from a judgement. The helped me to understand the only distinction: the existential element; the difference between the noun 'thunder' and the verb 'to thunder'. From there, I was able to move forward by myself. But I became so confused that I had to refer back to the textbook. I studied the logic of Benedetto Croce. And in the first few chapters, I found snatches of my own observations, which were rarely different to other conclusions. Croce was both clear and obscure. It was therefore necessary that I should gain a better understanding of Hegelian logic. From Hegel, whom I did not always understand, I came back to the moderns. I spent excruciating weeks with Gentile, Goblot, Enriques. One morning, confused, depressed, exhausted, I hid the books away on a shelf, without having come to any firm conclusions.

I decided to speak to the professor. He smiled encouragingly all the while. Sheepishly, I rambled on, without managing to reveal to him my disquiet. He interrupted.

'What a happy age, nineteen – so much ahead of you, no reason to rush. How should I put it? One understands such matters only after not understanding them for a very long time. It took me seven years to find an answer, although I have yet to understand the problem of induction. And there are questions I hope I shall never fully comprehend.'

We walked side by side, next to the university building. The professor spoke to me in a kind and friendly tone. I almost asked:

'Do you believe?'

But I knew that he could not answer me.

'We can't understand anything on our own. It comes to us, at a certain age, like the sexual urge or arthritis.'

'But I want to find an answer, through logic.'

'I suggest you first become completely and utterly confused. Afterwards, you'll begin to see clearly, to understand organically, effortlessly, without torment.'

'What should I do?'

'Waste your time L do you even know how to waste time? Grab a piece of paper and doodle on it with a pencil until evening. Then visit a tavern! But whatever you do, don't show off, and don't talk about philosophy – you'd ruin everything. Drink, my boy!'

I looked at him, stunned. The professor's blue eyes twinkled in their dark sockets. He was pale, very pale, with devilishly arched eyebrows.

'You are precocious. But what's worse, at your age, I drank all the time and I still turned out badly, a university professor. But what about you? Do you drink coffee?'

'Sometimes.'

I was hesitant.

'Don't be shy. I don't walk around on stilts, unlike some of my honourable colleagues. You don't seem to be completely disinterested, and my position doesn't forbid me from offering a cup of coffee and a cigarette to a young friend.'

What did he talk to me about at the coffee shop? About Mach, Pascal, the Italians, Poincaré, Descartes. About Descartes in particular.

'When you go to Germany, you'll understand Descartes. Over there, the people walk down the street differently. Do you realise how much you can learn in a city where people walk differently than they do here?'

For every author he had an exclamation, an epithet, a parenthetical aside, praise or invective. Whenever he gave me a friendly look, I was tempted to ask:

'Do you believe?'

He avoided the subject of religion. But he did make one regretful observation.

'I know a Christian who has two atheist daughters. Even though he's ascetic and spiritual, he still hasn't kicked them out. Whether or not he realises it, he's either insane or God …'

We parted ways that evening. As he shook my hand, he advised:

'If you want to understand religion, study logic, medicine and biology, textbooks on biology in particular. Religion wins the case only in absentia.'

On the way home, alone and confused, I fell to thinking.

My professor was a genius, or perhaps a practical joker, but how was I supposed to know which?

When I arrived home, I postponed my search for an answer, sine die. On my table were plenty of other books and blank paper to tempt me. On my table were also many incomplete thoughts, a burning desire in my soul, and black ink, lots of black ink.

When I told Radu about my meeting with the Logic professor, I made a surprising discovery: my friend and drinking companion felt a need for Philosophy.

After bragging about Nonora – who had still not let him get any higher than her thighs – he asked me the kind of questions that I, and all those not content with platitudes, could never answer.

I had never heard him talk about 'salvation' before.

'It's strange, but I've actually been thinking about it for a while. Through prayer, I learned that I'm going to be saved.'

'How exactly is it that you will be saved?'

'I'm not exactly sure. Maybe by being immortal? I know that even though I'm physically going to die, my soul isn't going to die. I'm sure of it; although, I can't offer you any proof, but I tell you I'm not making it up, it's not a lie. I know that even as a sinner, I will live forever. I'm not scared of death, but I am scared of death without Jesus.'

I was surprised as I listened to him. This insight into my friend's soul troubled me. I had never suspected that mysticism, which I had regarded as second-hand and jumbled, could contain such Christian simplicity. Radu was so Christian; and also so sinful.

'Please don't let any of our friends find out about this, or Nonora.'

I waged the bitter struggle of one who strives, against all odds, to bring his dreams to fruition. Winter came to a close with my soul having endured the storms of autumn and the promises of spring.

*

Now, as I write, I see all the disquiet: the impatience, the desire to know and master myself spread out before me. I am aware of my *what does this mean?*

actions, my work, my fears, my joys, my sorrows. But I understand nothing, and the uncertainty torments me, and no one can see the glowing embers in my soul, not even the professor with blue twinkling eyes and arched, devilish eyebrows. The professor was the only one who could help me. But he was also the one who told me to be disquieted.

This advice was more sincere and more profound than I could yet realise.

SIX: **SPRING**

nice description

That year spring descended gently, and lit up the city with budding chestnuts. Light invigorated the attic. And now I was compelled to spend less and less time at my wooden table. Spring always got the better of me. It was the only temptation to overwhelm me, break me, lead me down paths harmful to my soul. In spring, clouds were my salvation. Nice thick clouds that darkened the smile of the city with their call. I loved the clouds that filled the soul with solemn sadness and bore on their crests the broad sweep of destiny. I waited for them, my clouds, on perfumed afternoons, when I was tempted to punch the walls of my overly white and narrow room, and to arrange flowers on my bookshelves. I delighted in every interruption of the sun's rays: Darkness! Darkness! But then the sun would hold sway once more, and I cowered again, enslaved.

My spring was not the same as the one I had known in the lives of my friends and from books. Mine was bitter and wild. I was aroused by the warmth, the wind, the sunlight, the gardens, the women. The orgasm tormented me hour after hour; it mortified my flesh, haemorrhaged in my brain, and grieved my soul. If I saw a fruit tree without blossoms, I was overcome with anger; when I happened upon furrowed soil, I wept; by the side of the river; I howled; caressing a stone, I clenched my teeth; warm mist rising from the earth provoked me to kiss it, taste it, smear dense mounds of it over my bare chest, nestle my shoulders in the black soil and to lie on my back gazing at the sun. I never had the courage to leave the city, all by myself, on a cloudless spring day. Even the specks of spring glimpsed in the front garden exhausted me. In the presence of open fields, I might lose all control of my senses. Who knew what might happen? I experienced the beginning of that spring as if they were a series of nights in the boudoir of an insatiable lover. Not one emotion, scrap of sensibility, or particle of my brain escaped being consumed. My enemy knew all the wiles of perversity. She tormented me with branches of cherry blossom, with the shoulders of an unknown woman passing by, with an achingly clear sky, with the urge to wander. Even the pavement was a temptation: sinuous, clean, with the shadow of eaves cast at regular intervals. Children upset me, because I was surprised that I liked them. I did not want to like children. Birds invaded the ivy. Why did they not come up against crimson waves of deadly storm? At night I fell asleep exhausted, humiliated, like a slave broken on the wheel. I dreamed dreams of sexual tragedy. I awoke, trod the carpet of moonlight, dressed, took to the streets, wandering far and wide. But not even the companionship of unfamiliar bodies in strange rooms, no matter how prolonged, soothed me. Nor was I soothed by my walks through the city at night. Or by tortured reading. The only thing that soothed me was the triumph of darkness over daylight, cold and dreary rain, the monotony of the trees, the streets, the passers-by.

None suspected the defeat that debilitated and humiliated me. And I did not want to admit it. I knew that I was scorned by some, who considered me a dry and dispassionate soul absorbed in books. I took pride in this, but it also worried me. How could I explain to them that spring unsettled me, scourged me, humiliated me?…

I was not humiliated by the appetites, desires, urges, and mad escapades that tormented me amid the spring wind and rising sap. Rather it was because this exhausting dynamism was ordained to me, bestowed on me at the same time as the flowering fields and the returning birds. And because it was not mine, but was an alien body that replaced mine with the coming of the thaw. It was the alien flesh lent to me by spring that was the cruel, unforgettable humiliation. How was it that I was capable of mastering my body, emotions, and mind only in autumn, summer, and winter? Why could I not be master of my body and soul in the spring? Could the reason be that they no longer belonged to me but to my sex, species, and time of life?

Nights, nights of rage. Days without complaining, without the gnashing my teeth.

I felt that what I valued most about sex was temperance, and that this was ebbing away without me being able to do anything about it.

Now, as I recount these things that happened long ago, I am no longer afraid of spring. Painful answers have come to me, answers that have stifled the muffled revolt. Now, I wait for spring with the virile nostalgia that averted crises lend one, with the quiet, restrained sadness that comes from solitude. I now understand that what tormented me was not spring, but *something else*. I was afraid not of the torrents that coursed through my blood, consuming me, exhausting me, but of the new soul that was secretly taking shape. I was afraid to replace my own decisions with mediocre, but gratifying, decisions that I would regret in later, sad years. With Nonora, I was not afraid of her body, which I ached to clasp in my arms, to hold to my chest. I was afraid of becoming stupid and brutish through mendacious sentimentalism, time wasting, and my transformation into one of those countless, perfect tools of love, a perfumed, groomed, witty poseur.

In spring I was not afraid of the life of the flesh, of the brain, or of the soul. I understood that the fate of the sensitive soul is to suffer and that of the brain is to succumb to senility. I understood that flesh is doomed to insatiable desire interrupted only by disgust. I understood all of these things and was glad no one else seemed to think about them.

In spring I could fall in love with a creature that in winter or autumn would have remained simply a friend. Why should I love only at the command of the sky, the cherry blossoms, and the lilacs? Why be deceived? Why must I wait? Waiting for love and for spring humiliated me even more than all the desires stifling my breath and boiling my blood. To wait is a feminine attitude. I felt as passive and pensive as a sentimental virgin waiting, resigned, for her master to pick her. This defeat humiliated me deeply.

Springs past, and springs future: I no longer fear them. And here I am, writing, unbeknownst to anyone, in a notebook that I conceal among boxes of research notes. Here I am, writing in the middle of autumn. And how no one will be able to know whether I am sad.

And I am not sad, either about autumn or this account of my memories.

SEVEN: WORKS AND DAYS

In winter, the club met in the Society hall, where the chairman had made special arrangements. But members were never very numerous. Those who remembered the warmth and intimacy of the attic felt uncomfortable in a room so large, impersonal, and cold, with so many chairs, and official paintings between windows. The chairman was distraught at this withering away, which threatened to dissolve the club once and for all. The initiatives of that winter – funds collected by the choir, the festival, and the ball – were endangered. The committee suggested small weekly gatherings, but none of them wanted to take responsibility. Not even the university journal, of which the chairman had put me in charge, managed to rekindle the atmosphere of the Christmas holidays. I had to scour the corridors of the university to find the professor who had promised us a feature article all by myself. I wrote the book review all by myself, proofread it three times all by myself, and set the pages and sent it to press all by myself. I went to bed exhausted, after midnight, in an attic overflowing with draft copies.

The journal did not sell. Being neither anti-Semitic nor philo--Semitic, there was not any interest. People bought the first issue out of curiosity. But subsequent issues sat on the racks.

I did not despair. I had joined forces with an old friend from lycée – Petre, a second-year student of Law and Philosophy, feared at seminars because of his niggling dialectic. He knew everybody in the university. We also had found an accountant: the choirmaster, who bought a ledger and managed to make such a mess of the sums that he recorded a surplus of twelve-thousand lei.

With our third issue an incident occurred, after which the journal survived no longer than a month. We had published an impertinent review of an important book by an old and celebrated professor. The review erred in being well researched. A keen eye would have realised how dear the author of the book was to me, how highly I regarded him, in order to be so severe and unrestrained in the face of such disillusion. It should have been clear that behind the words of the untimely troublemaker lay a disciple's reproach, expressing more than just disappointment.

No one understood it. The offended party approached my professors, protested, complained, wrote several articles in his newspaper, so obsessed was he with the incident, although he never cited me by my name. Through Petre, rumours reached me that gave me food for thought: the journal was to be banned, and I would be hauled before the disciplinary council, risking expulsion. So as not to lose the journal, I resigned, promising Petre that I would continue to work with him under a pseudonym. The issue containing the news of my resignation was the last. Thanks to the intervention of a diplomatic and benevolent professor, the conflict was never brought before the university senate. In all logic, nor could it have been.

The professor of Literary Aesthetics accused me, in one of his journals, of ignorance and impertinence. I responded sharply. This delighted the author of the reviewed book and embarrassed the diplomatic professor, who intervened once again with the professor of Literary Aesthetics. I was confused by what I had learned. I thought it was natural to criticise, based on argument, an imperfect book, to pass judgement on it in a passionately engaged review, since the author had been a role model to me. The threats did not make me bitter. I was prepared to be sent down for a year from school, if thereby I avoided engaging in flattery. It was around this time that I began to suspect an idea that fully occurred to me only later: the purpose of life is not happiness, but rather heroic accomplishment. Every soul encompasses potential heroism, I thought. But every soul flickers for a few adolescent years with heroic visions, before resigning itself to mediocre values, before submitting to the lives of others, shrivelling, and finally perishing. Why should I not be a soul, which no matter what the sacrifice required, attained heroism? Who could know? Perhaps I would be victorious in my pursuit of heroism. But then the victory itself would no longer have any meaning, but only the tireless striving toward it.

In that warm early springtime, the greatest danger I faced was unpredictable urges. The day I read the article that the professor of Literary Aesthetics wrote against me, I worked like a madman, almost without getting up from my desk for twenty hours. The news came to me in the morning. I gritted my teeth and began to read. I took a fifteen-minute break for lunch. That evening, I contented myself with a glass of warm milk, drinking it at my desk, with my eyes still on the book I was reading. I read through the night until sunrise, lost to the world. Finally, I looked up, with a heavy head. I remembered a single word: 'Ignorant'. This gave me focus, and motivation. I was shaking in fury and disbelief. I could have screamed at the top of my lungs, still gritting my teeth and still with my eyes on the book I was reading. I fell asleep at day-break. I bolted the door. On the third day, someone knocked. With my eyes on the book I was reading, I did not answer. My muscles were trembling, my forehead was burning, my brain was throbbing, as if with fever. I was so tense that I was incapable of speaking a single word. On the fourth day, I felt drained, bewildered, weak-limbed, muddle-headed. I closed my eyes and pictured the Literary Aesthetics professor's lecture hall; 'He's soporific' I heard him say. Soporific? Look at me! Could I be accused of being soporific? My brain became as clear as it had been on the first day of my twenty-hour-a-day regime. And no one suspected a thing. I lied, said I was working on an urgent seminar paper and needed to eat at my desk so as not to lose the thread. But they did not know that I wasn't sleeping nights. I rose at eight, the same as ever.

A week later, I read a mocking short article in a provincial news-paper. I decided to dispense with sleep altogether. I was devastated by the thought that I might be an ignoramus. After a few hours of work, a stabbing pain shot through my heart. I doubled over. I could not breathe. Even the slightest movement made me feel like my knotted viscera were about to burst. I crawled into bed, pallid and cold. I was furious that I would die stupid, downtrodden, I who had wanted to abolish sleep! My breath was laboured, I was unable to lift my drooping head. I called for help. Panic, tears, cries. The doctor came with his emergency kit. When he lit the spirit lamp, I revived. I started to breathe again, very slowly. After giving me an injection, he took my pulse, which was fast and irregular. The fright and the heart pang had caused palpitations; a situation I never would have anticipated. Within a few hours, the crisis passed completely. I was alarmed at what I saw in the mirror: I was ashen, haggard, my hair slick with sweat, my eyes sunken in their sockets. Thenceforth, I would allow myself four hours of sleep, no matter how many insults I was dealt.

I was driven not only by the things that were said against me, but also, above all, by the things that were not said. They did me good, those months of silence in which I laboured with many a groan to complete that work. I thought to myself: 'Perhaps the gentlemen refuse to acknowledge my existence? Is it out of stubbornness that they ignore my writing? Then all the better. But soon they will have no choice, because that is what I will!' For me, to utter the commandment: 'I will!' was almost a magical rite. The verb was inextricable from so many years of excruciating adolescence, so many experiences, so many thousands of hours of silent study. My will was a reality to me, whose fruits lined my bookshelves and desk drawers.

The greater the silence around me, the more I wrote and read. I was saddened by the thought that in ten, twenty, thirty years I would no longer encounter the same hostility. To be praised was to be lost. When that happened, I would build a house with a terrace overlooking the sea and live all alone. I would read not one journal or newspaper. And I would work unceasingly. There were so many things yet to be explored: oriental languages, mathematics, ancient history, religion, the history of science, the sciences, philosophy, art history, occultism, philology. I would need time and self-discipline for all of that, I reckoned. And I would also need to write, but writing was painful and often laborious. How would I be able to accomplish everything without enemies or without silence?

At the time, I was intoxicated by the scent of heroism that blossoms only in disciplined, vast souls, and which reveals itself only in solitude. But heroism – the only justification for life – comes to fruition only through fierce and unrelenting sacrifice. It was not the escape from reality that tortured me, but the will to master it through sacrifice. I was not daunted by temptations. The only way in which I wished to live was to be winnowed by temptations, but also to know how to overcome them. I did not crave peace of mind, or the comfort of the misanthrope. I wanted the unsuppressed, relentless struggle that seeds in the soul a taste for the divine and the diabolical. The relentless struggle can only be found in solitude, where the temptations and memories are myriad.

My life, unbeknown to anyone, was a relentless struggle for heroism. I had an appetite for heroic austerity and despair, the same as one might have an appetite for a piece of fruit or the curve of a white hip. My soul smiled on me only once I accomplished some task that defied humanity. I dreamed of broad plains and harsh winds, and lightning-struck rocky paths leading up into cloud-capped mountains. I saw myself climbing, howling, stumbling, bleeding. I yearned for an austerity that would affright the forces of mediocrity in my city and in my time. Then I would be a hero. I wanted the heroic to live again, through me.

I was more than once defeated. From my soul, from my flesh erupted the temptations of sweet and immediate delights. It was then that a strange voice within my soul would say: Sacrifice entails disfigurement; I am complex, my desires are vast; how am I to choose? How am I to relinquish?

And I did not know what to do.

I honed the sharpness of my willpower through hard work. This much I knew: that I must discover and elevate all the powers of my soul and my mind. I was not afraid of cerebral experiences. But what about other experiences? What of life, the soul? Which should take precedence in me? The will, the mind, or the soul? I vowed always to be loyal to my true self, the self that none could know. But what if my inner life were revealed only through my soul, and not through my mind? Would I have the will to sacrifice my mind, my selfhood, my work, the writing forged in the crucible of my brain?

And I did not know what to do.

EIGHT: **THE TRIP TO THE MONASTERY**

On the morning of Palm Sunday, the Constanța train left us at the monastery station. We were under the spell of spring. I had become friends again with Nonora, and Bibi was giggling at Radu's whispered asides. Gaidaroff had fallen in love with Măriuca over the winter. A red-lipped, dark-eyed blonde, Măriuca had fallen for him too.

In the same train carriage, some other students were also on their way to the monastery. Oh, how they laughed and laughed. Among them, at an open window, I glimpsed the face of a girl. I gave a start. No one noticed, not even Nonora, who assured me that this spring would be fatal for me, and would end with me falling in love with her eyes, her hair, her breasts. We alighted in a noisy train station, with the chairman leading the way. We were not sure of our numbers, which made us glad; maybe there were a great many of us. We set off down the path that skirted the lake. The forest was in full bud. Among the trees there were flowering bushes, carpets of dry leaves and patches of tall grass.

The group of students came with us. Constantly and with painful clarity, I kept hearing the laughter of the girl from the window. Why was my heart pounding? I was tormented by the thought that maybe I had met her before, one summer in the mountains, long ago. But nothing came to me. And yet, her nostalgic green eyes, her violet eyeshadow, her eyebrows arched as if in astonishment were familiar to me. I did not know why, but when I looked at her, old sorrows, memories of a lonely holiday, and the melancholy of painful adolescence swept over me. Her laugh continued, clear, irritating, and full. Perhaps I was the only one bothered by it. It annoyed me because *a girl's laughter was always for the benefit of someone else.*

We piously stepped inside the church, making the sign of the cross. It was cold and dim in the candlelight. Through the windows could be seen the branches of cherry trees in bloom. And the girl with the green eyes kept whispering, stifling her laughter.

For a moment, all was silent inside the church. The others had left, tiptoeing out. The girl may have gone too. There was now silence. Turning around, I saw her gazing at the faint light coming through the window. Her lips showed a sad smile. Her oval face was pallid and at rest. Her eyes had filled with tears, or perhaps not, perhaps it only seemed that way to me. Her eyes looked so different beneath that web of sadness.

I pretended not to notice. And I was happy, delighted at the thought that she had remained behind in the church, alone. I knew that she was not a believer and that she was not praying. I sensed the sadness that enveloped her, because in that place there were shadows, darkness, the past, while outside there was sunshine, and the sounds of life; but perhaps she did not want to hear them. Who knows why there were tears in her eyes? Perhaps she was in love or perhaps she was waiting for something; and the passing years were beginning to squander her hopes. Who knows why she was gazing at the window dimming the sunlight? Perhaps she recollected something; or perhaps she sensed the pain of a life that demands it be lived to its fullest but at the same time allows only fleeting pleasures.

The others called for me. When I walked past her, her eyes were merry, without any tears. In the courtyard of the monastery there was too much light, and the boys were too noisy, and the girls laughed and laughed.

With Nonora, I visited the crypt packed with coffins. Yellowed bones, lustrous or putrid, dull, and old funeral wreaths with metallic foliage. Nonora was not sad.

'These skulls have taught me that I should take care of my complexion now, while I'm still young.'

We both laughed. She gave me an encouraging look and then, without understanding why, I kissed her. Nonora's lips overpowered my mouth like a suction cup. Her hair got in the way of my hand. I shook her free from the curls and again pressed her lips with my mouth. Her eyes beamed and she breathed with fiery nostrils.

'Look, you've wiped off all my rouge.'

How happy I was that Nonora's reproach, by reminding me of how many strangers had kissed her, allowed me to feel sadness.

In the courtyard, I heard the green-eyed girl's laughter again. Five boys were standing around her, and she recited lines of poetry to them: Codreanu, Minulescu, Iosif, Coşbuc, Arghezi. I was surprised, and confused. To the fifth, she beautifully and enigmatically recited a few banally earnest lines.

'Any guesses?'

'Victor Eftimiu?'

'Get out of here, you don't know anything! Here's another.'

'Philippide, Demostene Botez?'

'Wrong!'

Why were they unable to guess that it was a young poet, one who had fallen in love with her, and composed his poems while contemplating her eyes?

'What do you want? Eminescu or Topîrceanu?'

'Give us his ballad about the village priest.'

She stopped after a few verses, smiling melancholically.

'Choose something else, but this time about love.'

Nonora called over to me.

'You! Fetch the plum brandy.'

In the forest, we had our picnic on a white tablecloth spread over the grass and leaves. The chairman uncorked bottles of old wine, and rejoiced over the rebirth of the club. The two 'Florenţas' made coffee. Gaidaroff went hunting for crocuses with Măriuca. Radu walked down the path next to Nonora, smoking and whispering.

And then something happened, something I would never have expected in my wildest dreams. The girl with the green eyes came running. Her short curls shaded her face. When she brushed them aside, wearily, a few locks remained giving her a wild but delicate aspect.

Smiling, she approached 'Florenţa'.

'Can I get some coffee too? You must know how tired I am.'

She smiled so beautifully as she confessed how tired she was.

'I know you from school', she said to Bibi. 'And I know your name – we have a mutual friend, Viorica.'

Now Bibi remembered her.

'If you think you know my name', she added raising her eyebrows peremptorily, 'please don't say it.'

The boys jumped in with ironic observations. But the girl with the green eyes fired back as quickly as they came, laughing and winking. The chairman was enjoying himself. 'Florenţa' served her a cup of black coffee.

'Thank you, miss. The gentleman next to you looks Persian; perhaps he's even sentimental and amorous. In any case, beware.'

The 'Persian', a law student, gave a flattered laugh.

'I'm sorry miss, I don't understand.'

'And you of course, are consistent with your many remunerative characteristics.'

'I beg your pardon?'

'With you young man, the discussion is over.'

The 'Persian' merely shrugged at the *cozonac* the chairman had brought. The others were irritated by the casual and caustic language of the nameless girl. I tried in vain to imagine her in the church.

Predictably, they began to read the coffee grounds. The girl with green eyes wanted to learn what her future held, with disarming impatience.

'Do tell! Oh, is that all? Please, tell me something more.' she demanded, cajoled, commanded, wheedled. She was not much satisfied with any of the predictions. And then finally, it was my turn.

'Are you a friend of Bibi's? Do you know how to read fortunes?'

'Only palm reading', I lied, essaying a smile like a chiromancer's.

'Well then, what are you waiting for?'

She held out her hand. But how could I repeat what I had found out from her own words and her glances at everybody else?

'It would be better for us not to proceed. I do not wish to betray your true character in public', I said, attempting an honourable retreat.

She was incensed. She took my hand and led me away. Amused, the others commented on my terror-stricken gait. We found a log by the lake. The thought that I might look ridiculous gave me confidence. I spoke plainly, informally, and without blushing. I drew her hand close to mine, looked pensively at the lines of which I understood so little, and composed a portrait for her.

I knew her so well, felt so close to her, saw her so clearly. She listened attentively, with increasing interest. I went on and on. The soul of the girl with the green eyes – which I willed to be capricious and restless, weak but vast, wracked with aspirations, but paralysed by the mediocrity of her accomplishments – I limned more and more accurately, employing stark contrasts, light and shade, thoughts even she concealed from herself.

Everything I had learned from Freud, skilfully interjected, revolted her.

'And just where did you come up with that?'

I was at a loss, having finished reading the lines of her palm, so I moved on to her face. There I understood her even more profoundly, but what I divined was closer to the truth. At intervals, her face twitched, and the twinkle in her green eyes faded. When I finished, she did not know what to say. She smiled, awkwardly.

'From now on I'll have to avoid you! I wonder if you can even see into my dreams.'

We sat on the log until evening. I talked, talked openly and profusely about books, about dreams, about sex, about regrets, about triumphs undisclosed to anyone else. The girl listened. From time to time, embarrassed at my forthrightness and the profusion of my vocabulary, I asked:

'Am I making you uncomfortable'

'No.'

She stated this, without another word.

A change had come over her. She did not interrupt me, she did not joke, and she did not engage in wordplay like she had with the others. I divined everything that was going on in the soul of that naive sentimentalist who wore a mask of vivacity, and what I divined encouraged me. I talked, and talked. Occasionally, I saw her eyes stray over the lake, over the forest, far away.

And she still did not want to tell me her name; a misguided caprice, I thought.

'I'm afraid you wouldn't like it', she demurred.

I remember how evening fell, how the others left for the station, after calling out to us through the forest. I had so much to tell her that I had not shared with Nonora, or Bibi. I asked about her friends.

'They're a just a bunch of silly girls. I prefer your friends, I've heard about them through a friend.'

It was time for us to go, and yet she leaned against the trunk and asked me questions requiring long responses, and she talked, and talked.

As we set off for the station, the stars began to appear. We took the path that went around the lake, emerged from the forest, and came to the road. The night was cloudless and cold. I asked her if she was cold.

'No.'

I noticed that she looked nowhere but at me, that she was afraid to let her eyes stray from me, to look at the fields or the road. I wondered if she was afraid of the dark.

'Are you afraid?'

'Yes, very much so. I'm always afraid of the dark in the countryside, but if you're not afraid.'

'Me? No.'

A light breeze wafted the scent of damp grass, flowers, earth. We stopped every now and then to rest at the side of the road. Our hands were silver in the moonlight. She recited hundreds of lines of verse about the moon. I told her about the disorders of those who expose their craniums to moonlight. She was terrified.

'I'm scared, I'm really scared.'

At the station, we found out that the last passenger train bound for the city had passed through a quarter of an hour earlier. For a moment her green eyes pulsed with terror, and then she laughed.

'It's an adventure, really. What should we do now?'

I told her my idea: we would follow the road back and take the shortest route, which cuts across the tracks. The city could not be more than twelve kilometres away.

'How many hours away?'

'Three.'

'We'll arrive at one in the morning.'

'But only on the outskirts. I don't which district you live in.'

'No other solutions?'

'No.'

'Well, let's get going.'

In my briefcase, I still had some croissants and *cozonac*. My companion thought them the best thing she had ever eaten. I did not eat, instead telling her in great detail about *Martin Eden*.

'I haven't read anything', she despaired.

She was impressed by Martin Eden's strength. She told me how she could not stand dapper, charming, insipid young men. She revealed her favourites at the university, among the professors and students. I told her about the scandal with my book review in the University *Journal* and how I was happy that I had been in the right. How then did we get onto the subject of the Sistine Chapel and occultism?

Neither she nor I had a watch. We measured time by the moon and her fatigue.

'Do you think we have much farther to go?'

I was happy with her reaction when I employed the maxim, 'A journey at night ends only with the dawn; and when there are two, it is less of a yawn.'

'I'm starting to feel faint.'

'If you like, take my arm.'

We walked with the moon at our backs. The night grew colder, the fields ever more redolent.

She was shivering, causing me to slow my steps. Never had I felt less tired.

'Still not afraid?'

'No.'

And we walked on, I talked, and I talked, and she listened to me, with the cool breeze ruffling her hair. Behind us shone the moon. And ahead of us stretched a white road, leading toward a city with many lights in the night.

It was after two o'clock when we arrived in front of her house. The weight of her arm had seemed to me blessed. I felt stronger, my muscles invigorated. Her eyelids drooped, her feet dragged.

The city had briefly reinvigorated her. She confessed that when we had crossed that lane at the edge of town, with barking dogs and flickering street lamps, she had been frightened. But on the deserted boulevards, she had proceeded with confidence. But then we had had to climb a cobbled lane, and the effort had wearied her. She had gasped for breath.

In front of her house I asked her:

'Won't your parents scold you?'

'My parents don't live here. And besides, at my age, I am absolutely liberated.'

I held out my hand, bidding her a 'good night'. She stopped me.

'You never guessed my future. Shall I show you my palm again?'

'No.'

I had remembered all the goals and dreams she had confessed: she would conjoin her life only to that of a superior man, one able to overcome his parents' will and the prejudices of his time. Such a man would not necessarily be her husband, but perhaps only *le compagnon*.

I then predicted she would marry a man who would be a stranger to her and to whom she would be a stranger, a provincial life as a schoolmistress with a clerk for a husband, succumbing more and more to mediocrity, with each passing day, forgetting her ambitions and desires, stupefying herself with mindless work, with stuffiness, with lovers, with children.

'And that is how, young lady, you will be suffocated by life in a dead town, a spiritual wasteland. You will forget beautiful books. In autumn you will become lachrymose or perhaps even cry. Autumn will stir up so many memories. It's banal, but you will waste your time remembering the excitement of university life and you might even regret giving up your pursuit of originality. Although, there will come a time when you no longer have regrets. Nothing but a vulgar husband and children. You'll realize that your youth is over once and for all, that you have not seen the world, that you have not crossed the ocean, that you are doomed to nurture the family you agreed to in a moment of weakness or boredom. You will lead the obscure and mediocre life of all those who, like you, once had dreams in their youth. You won't even have any awareness of defeat. You will forget everything, everything, in a grey and invincible mediocrity.'

Why did it make me so sad to predict her future? And saddened by her fate, why did I sense the reality of the words I spoke to her so intensely?

When I looked at her again, she was crying. She was crying, of that I am sure: the tears ran softly down her cheeks, from her eyes poured the sadness of a dead sea.

She managed to speak, with a smile.

'You are joking. I will never accept a life like something from a Cezar Petrescu novel.'

'That's what they all say and that's how they all end up. It will be even more difficult for you, because you've planned on such a beautiful life and were born with higher sensibilities. That's all.'

Again her eyes filled with tears. Her eyes made me pity her, but I also felt a savage joy in predicting the inevitability of a mediocre and devastating life for her.

'To survive, you would need a level of determination and perseverance in the face of self-denial that you will never attain, because you are a woman, and you are sensitive and you are capricious.'

'I will find a man!'

I smiled. How was I supposed to respond? To have done with it, I made a joke.

'I bet that in three years' time you will be married, in the provinces, and that you will not be happy. Let me be clear, resignation is not tantamount to happiness, especially for a certain kind of woman.'

She slowly opened the gate. She was so exhausted because of the walk back from the monastery.

I continued by myself, down deserted, cold streets. A morning breeze was beginning to blow. I felt alone and powerful. With clenched fists and uplifted gaze, I ran. I was happy.

I could not sleep. I climbed out of bed and, before starting my studies, I wrote: 'Private spring diary; today, Palm Sunday, a new life begins for me.'

But when I asked myself: why? I realised that I was assigning too much meaning to one of many encounters. So I ripped the page out of my notebook.

Morning light lit up the gardens of white stone houses. I may have been the only person then awake. And I was happy.

a protagonist unlucky
in the certitude he
directs towards his own
thoughts

NINE: **HER NAME IS NIŞKA!**

At the beginning of Holy Week I met several members of the club, who passed on to me rumours about my disappearance during the excursion. The chairman had worried all the way back. He had waited for me at the station. Radu came looking for me the very next morning. He was astonished when I told him the story. He thought I must be hiding something from him.

'And that's all?'

'Yes.'

'You're either stupid, or in love, or insane. Not everyone has the chance of spending the night with a girl he likes, in the forest – you missed an opportunity.'

Since it was Radu who was upbraiding me, I tried to explain that in every situation I sought the most perfectly ethical, beautiful, original, and heroic solution. There was much more beauty in a chaste nocturnal journey at the side of a stranger, whom I felt becoming my friend, than in any other prolonged series of embraces, ending, perhaps, with sexual assault in a furrow. Anyone could do that. Why not experience a series of actions that only I could enact? Why must the hero always be interpreted as a brute, when the Nietzchean path toward the superman could be accomplished by fulfilling the most insane ethical standards? Why should I not acquaint myself on a daily basis with the tenants of heroism, so that my life might naturally unfold in an heroic existence?

Radu knew my sexual temptations and potential all too well; he could not suspect me of unmanliness, timorousness, or inadequacy. Therefore, my conduct was driven not by weakness, but by the spiritual forces that controlled my conscience. Whence a series of parables offered by Christianity: at which point Radu seemed to understand me and explained, or rather, added, that he could never do anything as insane as that.

'To those who have never engaged in the struggle to achieve the absurd, anything that goes beyond weakness and mediocrity will look like madness', I concluded, abruptly, looking at my friend.

A few days later, a little before sunset, I heard laughter and knocking at my door. Bibi and the girl with the green eyes had come.

'I can tell you now; her name is Nişka!'

When I heard that name, a memory flashed through my mind. I knew where I had seen her before: it had been at Sacele, on a cart path next to the railroad tracks, six years previously. She had been wearing a short adolescent dress, and had been running through a field of wheat. A grey-haired man had called to her: 'Nişka! Nişka!' That afternoon, I had decided to dedicate my life to chemistry. I had promised myself not to waste my time on anything else. On the first page of one of my *Diary* notebooks, I had written, that very afternoon, my cardinal rule: I will never fall in love!

The memory transported my soul to a solitary summer, in a small mountain village, amidst struggles and yearnings now long forgotten. My visitors looked at me without understanding the bitter, bitter shadows on my face.

'Aren't you happy we came? Nişka would like to thank you again.'

'Let me say it, I came to remind you that you conducted yourself very sweetly a few nights ago and you spoke to me very beautifully, although as you were leaving you got upset and made several false predictions that I'm sure you now *regret*.'

I mumbled a few meaningless words and invited them to sit down. Nişka marvelled at each bookshelf in turn. She pulled out books, leafed through them, complimented them, and made exclamations.

'Will you take me on as your librarian? Just wait and see how beautifully I'll arrange the books. Please say yes!'

'Strange hands cannot bring order to a library.'

'I'm so glad you know that!'

I thought she might be offended, but I glimpsed a smile on her face.

'I'm not sure how to conduct myself around you', I confessed. 'If I talk to you frankly, you get annoyed, but if I am reticent, you become suspicious.'

'Talk to me as if I were your friend.'

I blushed with delight, and pretended to be taken aback by the intimacy that Nişka displayed and demanded.

'Do you know what people are saying about us? That it was an attempted kidnapping. How about that! As if there had been any need for kidnapping! Bibi, how could your dear friend, who acted so abominably chaste, be accused of such abuse.'

Why 'abominably' next to 'chaste'? I told Nişka about my ethical urges. I explained to her that, in my conscience, my actions had been authentic and real, rather than borrowed from storybooks, or inherited from childhood. That ethics had been a discovery, a triumph of mine from last winter. I told her why she should not mistake an ethically illumined soul for dry, absurd moral rigour, for pedantic, false moralism, the same as anything else inculcated through fear by families and schools. Ethics should crystallise as the result of lived experience.

'But nobody does that.'

'Others have done it, before me. Why should I not experience it, over again? Do you suppose that to have a conscience with ethical values means to be unmanly, elderly, insensate, idiotic? Do you think that ethics cannot cohabit with sin, with temptation?'

'Stop it, stop it, I don't understand you any more! And besides, I feel so strange.'

'Women are not capable of experiencing ethics.'

'But you men are?'

'Not all men: only an elite. It requires a whole series of experiences in order for a masculine soul to ripen. How many would survive, especially when such experiences imperil life, sleep, tranquillity?'

Evening gently descended on the attic. It was the first spring evening when young women had lingered upstairs in my attic. And I was not about to tell them. Nişka asked if I had any cigarettes. She had never smoked before, but she felt a craving to smoke. Bibi refused stubbornly.

Eyes watering, smiling, rubbing her eyelids, moving her eyebrows up and down, she finished half a cigarette. Together with the rest of mine, I placed them in an envelope and wrote the date on it.

'What are you doing?'

'I'm keeping them.'

'Witchcraft?'

'No, memories.'

We laughed, amused by the accumulating sadness that would weigh upon the envelope with each passing year.

On her way downstairs, Nişka asked if she could visit again.

'You have the most adorable little room and so many books – it's comforting.'

I told her that on certain days, when I had less work to do, she could stop by for a few hours.

'And which days are those?'

'I have never thought to designate them.'

'In other words, you don't want to see me?'

'Don't exaggerate.'

'That's fine, don't worry. I won't come.'

They did see the shadows welling in my eyes.

'And all this time I thought we would become friends. And I wanted to introduce you to Viorica.'

I did not know what to say. So I said nothing, frowning.

'But we could sometimes meet.'

'Thanks, how nice of you.'

She left, with an insouciant laugh. Bibi turned to me:

'You ought to know that this time she really is upset.'

That evening, a note from Radu: 'Tomorrow Nonora and I are going to the cinema. She wants you to come too. Before five o'clock, my place.'

The note was my salvation. I had not seen Nonora since Palm Sunday. I thought of our impetuous embrace in the crypt, when Nonora's lips had pressed against mine.

TEN: *L'HEURE SEXUELLE*

I left the cinema in a daze; with Nonora at my side. Radu had got lost in the first few rows. For three hours I ran my hand over Nonora's flesh. I wanted to prove to her that a library did not kill the assurance of the act of vice. She writhed, trembled passionately. I divined her astonishment: 'Me, really me?' The question also implied a rebuke aimed at me; I did not want to respond, consumed with tension as I was. Nonora could be nothing but delighted by the discovery. She pretended to whisper to me, with her head bowed, and bit my arm. This must be a good sign, I thought.

We parted gazing into each other's eyes, hers ablaze, mine frowning. The next day Nonora returned to the attic. She redis-covered her armchair next to the tiled stove. She opened the little window to let in the spring. She laughed, with her dark hair and the dark rings under her eyes. She was too hot, and her knees too tempting, and the reservations in my soul willed themselves forgotten. My arms broke her body, my lips made their way down her shoulders and onto her breasts. Nonora trembled, without resisting. At a sound from the street, she gave a start.

'What if somebody comes?'

'Today is Good Friday. Nobody's thinking about me.'

'Lock the door, just in case.'

I had not expected her to keep her wits about her. When I came back from the door, she had unfastened her shoulder straps. This encouraged me, even though I knew how far Nonora would go.

'Mind that you don't get too excited.'

I kissed and kissed her. Her breasts were naked with delight, brown and warm. Her legs incited daring caresses. Nonora closed her eyes and bit her lips. I told her that I knew what she wanted. Nonora told me to be quiet. She demanded I behave myself, that I not get needlessly worked up.

'You're going to try something insane.'

I reminded her that I was a friend whose word she need not doubt. Nonora trembled, hot air whistled from her nostrils.

A spasm caused her body to arch, to writhe. Her breasts turned to ice; I nuzzled them with my cheeks and lips. They trembled, meekly, provocatively. I delayed, tortured, my eyes blinded by the heat of her belly. I prolonged the anticipation even further, with fevered muscles, with turbid light beneath my closed eyelids. Nonora's body was so close to me now, and more restless with desire. Hot, lingering kisses slithered over her thighs.

That evening, after Nonora left, I looked at myself in the mirror: My eyes sparkled grey from within dark circles, my face was pale, my hair damp. My head felt heavy, my limbs weary. I was shivering. I was not at peace, and I could find no serenity.

Nonora came nearly every day, closing the door behind her. She came at times when no one would venture to visit me. And the game would begin all over again, with the same fierceness, the same perverse innocence of a body that you will never subdue no matter how hard you pummel it. And then we would part, she serene, I in torment.

I had not spent any time with Nişka, nor did I wish to spend time with her ever again. I found out that her parents had lived in Bessarabia, then in Craiova, and then in Braşov. They had resolved not to meddle in the life and aspirations of their only daughter. A consumptive second cousin, while still alive, had given her a house, which Nişka had rented to a family friend. She had enough money to leave, but she was waiting to find her companion. She wanted to *choose*.

Bibi was now even better friends with her. She confessed to me, on a street corner, that Nişka was either adored or hated by girls, that she either irritated boys or made them fall in love with her. Bibi praised her with great enthusiasm. She spoke to me about the novels Nişka had read, about her exams, and about the degree she was now studying for. I gathered that Bibi adored her. I interrupted her.

'Why do you exaggerate all of Nişka's qualities? Do you think that, maybe I too will end up falling in love with her?'

'You never know', smiled Bibi.

Why was my soul awakened as if touched by an unseen hand? At that moment I felt old resolutions gain new determination, annealed by the years, by autumn, and by solitude. Visions of a marshy wilderness at dusk darkened my sight, visions in which I drifted in a boat with silent companions, with my eyes on the sky and my thoughts on the water. I remembered the smell of rocks under the stars, alone with the mountains, watching the sunrise from behind the junipers. I had got lost, grown wild, and all the unconfessed beginnings, disappointments, dead ends had rained down on a soul overwhelmed among other souls, among delights and disappointments. And they now awoke within me afresh, at the mention of the girl with the smile.

As much as Nonora allowed, I worked. I came to realise that I did not consider her caresses an irresistible temptation, but rather as something I commanded to happen, for the sake of an unfathomable disquiet. You might say that Nonora was no more than a body called upon to quench the desires of my soul. But she did not quench them; and they spread throughout me, constantly forcing me to remember my decisions in more difficult times.

I suspected that a crisis was coming to a head, but I did not want to acknowledge it. I did not want to think about Nişka. She had too much of what I had thought about for all those years. But now, the strange stirrings in my soul, which arose only when I was alone, and which would immediately have vanished when Nişka was near, could be nothing but a hindrance to me. I wanted her as a girlfriend, but I was afraid. Not for my own sake; I was incapable of falling in love with her. I was afraid that the springtime, our *tête-à-têtes* in the park, the moonrises, and the austerity of the sentiment in which I had thitherto lived, would endlessly prompt questions, desires, nostalgias, which it would take me great time and effort to dispel.

I did not know whether he did or not, but what if Radu loved Nonora? I would be breaking up a friendship, without even the solace of knowing that it was broken up because of love. I felt awkward when Radu looked at me. I felt guilty, not because I was seeing Nonora, but because I was seeing her without wanting her and without feeling my erstwhile lust for her dark burning flesh.

One day, when Radu smoked heavily and was largely silent, I noticed his sad, downcast eyes. I laughed, realizing that he was in love.

I had to laugh. Ever since high school, Radu had fallen in love with the sisters of all of his friends, with Petre's English teacher, with the three 'stars', with an actress. In Brasov, he fell for the nostalgic eyes in cabarets. In autumn he fell in love again, without revealing her name.

'How many times have you fallen in love now?' I probed.

'I don't know; I just love.'

He spoke this secret with an impudicity that made me blush. I believed that certain words should be uttered neither to a close friend nor even to oneself.

'Are you in love with Nonora?'

'No. I was in love with her this winter. But I was wrong; she's perverse and capricious.'

And I thought: if my friend condemns caprice.

'Viorica!'

I laughed and congratulated him. Nişka's friend was petite, delicate, with large, clear eyes, bright, and a white forehead framed by hair bunched at the nape of her neck. I met her in the library, in front of a collection of philological journals, next to Bibi, who was dreaming about Andrei. She nearly turned red when she introduced herself to me. In the daylight filtering through the cold windowpanes, she appeared to me as the most natural and authentic virgin. She had warm, pointy shoulders, white arms, and gentle gestures. Her eyes and brows smiled. Her lips always listening.

And Radu was in love with her.

'Are you going to tell her?'

'No.'

'Then?'

'I'm waiting for it to pass, Isn't it true that it will pass?'

'I know from Heraclitus that everything passes. But how did you fall in love? When did you meet her?'

'Bibi introduced her to me. That night I dreamed about her, even though I was drunk. The next day I thought about her. "It's very simple", I said to myself; "I love her!" When I sang her name to a sad melody, it made me sad. I know; this is love.'

I joined Radu in thinking about love and I was happy that I had never sung a name to a sad melody, only spoken them. Seeing that

I was resigned to listen to him telling me about love, Radu asked the question that had been tempting him for years.

'Have you ever been in love?'

In response, he received my usual inscrutable mask.

'I don't think so.'

'Then you will be happy.'

'I know', I lied, with a sad smile.

Radu noticed that smile.

'Forgive me, you're going to think that I'm stupid for saying this, but I don't understand you; for nine years, ever since I've known you, you've loved only one girl, with an intensity that frightens even me. Aren't you tired after nine years? How have you not grown bored waiting for her?'

I laughed heartily at my friend's joke. He confessed that he had suspected a secret love from the very beginning, perhaps an affair from my adolescence. But I had never given away a name, or a memory. And yet, my whole being told him that I was in love.

My face maintained the same mask. If my friend had set a trap for me, I had eluded it. He would never know the truth. Why should he know?

One afternoon, in May, Nonora forwent unfastening her shoulder clasps. We set off down the boulevard, heading for the park. I spoke to her in an unrestrained flood. Nonora listened with moist lips.

At the corner of a street with an empty pavement, Nişka saw us crossing. She took a long look at us, and smiled.

Why was I so pained by the encounter? Why was it that I had nothing else to say to Nonora, who was overjoyed at Nişka having seen us? I was so downcast. Devastated. It was as if some hope of mine had shattered, some yearning unknown to anyone; not even to myself.

Nonora went on and on. I listened, walking at her side along the path. Later, she kissed me behind an empty bandstand. I accepted the kiss with wild passion, biting her lips. Nonora swooned. I wanted to laugh, I wanted to kiss her. So I kissed her, and kissed her.

Leaving the park, I was overcome by remorse: I had to run after Nişka to tell her. Surprised by my thoughts, I asked myself: should I tell her *not to believe*?

This was all just sentimental capriciousness, I told myself. And by commanding it to go away, it went away.

I told Nonora that my exams were coming up. She understood, because she gave me a mocking look.

After which we did not meet again.

ELEVEN: MY FRIEND IS IN LOVE

I have a new friend, I have a new friend!

We were at lycée together. We were classmates for so many years. And since this spring, which is coming to a passionate close, he has become a new friend to me. His name is no other than: my friend. I have many friends; but he is my new friend. He is my only friend.

I share with him my thoughts on both poetry and prose. He doesn't always follow, but he understands me. We spend the May nights talking and talking. I reveal to him manuscripts no one else knows about. He recites poems to me that he will never publish. Whatever I think, I share with him; whatever he feels, he shares with me. I feel so many other things and I will share them with him. Perhaps he too thinks thoughts that I will come to know.

We had a candid conversation one evening, at my place, in the attic. He was in love. And I told him things no one else had ever said to him. I met the woman he loves in a bookstore. She read a lot, worshipped Beethoven, vanquished sleep throughout lonely nights at a white piano. They had met in the mountains and fallen in love. The woman's husband was an architect. Perhaps she realised that there was something more to the friendship of that tall fair-haired youth who listened to her glorifying the Sonatas.

My friend was a student like all the others: blond, tall, pleasant, well-read, talented. But he loved a woman, and he loved Beethoven. Waves of potential were unleashed in his soul. I realised this the afternoon we met. He spoke with so much restrained passion, and with so much belief in his strengths and his capabilities regarding the love of the woman.

Through loving, the fair-haired young man became my friend. I no longer recognised him. He was so exalted, restless, determined. We got along so well; I, who was not in love.

He rarely spoke to me about his love. He spoke to me of his agony at first, of how he struggled to forget her, but did not succeed – because once you are in love you never forget – of how he agonized thinking about the woman in the company of her husband, about her whom he could conceive only in the company of Beethoven. And he spoke of the woman who did not believe him at first, and then of their first kiss seated at a piano still resonating from a minor arpeggio, and of their evenings, when her husband was out, on the fur rug in the salon, he dedicating poems to her, she creating improvisations somewhere between Tchaikovsky and Grieg, and of their promises to each other, in which he believed.

He found himself and was fulfilled in love. Henceforth he wasted no time. He worked at the library, and in the evenings went out. He wanted to finish a series of promising papers. Everything had become a calling, an impetus for life and work, because of love. He believed in himself and the love of the woman. He believed in me after he was convinced that I understood him and envied him. I told him that I sincerely envied him. His lady was such a rare specimen, I lied.

Hot nights, at the beginning of the summer, with my new friend. How they passed, and how they cannot, ever, return. Here I am, writing the first book of my youth; there he is, in the middle of a western country, carrying his tortured soul that had wanted to discover the horizons of love. Love that had kindled within him ambition and desire, and given him an unexpected capacity for work. That which was destined to happen, happened, and so quickly. The lady with her white hands on the keyboard said that she loved him, but that she was no longer in love with him. Who knows, who knows?

My friend was carried away by the sails of despair that darken and destroy. I supported him, wept with him, and then berated him with harsh injunctions.

He has run away. He will waste years of his life: we both know it. But all that he gleaned from the love of the woman will become seed that bears precious fruit. I shall wait for him.

Why have I interrupted the thread of my story with this fleeting sadness? Because at the beginning of spring, my friend had been happy. And I thought: If for him closeness to that lady had created him anew, endowing him with manly spirit, what would happen to me, with the happiness I might encounter in the love of a woman's soul ? I caught a glimpse of myself in the glory, the glory of increasing happiness.

And the thought of having to wait, made me anxious, but also brought me comfort.

TWELVE: **STORM AT THE HERMITAGE**

In the middle of summer, my new friend and I went to the hermitage within a cave. We arrived in a cold, hard, cruel rain. We hurriedly descended the White Crags, without speaking, straining our legs as we made long strides.

We slept in a small chamber with white walls, lit by a candle made of yellow wax. Outside, a storm raged through the mountains. We slept with a chill air above our bedclothes. In the chamber hung the scent of dried rhododendrons. Our eyes were clear, and we found pleasure in our toil.

The storm grew over the mountains, throwing the night into disorder. Lightning flashed blue on the walls; we heard the rain, and mountain streams. But in our dreams, we heard the howling of ghosts.

A clap of thunder in the forest woke us. Our little window trembled meekly in the driving rain. The wind muffled the shrieks of the forest, and the rushing water thundered as if possessed by demons. We imagined the mountains around us laughing. And it was as if the forests were the living dead. And from the hollows, long grasping claws snaked out, only to be crushed under rocks like worms. The mountains, and the hollows, and the living dead, and the rushing water, all descended upon the hermitage. Our proximity to the cave frightened us. We imagined it might be bottomless, full of dark and humid recesses, echoing loudly to each droplet of water.

My friend was pale and shivering, and over the little yellow candle, he recited the prayer of Saint John.

The little candle flickered, humbled by the winds. The same winds bore away the clouds and the thunder and lightning deep into the wilderness.

How long did our silence last? Neither of us dared look up at the other.

The storm cleared. We saw shining stars emerge. The night softened the mountains, which now lamented their defeat. The rushing waters raged with a savage enmity, passed down from the Ice Age.

I opened the window without saying a word. I sat on the white bed. I was exhausted, and my soul shook with the same joy and fury that spread through the darkness.

We kept vigil. My friend sighed, trembling. Then he looked through the window into the night. Up above, on a cliff along the ridge of the hermitage, a tree struck by lightning, humbly awaited the rising sun and the astonishment of the monks.

ideal de inspirație legionară

In the morning, after we sipped milk from earthenware mugs, we set out for higher ground. Together we praised the blue sky, the flowers, and the subsiding wind.

Along the path, we met a pallid young man, with a surprisingly broad forehead, and domed temples. He had come, as we had, to stay at the hermitage for a week. He was a student of Mathematics and Philosophy but, because of a chest ailment, had not sat a single exam.

We reminisced about the storm and our fear. The student had kept watch all night in the small chapel, praying. He did not hesitate to declare himself a Christian.

'My conversion took place due to rather stupid circumstances. I was suffering terribly with my chest, and I was too much of a coward to not be afraid of death. I didn't even have the courage to die. Nothing remained but the desire to live. And then I sought a cure through Christian Science. I believed in order to be cured. This all happened in Geneva, where I spent all of my money. My lungs improved month by month. The miracle, with the force of animal magnetism, brought me to the New Testament, to Catholic Theology, and now, finally, to the Orthodox Faith.'

My friend was exultant. He spoke about a simple and redeeming faith that comes from grace. He was against books, theology, and religious philosophy. He wanted a pure, absolute Christianity, faith without any connection to the dogmas of the church.

'I see an evident contradiction in your arguments', interrupted the student; 'For, the faith in the Church that you profess is far more than faith in the New Testament, which you also profess.

what is his purpose in showing us the preoccupations of people in this world of years ago?

Moreover, you must accept theology, and even philosophy, as soon as you accept the Church, based not only on the New Testament, but also on the teachings of the Church Fathers and Ecumenical Councils. If you were purely Orthodox, you could not discount philosophy and theology, even if the raw data of Christianity cannot be known, or discovered through rational processes, but only through experience.'

I foresaw an interesting discussion, albeit one that was out of place. We were climbing a rugged slope, under a clear sky. Before my friend was able to reply, perhaps in an attempt to defend himself against the protestant accusations insinuated by the student, I spoke up.

'I don't believe in God. And furthermore, I don't always think that Christianity requires faith. Christianity is an unworldly spirituality, intended to guide man's evolution toward God, by overturning worldly values and enthroning divine values. Wouldn't you agree?'

'Yes. The Christian dies and is reborn in Christ, transforming himself from man into man of God, and the polity of man into a polity of God.'

'This transfiguration happens through mystical experience, not through dogma.'

'But experience is faith.'

'No. Here is the distinction and herein arises my greatest doubt. I do not believe, and yet I have still had a religious experience that filled my soul with a Christian vision, transfigured me, and made me a Christian.'

'I think you're mistaken. What you call "religious experience" was the certainty of redemption, or the certainty of grace, or in other words, faith.'

'And yet, I still don't believe in God.'

'You confess this now, because you are ruled by reason. But you yourself said that experience is a transcendence of rational consciousness. You believed that then, when you experienced Christ. But now, faith seems absurd to you because you judge it. Actually, if you acknowledge a transfiguration of consciousness arising from the brain, then you also acknowledge faith. Transfiguration is a transcendence that can occur only through grace.'

'As for myself, I do not believe in grace', I confessed.

'It only appears to you that you do not believe. It appears to you that the vision, which you possess of man as coequal to God, is one that you acquired by yourself. But it can only have been given to you.'

'Then why was I not also given unwavering faith, like my friend's?'

'You have it, but you are afraid to acknowledge it.'

'Here you are fundamentally mistaken, but I won't dwell on it. I want to tell you about my understanding of Christianity.'

'It is Protestantism. Why do you need to have an understanding of a new Christianity? There is one alone, eternal and infinite.'

'It is a Christianity brought up to date, one that is more than just ritual and faith, one that is a guide, a criterion, a validation.'

'One that can only be personal.'

'Which is to say, heretical', interjected my friend. 'Within me exists a single living, fecund Christianity, a Christianity that creates values, and I acknowledge it as orthodox and ecumenical. There is nothing personal in it.'

'Now, you too are mistaken', said the student. 'Any authentic Christianity is also personal, by the very fact that it is at work within the viscera of a personal spirituality.'

'Gentlemen', I implored, 'theological discussions are always interesting. As a matter of fact I would recommend the study of dogmatic theology to any young man; one encounters there a spirituality so pure and well-structured that even those who will never believe, those who study philosophy or mathematics, will profit from contact with the forms and functions of a mode of thinking completely purged of the thinking to be found on lower planes, such as the historiographic or biological.'

'Then why do you interrupt?'

'Because what we set out from was *my* Christianity. I accept your accusation of Protestantism, even though I sense that through its austerity and sobriety, it is purely Orthodox. But I would rather be a Protestant and a Christian than a hypocritical son of the Church. Up till now, the only living Christianity I have been able to know is a personal one.'

'In other words, a Protestant one. Naturally, it's preferable to be a Protestant than a Buddhist or an atheist. But do you understand the consequences of such a faith? I don't need to look for examples in history: I recognise them in you; you are not Christian, precisely because you consider yourself to be a pure Christian. Your religion is pragmatism and magic.'

'You're contradicting what you yourself were saying just now.'

'I didn't comprehend the extent of your heresy.'

'But even so, let me tell you what constitutes this heretical Christianity.'

'Please be brief, so that I'll be able to keep in mind all your mistakes.'

'It is my belief that a Christian is any hero of the spirit. Any soul who lives a heroic life is a Christian soul.'

'I don't understand.'

'Then let me explain. Does the Christian transcend the human, the physiological and the social?'

'Of course.'

'Does the hero transcend it?'

'That depends: what do you mean by "hero"?'

'One who struggles with all his might to make certain spiritual values that greatly transcend the common spirituality become tangible, flourish, and spread. One who goes beyond the human. One who renounces the way others live, in order to live ascetically, like a saint, all because he has sworn to achieve those things he has set out to do.'

'In this way the Christian is also a hero; but not every hero of the spirit is a Christian.'

'I too had the same doubt, when I thought about Indian asceticism and Buddhist abnegation. They too achieve a life illumined by certain spiritual values, which go beyond the spirituality of the merely human. But my heroism validates and brings up to date the premises of Christianity.'

'Which are?'

'The primacy of the spirit, leading to transubstantiation, through Jesus.'

'But you are forgetting one essential element: grace.'

'Grace is essential for theologians.'

'Yet another mistake. Grace can be found to predominate throughout the New Testament.'

'I can't believe it.'

'You don't want to believe it; you are still under the sway of paganism. Your heroism is pagan, despite your abnegations for the sake of the primacy of the spirit.'

'A heroism built on abnegation, on self-restraint, on the exultation of a Christian ethic, cannot be pagan. But this discussion would lead us on a tangent. Thank you for helping me discover what I want to be: a hero. Now I understand you completely. I want to transcend myself, to transcend myself through experiences and suffering, to the point where I am no longer a man, but a hero. I want to achieve a vast, harsh, terrifying life; I want nobody else to reach my level, I want to surpass everyone with my accomplishments, all of which will be impenetrable in their meaning. I want to achieve a tangible, Christian heroism, not one that is to do with words, aspirations, nostalgias. This is why I am not pagan: I want heroism to spring from my flesh and blood, for them to be crucified for the sake of a madness of the spirit. I want to be mad, like Dante or Don Quixote. I want to lower the will of my ideas down into the viscera, to dwell in the world, the way others are content to dwell in the clouds. Let nobody else understand me, but let me be a hero. Let me keep the great mystery hidden, multiplying my heroism a hundredfold through my silence.'

'Beautiful', said the student, saddened. 'But you are an authentic pagan in your heroism, which you desire to attain solely through your own will. The will of man, when not assimilated by grace to divine will, is diabolical presumption.'

'But even so, if you abolish the personal will in Christianity, you go the way of Luther. Otherwise, the foundation of religious experience, in general, is the will. You're contradicting yourself again.'

'I am not abolishing the value of will, but I demand that it be illumined by faith. You believe in your own powers, in your own spirit, that of an exalted youth. But you will never accomplish a heroic act.'

'I will, because I want to.'

'Now you are speaking like a child. If God wants to redeem you, helping you by His grace, then you'll become a hero.'

'I don't believe in God. I believe only in Christ, the first and greatest hero of Christianity.'

'So much the worse. But the grace of God is large. Don't congratulate yourself after the victory; it was not you who prevailed, but God. He helped you. Otherwise you would have been vanquished.'

'But the temptations I overcome, the suffering, the tears, are they not proofs of my actual, personal will?'

'Don't you understand? It's merely a divine instrument.'

'Predestination?'

'No, grace unmitigated and infinite.'

The three of us sat on the ridge of the mountain, under a blue sky, cloaked in the wind. My friend had fallen silent.

'All of this talk is meaningless. Only one thing exists: Faith.' The student repeated emphatically.

'Faith makes you happy without heroic exertions.'

'But I don't want to be happy. I don't believe in happiness, just as I don't believe in God; even though I want to believe, the same as I want to believe in God. I'm even afraid of happiness. I can't sleep peacefully unless I'm in danger, in jeopardy, in pain, in abject boredom.'

'Why do you want to be tormented your entire life?'

'Because that way I will be able to become a hero.'

'A simple experience of faith would have brought you nearer to heroism than all the sufferings of a pagan life.'

'I don't think so. The Christian is optimistic and serene.'

'The nearer you come to a Christian solution, the more serene you will be. But you are nothing more than a simple pagan tortured by your inability to convert. I pity your sufferings. You are advocating a paganism so wrapped up in its own zeal that even

I would now be tempted, were you to ask me, 'Do you believe
in grace?' to answer, 'No!' I must confess that I doubt grace not
because of my discussion with you, but because of the experience
of your company. You are demoniacal.'

'I want to be Saint Francis.'

'One last piece of irony?'

'No. But I do want, whatever the cost, to be a hero, and therefore
holy. That is my final position. Maybe I will evolve from there. But
in the direction of going beyond heroism experientially, having
accomplished at least one heroic act. A Saint Francis without grace.'

'God help you. If I'm not in a sanatorium or six feet under, I'll
rejoice with you.'

'Although the rejoicing will be greeted with tears.'

'Behold, the eternally nostalgic pagan.'

Standing up, my friend said, 'I'll pray for him, that he may
believe.'

We went back to the hermitage. All three of us ran our hands
over the pine tree sundered by the lightning bolt. Then, my friend
retired to the cell. I sat with the student of mathematics on a tree
stump. His face lighted by a smile, he mused: 'What's really tragic
is that I don't believe either. I know what and how to believe. I don't
believe, but rather I am waiting for grace. Good night.'

I said nothing of this to my friend. When I entered the cell, he
blushed and concealed a half-written page.

'I was writing to her. I miss her.'

We stayed a week longer, reading from the Gospels and the
Apocalypse. In my backpack I had a white notebook, intended for
a story I was not able to write. Next to the notebook, Saint Francis
and Pascal.

After a week, my friend felt oppressed by the solitude. The
student had gone over the mountains into Transylvania, to a
relative's. He had given me a copy of *Gracian*, with a bleak dedication. My friend had become even more distraught and even
more obsessed with the memory of that lady. One morning, he
said goodbye to me and left. I walked with him part of the way,
through the forest. He was so happy that soon he would see her.'

When we reached the plateau, we parted. I turned back to the hermitage, while he went back down to the town. The day was clear, hot, tranquil. We remembered our climb, in the rain and the dark, one week before.

'Henceforward, each to his own path.'

Days passed, unrelenting, difficult, and unmerciful with their doubts. I dwelled in the wild solitude that I had yearned for in my library. I met nobody but the monks. Taking my white notebook, every day I set out alone, heading for the crests, the ridges, the paths that descended into chasms. I loved the wasps that gathered honey from the bushes. I loved the birds, whose voices I often seemed to fathom. I loved the rugged mountains, the forests, the leaf mould between the trees.

At night, questions tormented me. The answer was always the same, and the torment led me to believe that I was on the right path. I did not forget for an instant that I wanted to be a hero.

But the questions were relentless and biting: What should I tell Nonora? Should I shun girlfriends? Should I shun Nişka? What if I fall in love with her? Should I break off the love affair? Should I mutilate myself?

There were nights when the struggle humiliated me to the point of tears. The crisis swelled, swelled in my solitude. I felt abandoned by all, forgotten, in my death throes in the wilderness. My soul wallowed in the mire, in mute desperation, in weaknesses. Everything demanded that I return to the city, that I be among people. I would have liked to see Nişka, to beg her to be my good friend. I would have liked to talk. There was nobody around. I was lost, and Pascal seemed cold, Saint Francis incomprehensible.

Every morning I said to myself: Today I will attain the peace I came to find. I fell asleep to humiliating visions of happiness. The greatest temptation was the love and happiness of my friend. I would say to myself: My friend is happy. Why should I too not be happy? I did not believe in happiness, but I lusted after it like a fruit.

Whenever the sadness of harsh solitude overwhelmed me, I said to myself: It will pass, this will pass. I resented having to wait with such uncertainty for that moment, a moment that had to come.

Was not this tortured, hopeless wait the beginning and the defining image of my entire life?

A sunset that tinted the forest blood red calmed me in a matter of seconds. I cannot describe the tranquillity of the solitude. It was faith, and despair, and love, and a yearning for self-sacrifice, for abnegation. I tasted the bittersweet, soothing happiness of overcoming.

That evening, in front of the candle that my friend had lit but once after the storm, I opened the blank notebook and wrote on the first page:

Here I shall set down my crises and their resolutions. A notebook for the soul, in which people will be temptations, and events attitudes. I cannot reconstruct the experiences that have haunted me over the last ten days, since my friend left. But now that the crisis has passed, I feel stronger, more cheerful, more confident. I know now: the more I am overcome by sadness and anxiety, the more I should rejoice. Victory will bring a painfully serene clarity and will hone my powers.

Thus, there is no reason to avoid danger, whether sentimental or intellectual. I owe it to myself, to attain heroism, to overcome great and vast temptations. To find fulfilment on the road ahead of me, shared only by the student and by my friend, I will have to renounce happiness. I shall put into effect my abnegations once I have gone back down into the world. Abnegation does not mean living the life of a hermit. My asceticism will be purely ethical. I will only renounce a thing when it endangers my journey toward heroism. Thus, not absolute abnegation, but deliberate renunciation.

I will be friends with Nişka. But if the danger becomes too great, if I fall in love, I owe it to myself to nurture that love until it completely consumes me. And then I will renounce Nişka and any other kind of love. I mention her name, because it is by her that I am the most sorely tempted. I am honest; I am not afraid of danger.

My only concern is heroism. But no one need know it. I will live the same life as before. If certain abnegations might seem insane, then all the better. Only the fool survives mediocrity.

In important moments, let me not be sad, but serene. I accept nostalgia only in memories. But in deeds, the same steadfastness and manly confidence. The deed must be subservient to the hero. All life must give way beneath his madness.

THIRTEEN: **DEPARTURE**

I descended at peace.

The city was baking beneath a blazing sky. At noon, the deserted streets glared white. People crept close to the walls, sniffing out shade. The sun poured into the attic, yellowing the white of my books.

I left once more, this time for a village whose cottages were scattered along the seashore. There, sunrise was blinding above the watery horizon. Noon shone like a glassy dome above the naked bodies on the burning sand. Sunset bled over the clayey hills. Evening set in only with the rising of the moon from the briny wastes. And night radiated a lofty blue.

At the train station I bumped into Marcu, who was accompanied by a dark-haired young man and a young lady. I had not seen him since winter. In the midst of the hurried couples and the porters, we embraced. He introduced his new friends: the young lady, who had a complicated Jewish name, was a student of the Natural Sciences; the young man was a medical student and an anti-Semite. Marcu laughed, and I would have thought he was joking, had I not seen a silver swastika on his friend's lapel. There was no time for surprise or questioning. We still had to find seats in a compartment that was not too crowded, so that we might travel and talk in peace.

We had to settle for leaning against the windows in the corridor of a carriage. Marcu and his travel companions were headed for Constanța. He was going to stay there until September, and then to travel by sea to Marseilles. In Marseilles, his father has relatives. He would holiday there and then go to Paris for six or seven years, to attend Medical School.

He told me how he had passed his baccalaureate that summer. His failure to do so on his first attempt had made him even more determined. He sat out a year; and did not even have time to do his military service. He had begun to feel that he was discriminated against, that he had failed because of the examination board's anti-Semitism. Only then did he begin to study. For eight months, he had studied hour after hour, just like we had the year before

98

in the Foundation Library. The two of us recalled the winter and spring we had spent together, with thick books with grey bindings. I remembered so many details about time spent with my friend, who was now going away.

I asked why he had not come to see me. When I had gone to visit him, a neighbour told me he had moved without leaving a forwarding address.

'Radu told me that you had become an anti-Semite, that you had opened your house to a Christian student association, that you were working on manifestos and conspiracies.'

We laughed, and laughed.

'Naturally, Radu told you nothing of the sort. It's true that my attic was the headquarters of the club for two months. Many of the students were anti-Semites, but you know me: I've never been an anti-Semite.'

'How unfortunate', interjected the student with the swastika. 'As I've told my friend Marcu many times: any enlightened Romanian student who is not an anti-Semite is either a coward or a fool. An enlightened student has to be nationalist.'

'Absurd', smiled Marcu. 'An enlightened student must be a citizen of the future: a Communist. If we don't abolish the super-stitions of nationalism, borders, and blockheaded ethnic theories, then who will?'

'You're a Semite and a poseur. The abolition of which you speak of doesn't seem to prevent you from being a fanatical advocate of Judaism.'

'We have to leave ourselves the final law, because without the law we have nothing.'

'You exaggerate; you have too many qualities. As a matter of fact, what persuaded me to be your best friend was precisely your intense and sincere Judaism, combined with your trite and insincere Internationalism.'

'Internationalism can be achieved only through Judaism.'

'Gentlemen', I pleaded, 'this conversation makes me feel awkward. Marcu is my good friend, and besides, there is also a young lady here.'

'The young lady won't take offense, because she's my fiancée.' smiled the student with the swastika.

All three laughed at my surprise.

'Can you believe it?' asked Marcu. 'This renegade young lady.'

'I beg your pardon, but assimilated', clarified the young lady, with a laugh.

'When you become assimilated with an uncivilised nation you are a renegade.'

'The nation is still young', the medical student continued. 'And this foreign girl now finds herself in a country of her own. Two thousand years ago she would have been a slave: and now she is a wife and sometimes a mistress.'

'But now she's a slave to Christianity', I said.

'Unfortunately.'

'Don't even start', said Marcu, interrupting him. 'My friend here is an authentic Christian.'

'The gentleman can't possibly be Christian. From what he's written, I'd say he's a pagan, torn between Apollo and Dionysus.'

'Please don't forget about Jesus too.'

'If you like, but I consider you intellectually evolved enough still to retain a primitive mentality. Christianity is religiosity, which is to say, condensed polytheism, which is to say, animism, fetishism, magic, savagery.' *amusing intellectualism*

'A thousand mistakes in a single sentence', I said, in annoyance. 'First of all, monotheism was never condensed polytheism, but the exaltation of the supremacy of the sky god taken to the point where all the other gods were abolished and disappeared. A single god therefore becomes the Lord God, rather than hundreds of gods being reduced to a single synthesis, as the school of Mythology would have it. Your second mistake is so egregious that it lowers you in my estimation to the level of any other mediocre, puffed up, uncultured, impertinent medical student.' *hah!*

'Oh! What compliments!' exclaimed the young lady, in irritation.

'Because only a medical student of that ilk could possibly confuse the experience of Christianity with the origins of the religious. Don't you see the terrifying absurdity of what you are saying? If you invert the phases of evolution like this, then can't you see how I might just as well say to you: Einstein is a savage?'

'Let's hear it, let's hear it!' rejoiced Marcu.

'Because I too have the right to move back down the levels, as you have done, descending from three-dimensional to two-dimensional geometry, from the Greeks to the Egyptians, then the Chaldeans, then the lines scrawled by savages on cave walls. Given that Einstein's theories originate in three-dimensional geometry, which originates in cave painting.'

'The savages' paintings were not a science.'

'That's precisely what I am accusing you of: magic, fetishism, polytheism do not comprise authentic religiosity, but only a series of spiritual phenomena that have nothing to do with Christian experience. Your conflation of Christianity and primitivism is downright absurd. In conclusion: Christianity excludes neither science, nor philosophy, nor civilisation.'

'Perhaps you're right. In any event, you cannot be a Christian – your duty is to be an anti-Semite.'

'Idiocy. I cannot be party to a solution so long as I have not studied the question.'

'Who prevents you from studying it?'

'Anti-Semites. Do you think I can be objective when they break windows, when they beat up their Jewish classmates, when Christian colleges are barred to them, when they no longer have student canteens or halls of residence?'

'Even more reason for you to take a stance. To wait and see what happens is cowardice.'

'Well said', smiled Marcu. 'I've always admired the politics of force; it's the only kind that gets results. I'm no longer a socialist, because there were too many theories and too little courage. In Paris, I won't be organising demonstrations against Romania, but attacks against the government. For every deputy killed – I'll drink a bottle of champagne!'

'Marcu', I pleaded, 'You're goading me gratuitously. I have always avoided talking about this issue with you.'

'You don't have the courage to take a side', insinuated the student.

self-seeking is a good thing

'I have far more courage than you might suspect. I have the courage to wait. My duty is to achieve equilibrium and the enlightenment of my consciousness.'

'And let the country go to hell.'

'You are mistaken; the country won't go to hell because five students avoid the Jewish question, preferring first to discover themselves, to create their own criteria and values.'

'That's an example of disorder. If I were a dictator, I would have you shot. What does the country care about your consciousness?'

'Maybe my consciousness will, after much struggle and progress, come to reflect the soul of the country.'

'It's obvious you're a philosophy student, what with your talk of "the soul of the country".'

'And as for you, it is obvious that you're a medical student. You contradict yourself with every sentence. You've forgotten that you were defending ethnicity. What is this ethnicity of yours: blood, or skin, or soul?'

'There's no need for you to quarrel', interrupted Marcu.

'What the gentleman says is interesting; he's trying to defend the young lady. I like talking to literature students; they are naive and sentimental.'

'Sadly they've changed. They're too interested in medicine.'

'Oh! My mistake.'

'Literature students borrow the freedoms of Medicine, without borrowing the mentality and the subject matter.'

'It would be interesting to know what you mean by the freedoms of medical students', inquired Marcu.

'Fundamentally interesting', said the Medical student, sarcastically. 'But perhaps the gentleman also believes in love?'

'While your indiscretion is embarrassing, I take no offense. But neither will I be able to provide you with an answer.'

'Naturally, we wouldn't understand', laughed the girl.

'That's not what I said. But you're mixing up the sex drive or cohabitation or "*sympathie amoureuse*" with love. I won't even attempt to go into detail about the levels of authentic love.'

'Now that would be interesting', smiled the girl.

'What would be interesting for me, despite the gaffes I am quite aware I am making, is to discover the motivation for the liaison between you', I said.

All three blushed. The girl looked out of the window. The student tried to make a joke.

'Perhaps you believe we're in love?'

'I don't believe anything; I await your explanation, should you choose to confide in me, of course.'

Marcu spoke up.

'They are students of the future: they are building a conjugal life founded on the communality of interests, losses and gains.'

'It's not exactly like that', protested the young woman. 'I'm studying biology, he medicine. We're very good friends, we get on well with each other.'

'Except for one thing: she believes in neither nationalism nor internationalism.'

'I believe in Science and in you.'

I gave a start. They had said they were not in love.

'That resembled a declaration of feeling, but I'll allow it as an exception.'

After stepping out of the train carriage at a station to buy fruit, the couple found seats by the open window when they returned and sat whispering to each other. I talked to Marcu about our lycée years, about his future, about my future. He was thinking of remaining in Paris permanently. I was saddened by the thought of parting with a friend forever. To me, Marcu embodied all the most arduous, intrepid, and sombre experiences of adolescence. Marcu reminded me of ambitions, defeats, books read, and my painfully precocious growing up, throughout experiences sought after and exalted. Now, he was leaving. Who could tell whether we would see each other during the next five years, as long as Marcu was to be out of the country?

Smiling, we both gazed at the fields in the sunlight. Then we fell silent, he alone with his thoughts, and I with mine. Perhaps he was saying to himself, 'This man will soon be a stranger to me.' I felt sad. I understood Marcu less and less, he with his medical studies and anarchist books, I with my inner life. I thought him stale, simplistic, 'a pharmacist'; he saw me as mystical, historical, hallucinatory. Which one of us was right?

'Only me', I answered myself. An innate epicurean, Marcu had avoided spiritual conflicts, forays down unfamiliar paths, the courage to accept absurdities, the madness of accepting contradictions and deadly experiences. I was right, because I had suffered more. My serenity was bitter, but effective. His was false and littered with doubts that had never become intense and absolute. Marcu was a friend who was leaving. I was a young man who was still waiting, confronting himself.

I thought all this, but said nothing to him. The train sliced through the plains trailing white smoke. We glimpsed stations, people bent under the weight of summer, wells at crossroads, carts nudging the horizon. 'This is my land', I thought. Marcu gazed, and gazed. Perhaps he was moved by his departure from the country where his parents were born and fell in love, where he grew up, on a sunny street, in a city with factories. Perhaps he was thinking about lycée, his friends, the girls at the library, all the sacrifices he had made, the nostalgia you feel when the party is over, Purim nights, when the two of us roamed the streets wearing black dominos capes, and a delicately smothered romance, and the death of his grandmother Esther.'

Both of us were silent, almost until evening. Marcu smiled and started to tell me about the life he would live in Paris. Then, of the couple whispering by the window, he said: 'I think they're both insane. He says he's an anti-Semite, and she brags about her science. In fact, they love each other, but neither of them wants to abandon the lie. Perhaps, to each other, they've confessed. They're like two love-struck, sentimental teenagers.'

He gave a malicious smile.

'Will you ever fall in love?'

'I won't run from it', I admitted. 'But I won't tell you my thoughts on what comes after love.'

'Since when have you been a convert?'

'We haven't seen each other for so long.'

'Although in lycée it always seemed like you were in love. You too have fallen: mediocrity, mediocrity.'

'If the love of Dante and of Don Quixote is a fall, then I have fallen.'

'I don't understand you, and you still bore me with that literature of yours.'

'But it's not literature.'

Marcu shrugged, with a weary smile. We lapsed into silence once more, he reading the newspapers, I waiting for the night.

In the station we embraced. I was tempted to cry.

'Marcu, it's as if you were going away for good. I can barely hold back.'

'I'm flattered, but I've still got three weeks in Constanţ. If you like, come to visit.'

'No, it's better we say our goodbyes now.'

I shook hands with the couple, who regarded me cheerfully. As the horse-drawn cab pulled up, Marcu called out to me.

'Don't forget to write! I'll send you my address. Write to me about Robert, about Radu, Dinu, Fănică. Write to me about our parents and our teachers – about everybody.'

I promised. 'He'll take the whole country with him, to France, through my letters', I thought. Old friends, and classmates from lycée, and the faces of teachers thronged about me that night. And my soul was beset with the sadness of a desolate adolescence.

FOURTEEN: **END OF THE HOLIDAYS**

From the veranda of my cottage, my eyes lingered on the sea. Ever more often, I found myself looking at the sea, while the wind riffled the pages of my books. For the first few days I did not want to meet anybody, in restaurants, the park, or the casino. I suspected there were people I knew staying in that village of isolated cottages; Bibi had told me she would be there with Andrei until sometime in September. I blushed whenever I thought about bumping into Nişka. I commanded myself to read; but then again, every morning I also commanded myself to go down to the beach to search for her among the bodies stretched out in the sun. I had to confront the danger. But Nişka was not a danger. I wanted her to be my girlfriend; I was not always able to conceal from myself the bitter sadness of triumph. I told myself that a girlfriend endowed with a lofty soul would soothe the harshness of my soul.

I wandered off at twilight, alone, on the path leading along the bluffs. My host thought me a precocious misanthrope. I wished only to draw down within me the mysterious spell of the setting sun. I had long since discovered the ritual; the dying sun was my impulse, my regeneration, my whip. I returned after sunset, as the stars rose. I ate what my host provided, who was happy that I paid what she asked and did not complain. Then I would go out again, into the night. From the casino, tempting strains of music wafted among the cottages. I imagined the lights, sounds, and scents that music accompanied. Why did I stay on my own?

I was fond of a certain spot where the bluffs jutted out into the sea. The water was calm under the moon. The rocks were cold, the sky lofty. It was there that I waited for the wind. I returned home shivering, with the collar of my jacket turned up. I lit a white candle and every night read the one page I had written in my *Diary*. I saw strange visions as I fell asleep: oceans, islands, deserts, towered cities, the rising sun, the scorching heat, before and behind me. I wandered alone, breasting the wind. After a week, one evening, I went down to the beach. There were a few couples there. The wind was blowing inland from the sea. I buttoned my jacket and walked towards my bluffs. I quickened my steps, without knowing why. I crossed paths with a young man, wearing smart white trousers. I could not understand why he gave me such a suspicious, mistrustful look. I walked faster to distance myself from him. The young man hurried after me. 'Maybe he knows me', I thought. I turned around and waited for him. He walked past me, glanced at me; he was a stranger, most likely hurrying to some rendezvous.

I slowed my steps. The bluffs came into view, black against the silvery white of the water. I thought, 'There's no reason to go the bluffs, now that I'll disturb that couple.' I wanted to go back, but strode ahead.

The boy in the white trousers had come to a stop, standing half in shadow. I saw he was with a girl. My heart sank. I walked past them without looking. But my eyes rebelled and looked behind.

'Nişka!'

The blood drained from my face. It felt as though I were climbing exhausted from a sickbed; it was as if I no longer had any reason to live, as if my life were in vain, and all my decisions childish.

Nişka ran up to me, took me by the hand, talked, laughed, spoke my name, introduced me.

'Paul, this is my best friend.'

I blushed; the lie delighted and consoled me in the night.

Nişka was thrilled at this twist of fate.

'If you carry on with *The Diary of the Short-Sighted Adolescent*, please don't write about our encounter. It's hopelessly novelistic, and no one would believe you. One night, on the seashore, with a gentleman in white. Who knows what readers might think. But Bibi will be happy; we've been expecting you since July; we'd given up hope.'

I lied, claiming to have arrived the day before. I asked how much longer she would be staying.

'For as long as my fiancé wants.'

I gave a mechanical smile. Then gaining courage, I congratulated her, and chivalrously kissed her hand.

'On such a momentous occasion.'

'Are you really so glad that I'm engaged?'

'Of course I am. In a few months' time I will have won our bet.'

Nişka gave a start. Paul was bored and annoyed.

'Nişka, what bet is this?'

I was about to explain it to him, impelled to remind Nişka of her weaknesses, but I stopped.

'My friend here is a pessimist. But you'll like him.'

She laughed.

I remained silent.

'And besides, you haven't won the bet. Our engagement is set for two years time.'

Still silent, I smiled. Why had Nişka grown sad? She started to talk about Bibi, and Andrei.

'Bibi is staying with me, Andrei at a relative's. They are both completely black from the sun. You won't even recognise them. But you haven't changed.'

It annoyed Paul that she addressed me with the informal *tu*.

'What are your plans?'

'I came here to rest for two weeks. And then I'll go back, for the exams.'

'Why Paul, we're also staying for two weeks!'

'What a coincidence, *chérie*!'

What a prig! *haha !*

The three of us walked back over the cold sand, through the night. I was in such high spirits I could have burst. I had grown so vivacious it disquieted me. 'Probably because I haven't spoken with anyone for a week', I told myself.

'Monsieur Paul will hold it against me. Perhaps I interrupted him in the middle of some declaration induced by the moonlight.'

'He did make a declaration, but badly.'

I waited for retaliation.

'Can you imagine? He met me at a dance here and spread the rumour that he would shoot himself if I rejected him.'

'You exaggerate', protested Monsieur Paul.

'But anyway, now I can ask you about your personal impressions on love.'

Nişka smiled, amazed.

'My impressions?'

'She's discreet', Paul observed.

I blushed. I lied, saying that I was dead tired, and ran home, whistling. I fell asleep toward morning, having read the only page in my *Diary* five times. I added: 'Nişka is engaged to some fellow named Paul who is insipid and handsome. She doesn't love him. All the worse for Nişka. She accepted the young man's hand out of cowardice. She is just as mediocre as any other sentimental girl. Nişka will follow the exact path I predicted for her: spiritual suicide through marriage, weakness, provincialism.'

I had not told Nişka where I was staying. For a few days I gazed at the sea from my veranda and wrote. I wanted to see her again, I wanted to talk to Bibi, to ask her about Paul, but I was waiting fully to regain my composure.

By night, I wandered the fields, amid the vague shadows of the haystacks. I lay down between the wheat sheaves, gazing up at the sky of Dobrudja. Night and solitude revealed in my soul unsuspected strengths, impulses, desires. I gathered them up and stowed them away inside me: 'One day, I'll need them.'

I met Bibi one morning in the garden of a restaurant. She was waiting for Andrei. She was dark, beautiful, and happy. She told me that Nişka was upset with me. My heart gave a throb.

'But Bibi, whatever for?'

'Because you went off without asking for her address; because you told her fiancé about that absurd bet.'

'Bibi, I stand by what I say. Paul is an imbecile. And Nişka won't be happy.'

'You're talking like a schoolboy. They still have two years; that's plenty of time to get to know each other.'

'But Bibi, a bride only loses her virginity once.'

'Do you want me to get annoyed?'

'I'm just speaking openly. I don't understand what can have persuaded her.'

'He did. He pestered her with his declarations of love, his threats. Other than that, he's not a bad fellow. He'll gain his degree next year. He'll teach maths until Nişka graduates and then they'll both go to Paris.'

'A mediocrity.'

'You judge things differently, like a novelist, or a philosopher.'

'Don't tease, Bibi.'

'But it's true. You want everyone to be like you.'

'You're mistaken. I want Nişka's life to resemble Nişka. She wanted something different. Paul is a confirmation of the predictions I made on the night of Palm Sunday. As a soothsayer I'm thrilled, but as a friend.'

Then Andrei arrived: darker, stronger, more congenial. He seemed happy to see me.

'Now that we've found you, you'll dine with us.'

Paul and Nişka had gone to Constanţa, in a motorboat.

'Their first voyage together.'

'How edifying' I remarked.

'How risky', Bibi opined.

'How expensive', Andrei concluded.

Thereafter, we met every day. Nişka grew friendlier and friendlier, and I worked my way deeper and deeper into her heart. Paul would grow bored and employed brainless ruses in his attempts to avoid me. One evening, Nişka whispered in my ear:

'Tomorrow, before we go to the beach, I'll come to get you from your cottage. I don't want Paul to know.'

I accepted gratefully, with a joy in my soul that Nişka could never have suspected. She came the next morning. We walked through the fields together, talking. I had one nagging thought: 'What if I lied to Nişka, intimating that I love her?' The commandment of that thought came as a relief. Among the wheat sheaves, we walked down to the water.

'Nişka, you'll have to get used to the idea of never seeing Japan.'

'Oh, and you will see it?'

'Yes. Do you love him, Nişka?'

We both laughed, and looked at each other.

'I will only ever love a great man.'

'Then you must elevate Paul.'

But neither of us believed her fiancé would ever rise above mediocrity.

'Nişka, you contradict yourself from one month to the next. I'm not being a good friend in asking you this, but I must. Didn't you think about your dreams when you accepted Paul's proposal?'

'I don't know, I don't know. Let's not talk about it. I have two years to decide. Then again, I'm already annoyed now, what with his whining.'

'Nişka, mediocre women always do things they are then unable to undo, simply because they didn't know how to hold in check their boredom or annoyance for a day or even one second. But you?'

'I don't know, I don't know. I was so disappointed when I found out you didn't want to be my friend. I was left without any kind of support. I abruptly lost weight.'

'This is just what I was telling you about, Nişka. You are easily led – you young women lack spiritual endurance: after your first defeat, the downward spiral can no longer be arrested.'

Nişka was silent, drained. We slowly walked down the rocky path. She was thinking. Before the choppy water, we sat down to watch.

'If I listen to you too much, I'll change my mind. Everything you've wanted, I've always wanted too, but even before. If we hadn't met, I would have forgotten those things, and your predictions would have come true. But now there is no way that they will come true.'

'If your fiancé could hear you now.'

'But remember this one thing: from now on you really must be my friend.'

'Happily.'

'But before you start with the compliments, do you promise to always help me to be myself?'

'While somewhat enigmatic, I promise.'

Nişka had a strange glimmer in her eyes. She yanked the ring off her finger and tossed it into the rock pools. I gave a start, over-whelmed with joy.

'From now on you are betrothed to the sea.'

'From now on you have to let me come over twice a week to borrow books.'

I attempted a joke: 'Which means you'll have to fight against my predictions.'

Nişka cheerfully took my arm.

'I'll just tell him that I lost the ring – that it's a bad omen, and that when all is said and done, our engagement is as good as broken off and if he attempts to make a scene, I'll leave.'

At home, I wrote in my *Diary*: 'Nişka contradicts herself. She broke off her engagement; all the worse for me. Nişka wants to be saved from her mediocrity. I owe it to her to help her. But what if I am forging a weapon against myself? What if I, in creating Nişka anew, in fact create the greatest threat to my heroism? Nevertheless, I must.'

Afternoons of scorching heat scattered by the salty wind, up on the cliffs, on the path leading up the spine of a hill in Dobrudja, with Nişka. The sea grew calm toward evening, and we returned over wet, smooth sand, cooled by the stars. Over the course of those two weeks we were always together. I did not want to think about the decisions laid out in my *Diary*, about exams, about stories to be copied out and books to be read. When I returned, alone, around midnight, I would ask myself: 'Do I love her?' and I would discover that I did not. She was my friend, and I needed her friendship like I needed the friendship of my fair-haired friend. What bound me to Nişka was the passion with which I revealed her to herself. She would be lost, smothered by mediocrity, without my help, I told myself. I worked on her soul, the way I worked out a story on a blank page. I anticipated her desires; awakened them, illumined them, aroused them. I wanted the Nişka I had seen on the way back from the monastery: proud, free, restless, searching for a sense of the greatest originality, spreading distain and that indefinable virtue of inciting pride, of directing the heart and mind to overcome, and incubating powers until they burst forth as an opus. That was the Nişka I wanted. She submitted to the chisel of my thoughts and desires without hesitation. I felt as if I were beginning to possess her, that her caprices were becoming malleable, that I was whetting her appetite for the elite. You might say that the furrow of her soul ached for my will as for the sower. In secret, I watched her trans-formations, her joys, and her sorrows. I foresaw that there would be nights of crisis, when she would find herself hating the faces, the books and the memories that had thitherto been dear to her. I was happy that fate had brought me a friend with so many virtues. And I was glad that Nişka's enlightenment happened so naturally, without self-suggestion, and without the fatal affectations of other sentimental young ladies. I was not easy on her, or with myself. Day after day, I forced her to relinquish her little gods of clay, her favourite schoolgirl authors, perfumed poets and clever essayists.

One evening, up on the crest of a hill, with a thunderstorm brewing, I spoke passionately to her about Brand. I shared my love for the harsh masculine spirit of the Shepherd. I illumined to its innermost recesses his tortured Nordic soul, with a depth of appre-ciation that had eluded lesser minds. Nişka listened, invigorated by the wind, the stormy sea, the night, and my voice as it uttered stern words with frowning eyes. I asked her what she was thinking.

'Of Brand – wouldn't I freeze alongside such a stern and austere soul.'

'The male soul controls as many compassionate attributes as the female. But sober and implacable, it restrains them. Once you know that they exist in him, there is no need to be frozen by his severity, no need to be frightened by his commandments. Know that he always suffers much more than you, because he also thinks of his female companion.'

'Maybe you'll think I'm being childish, because of the approach-ing storm, but I want to be the female slave of a man like Brand. I would look upon him as a god – only such a man could I accept as my master.'

'Nişka, you'll never find a master like that.'

Why did Nişka look at me and smile, and tighten her grip on my arm?

In my *Diary*:

'Nişka is growing dangerous. She's threatening to become the woman of my dreams. For the most part I understand her motivation to be authentic. I find myself wondering: with her by my side, would there be anything I could not accomplish? I forget that my life has another purpose, something more insane, darker, more heroic. I know Nişka expects me to fall in love with her. One evening, both of us were watching the sea, when she grasped me by the arm and whispered excitedly: 'If you were to say to me now: "Let's go!" I would follow you to the ends of the earth.' Nişka's eyes were green, her eyebrows were raised, her nostrils were quivering, and she was smiling through her tears. Nişka was trembling in the evening wind. I was scared: I was tempted to kiss her, to tell her that I loved her, that I would travel with her year after year to distant shores, up great rivers. I got a grip on myself and smiled. The danger is increasing. All the better for my heroic destiny, I thought. But what if the increasing danger is simply a sign of my weakening willpower or proof that Nişka is gaining control over me?'

Bibi and Andrei had left. Paul openly hated me; he spread the rumour that I had been seduced by Nişka, that he had felt sorry for me and broken off the engagement.

He felt sorry for me? For me, who dominated his fiancée more than a lover could, shaping her as a father would, by the will of my flesh and spirit? I could not bring myself to hate Paul. I laughed when I compared the two of us in my mind: he, a mediocre mathematics professor, aspiring to a rich, beautiful wife, someone to wait for him at home on rainy nights with soup and a warm embrace; I, moulding Nişka, pushing her to accomplish her dreams, to overcome weakness, to illumine all the qualities of her choice femininity.

The three of us spent the final evening together, up on the cliffs where we had first met. Paul smoked, affecting a veiled sentimentalism. Nişka was sad, but also gay. She smiled, and said: 'These cliffs are the past for all of us.'

'Therefore they should no longer concern us.'

'Have you no love for memories?' insinuated Paul.

'I don't let them control me. It would be stupid for you to leave here upset, because we have spent two weeks here that will never return.'

'Your sensibility is of the barbarous kind', smiled Paul. 'I cultivate memories, sentiments, flowers, even if I am a student of mathematics.'

'I let them enrich me, but not undermine me. I think the real man is he who can delight in his memories but nonetheless keep them in rein.'

'That's exactly what I haven't been able to learn from you', Nişka lamented: 'Not to let myself be consumed by memories. I just don't know how to avoid them.'

'Just think that they no longer exist, that they will never return, and that their laments hinder your life and prevent other memories from accumulating in your soul.'

'Mere words', interrupted Paul.

'True, they do have the drawback of appearing to be mere words, to those unable to penetrate deeper than appearances. I believe the struggle with memories to be one of the most indispensable exercises for the heroic mind. He who is tempted by memories proves himself sensitive. But he who serenely overcomes himself, transcends the sensibility of the elite.'

'Can be a hero, can he not?'

'Naturally, a hero adapted to the sensibilities of the contemporary mind. But even more precious and rare is the hero who knows no glory.'

'Like the one you're hoping to become?'

'We all are required to become heroes. As for myself, I have made the decision and I strive.'

Nişka looked at us, impassionedly, then looked out to sea, shook her curls and pronounced:

'And succeed he will!'

I gazed up at the Evening Star so that she would not catch sight of the look in my eyes. We were silent, strangers to one another. Perhaps Nişka had understood the pain that awaited her when her lofty prediction would come true.'

The next morning, as I awaited the hour of departure, I wrote in my *Diary*: 'Nişka hopelessly contradicts herself. She elatedly predicted something that will cause her difficulty. Perhaps she doesn't quite understand: our happiness together is unattainable; one of us must perish; inner fulfilment is impossible for us together. But how can I tell her that she dreams dangerous and impossible dreams? For, I feel stronger and stronger, but also more tempted. I shall never be vanquished. I write this on 2 September, in a small room whose window opens on to the sea, leaving behind me a holiday of temptations, without any regrets.'

FIFTEEN: **MYSTERIES**

Weeks spent reading for exams, alone. I did not want to see anybody, and I did not let anybody see me. I worked in the attic, feverishly, not because of what professors would expect me to know, but because of the fields of darkness I discovered ahead of me and surrounding me. For every page I studied, I found I craved further pages, further books, further ascents. But the more I studied, the deeper I was plunged in despair. In silence, I worked on. 'They all fall defeated by the breadth of science; they all lament the impotence of the human mind when confronted with the truth scattered throughout thousands of books and realms; and they all end bewailing the bankruptcy of the encyclopaedic. I have sworn to become a hero of ethics; why not also a hero of knowledge? Why not turn myself into a masterpiece? Why not make my spiritual life the mirror of the age? I should not be daunted by the fail-ures of my forerunners; their work was passionate, disorganised, impetuous. A heroic spiritual life, not one of rhetorical exaltation, or stultifying study, but rather a life of calm, method, discipline. I have been influenced far too much by the bankruptcy of Papini's Universalism. I must shake off unbelief. Once I have achieved the asceticism of ethics, why should I not also master the asceticism of universal erudition? Of course, it is not possible to master everything; but it is possible to gather and assimilate the essence of human genius. I will require five, ten, fifty years. And then I will be able to say: I have recreated myself, through assiduous labour, toiling in obscurity; I have transcended my species, because in my soul and in my mind are gathered together all the fruits of human labour; from whose seeds will grow forests, fields of crops, gardens.'

I redoubled my efforts. I received nobody; I desired to see nobody. I woke at sunrise, and on long strips of paper I outlined everything I needed to know; day by day the strips grew more and more numerous. But I did not despair. 'Any crisis must be resolved through hard work. No obstacle can withstand the power of determined, tireless, calm work. Those who have fallen were weak. I must attain my goal. I will succeed, without praise, without glory, without special gifts. Thoughts of madness and death may frighten the mediocre. But not me!'

I discovered my gaps: mathematics, Greek, Hebrew, Slavonic, Sanskrit. I drew up a schedule for myself and, labouring in obscurity, hidden away in a city of factories, I followed it day after day. I studied geometry, Euclid's *Elements* in the Italian translation by Enriques. I experienced shivers of delight when deciphering early thinking directly from the source. I gnawed my lips because I was unable to grasp Theon of Smyrna's *Expositio rerum mathematicarum ad legendum Platonem utilium*. For two whole days and nights I pored over Plato's *Timaeus*; and then I returned to Theon after filling with notes the margins of several pages on the textbook on the history of the ancient sciences that Mieli had given me. To gain an even better understanding, I read Plutarch (*Quaestiones conviviales*, VIII, 2 and *De animae procreatione in Timaeo*) and I plunged into the first part of Gino Loria's voluminous *Le scienze esatte nell'antica Grecia*. Evenings, I interrupted my work on geometry to start learning Hebrew. I had a grammar and a dictionary. My eyes watered as they strained over the thick letters speckled with dots. The work was hard, because I laboured alone, without asking for help. 'The only way to avoid being accused of plagiarizing Giovanni Papini is to surpass him, by attaining universal knowledge. All the gentlemen who claim that knowledge is immense are wrong; it is only immense because they study it for only a few hours a day, cursorily, or because they seek the easiness of depth. But before gaining depth, knowledge must have breadth.' So I told myself and I worked. I ordained for myself countless rules, from which I did not stray: to study only the essentials, the sources; not to share my discoveries with anyone else; to publish only ideas extraneous to my experiences, until my own thinking was completely matured.

The exams came and went. My friends had become importunate; they would not leave me in peace. After Niṣka's first visit, my eyes strayed from my Hebrew text, forgetting the meaning of the characters; I confused *maqqef* with *pasek*, and I mixed up the *Segolta* with the *Telisa qetanna* accent. The simplest of verbs seemed impossible to commit to memory, particularly the *Hifil* and *Hitpael* forms. After an hour of confusion, I felt an emptiness inside my skull and then the sensation that I was a stranger. I have forgotten everything else that happened that night. In the morning I awoke with a clear head. 'It can't have been tiredness. I am incapable of being tired. The memory lapse struck me because of the strain, nearsightedness, and the characters.' I moved my hour of Hebrew to the mornings. Thitherto I had studied Sanskrit in the morning, using a textbook by Fumi. It took me several days to grasp the eight classes of consonants. I enthusiastically deciphered the *Mahabharata*: '*Asidraya Nalo nama Virasen asuto bali upapanno gunairistai.*' ('I was a powerful king, by the name of Nalo, son of Virasen.')

After day ten, I realised that I could not learn two oriental languages simultaneously, singlehandedly. I had to choose. But I did not have the courage to part with either of them. So I set aside both and began to study Persian from the book by De Martino. I spent an entire afternoon pacing up and down the attic, studying the alphabet: *elif, bey, pey, tey, sey, gim, tim, hey*. On pieces of paper I practiced writing them in their isolated, initial, medial, and final forms. My eyes strained to tell the difference between the initial and the medial *zad*. I spent an hour studying *Ghiaf*, made up of two complicated signs that were painful to memorise. That night, completely exhausted, I thumbed through the textbook and realised I still had to learn the vowels and diphthongs. The four *izafet* sent me into despair. I closed the book and wrote in my *Diary*: 'For the time being, I am abandoning my study of the oriental languages, and will make do with translated texts. This is not a defeat, but rather an experience. There are other essentials I must first assimilate. I will start Greek again.'

The next morning I woke up with heavy limbs. I gazed out at the autumn through the little window. 'If I don't get up now, when I command myself to, I'll lose all the self-confidence I've built up over the past four weeks of work and solitude.' I winced, climbed out of bed in a stupor, washed, and sat down at my table. I was dissatisfied with this act of will. 'Why am I so tired?' I stopped feeling tired. I picked up an unread book by Simmel. 'Why read Simmel instead of starting over with Ancient Greek?' I opened my Greek grammar and my vocabulary notebook. I studied; and I was dissatisfied. 'Why did I sleep for eight hours, rather than four? Why did I give up Hebrew? Why didn't I slap myself in the face when I caught myself looking out my window at the autumn?' Why do I allow myself to be dominated by the thought that I will fail, like Papini? Why do I allow myself the self-indulgent consolation of failure? And why am I wasting time thinking about all of this, now?'

With clawed fingers I pulled my hair out. I wept with fury. I pictured myself as an adolescent once more, tortured by the same struggles with autumn, nostalgia, and weakness. 'I won't have made any progress, if I am still depressed', I yelled at myself. 'Enough! Enough! I'm going mad!' And again the thought: 'A reason to sleep eight hours and not study Hebrew.' I was crying. 'Crying is stupid and enervating. It won't solve anything.' I stopped crying and rested my eyes. 'I won't accomplish anything heroic without shedding a few tears.' I soothed my eyes with the autumn outside. I regained my composure. I was sad, sad, in despair. 'This too shall pass, this too shall pass.'

I realised that I still needed to understand one element vital to my life's work, the achievement of a heroic life: how much to demand of my will. I was reminded of the discussion at the hermitage. What if God did not want to bestow his grace upon me? The thought made me even more determined. 'I will succeed without God!' And I worked day after day, night after night.

One night I felt overcome with exhaustion. My whole body was heavy and felt alien to me, and my joints ached. I was pale, I had dark rings around my eyes and inflamed eyelids. My forehead looked odd to me. I looked at my hands on my desk, and did not recognize them. I was struck with terror: 'What if I am going mad?' I grimaced: 'This thought is just a temptation to convince me to come down from the attic and sleep for eight hours.' I felt ever more acutely the confusion that was taking hold of my brain and

soul. I found myself trembling. Then, all at once, I lost all awareness of why I was in an attic full of books. 'Who am I?' I smiled. 'So
this is mental overexertion', I answered, 'I don't believe in mental
overexertion.' Whose voice said that? I did not recognize the words,
I did not understand the meaning of the word *in*. 'I must go to bed
now; all this will pass.' The thought came to me, 'To sleep before
the appointed time is to accept defeat. Fatigue and the feeling of
losing consciousness are mere temptations.' In terror, I listened to
the dialogue between the voices within me.

I was tired because I accepted the idea of being tired. I needed
to shout out: 'Tiredness doesn't exist! Shout it loud!'

I was shaking, with my arms resting on the table.

'Tiredness does not exist!'

'That's stupid; who was that shouting?'

'I was!'

'Who am I?'

'What if I have gone mad?'

'Why do you ask?'

'I'm going to bed.'

'I don't have the will! Yes I do!'

Vortices of cold pierced my ears, rushed inside my brain. I felt
the pain only for an instant; and then a feeling of utter faintness.
And I wondered, 'What does *chair* mean?'

'Pray to God.'

'God doesn't exist.'

'What if I'm the devil?'

'Stop that! I'll go mad!'

'I'm going to bed!'

'If I go to bed, it means I'm ill.'

'Maybe I have gone mad?'

'Oh God! Oh God!'

'Calm down! Calm your nerves!'

I commanded myself, but my flesh no longer served as a vehicle
for my will. I was in a state of confusion. I contemplated death, and
insanity. 'What if I *never* feel normal again? What if I stay like this
for the rest of my life?' I yanked my hair out in desperation. I began

to pray, on my knees, with my palms pressed together: 'Oh Lord! Oh Lord! Oh Lord!'

I could neither *think* nor *feel* the word *Lord*! I uttered it, but it was voided of meaning. One thought lacerated me: 'I cannot pray because I am the devil!…' I wanted to laugh: 'The devil! The devil!'

I slept fitfully, after smothering myself with a pillow. I woke at sunrise. Everything had faded away. I reread the lines in my *Diary*. I added: 'Merely a scare. Next time, more discipline required. Today I will sleep a bit longer; but I will not go downstairs. God may or may not exist. I do exist!'

SIXTEEN: THE NEWSPAPER OFFICE

My professor of logic was now also a journalist. I met him in a newspaper office filled with cigar smoke, with threadbare sofas and walls garbed in colourful posters. He flicked through my manuscript with a well-meaning eye.

'We'll publish it. Drop by tomorrow and speak with Trăznea.'

Trăznea, or Thunderer, was an opinion writer and man to be feared. A while ago he had written a few good lines about me. This encouraged me. I waited impatiently for the day to pass. Once again, I climbed the stairs to the newspaper office. On the secretary's desk, a swarthy, impulsive man, with unruly hair and gestures, was speaking. Timidly, I remained next to the door. By his manner of speaking, I realised he must be Trăznea. He recounted a quarrel he had had with a cabman. He insulted the cabman from the beginning, and every time he brought him up, he piled on a new insult. When he mentioned the cabman's horse, the horse became the object of lewd insinuations. He described the cab, the road, the rain. And he cursed them all in turn. The cabman had refused to take him. So, in the newspaper office he recounted everything he had said to the cabman. On hearing the cabman insult him, he had turned around and insulted the cabman. Naturally, the cabman had responded in kind. And a quarrel had ensued. He had ended up giving him a ride, soaked to the skin.

He winked at me. The professor introduced me.

'And you are? We've given you a job in the newspaper office. You can write whatever you like, except politics or reportage.'

I was flustered and not sure how to thank him.

'Let me give you a tip: never offer praise. Defame! In my experience I only ever get respect from the dramatists I besmirch in my reviews.'

He launched into another anecdote. And then he remembered he had not written the editorial. He broke off his anecdote to muse on what the subject should be.

'Something that will draw blood.'

He snarled, with wet lips and white teeth. The doorman brought him a letter and news that a woman wanted to see him.

'Is she beautiful?'

'No, old.'   *haha !*

'Why even bother to ask, then? Don't you realise that I'm not here for anyone until I've written my article?'

He continued with his anecdote while reading the letter. I am not sure whether he finished the letter, but he did not finish the anecdote. Hitting on a subject, he stormed off into the next room. I remained and was introduced to the others: the secretary, a tall, brown-haired man, was absorbed in reading letters from the provinces. He did not acknowledge me, would not answer questions, and did not take his eyes off the manuscripts before him. Not for one moment did his right hand, stained with blue ink, let go of his pen. He erased, added, pasted correction slips in the margins, rang for the errand boy, sent bundles of manuscripts to the printer's, ordered corrections, sent for the editor-in-chief's article, upbraided reporters, harshly pressed the editors for their articles, requested a glass of water, demanded silence, and inquired of the cashier if he would give him an advance on his fortnightly pay.

I sat on the end of a sofa, overawed by the feverish activity of the newspaper office. In the next room the typists were at work. Telephones rang, doors slammed, buzzers jangled, apprehensive strangers came in and out. I asked the professor whether joining the newspaper staff might not be risky for me.

'Journalism is fatal to people of your age, but you won't be working as a journalist, merely gaining experience writing opinion pieces; you'll learn to write succinctly, simply and to the point. This will be useful to you. If I see that it is warping your development or preventing you from studying, I'll be the first to throw you out.'

After arriving home, I spent the evening writing for the newspaper. I promised myself that I would publish articles unlike anything usually printed in newspapers. But I would avoid revealing my own inner truths. 'Some truths are for the newspapers, others are for books', I told myself.

I delivered my articles twice a week, in the evening. That was when everyone assembled in the newspaper office. The professor of logic would listen to 'Trăznea' and smoke, with a choking, hacking laugh. Both directors would come; one with an amber cigarette holder and a stack of German newspapers, the other with a monocle, a white waistcoat, and an aloof manner. One greeted people with a *'servus'*, fiddling with his fingernails and narrowing his eyes. The other had a solemn gait, shook everyone's hand, and smiled suspiciously.

A short, stout, red-headed reporter had taken a liking to me. He used to call me, 'Kiddo' and clap me on the shoulder. He knew everything that was going on in the city and knew the whole country. Whoever might be the topic, he could dish up details. He knew every plan, thought, and meeting of government members. He had read every private letter exchanged between the leaders or representatives of the opposition. He knew every intrigue from every important boudoir, every lover of the actresses at the national theatre, and every mistress of the heads of the other theatres; he knew every police chief, prefect, priest, and literary café. One morning I brought up a name completely unknown to the public, that of a colleague who had written an opinion piece yet to be printed. The reporter knew the article. And he knew whether or not its premiere that week would meet with success. He knew every train that was running late, just like a railway clerk. My admiration for him was honest, expansive, without envy. I thought how interesting it would be to study his visual and auditory memory, his associative processes.

At the newspaper office, my eye had also been caught by a stylish, seductive young man who had inaugurated a series of successful 'political investigations'. He usually arrived around lunchtime.

'Your copy?' the secretary would inquire.

'How many lines?'

'Twenty-six cursive, twenty standard, one photographic plate, two subheadings, one two-line headline.'

'What did the boss write?'

'A "review" of foreign borrowing.'

'Trăznea?'

'Taxation.'

The reporter would seat himself at a desk, cracking jokes, lighting cigarette after cigarette. The next day I would read his 'investigation', in which he would state his case, draw conclusions, hint at doubts, launch his attack, foresee the fall of the government within the month. I admired his confidence, but could not divine who informed him so promptly and accurately.

'Our people, boss! We have them in the Palace, the Patriarchate, the Parliament, the Prime Minister's Office, the Capşa Restaurant, the Ministry of the Interior, the Customs Service, the Secret Service.'

The fat, red-haired journalist often became embroiled in arguments with the author of the 'political investigations.'

'*Mon cher*, I heard it from the ministry.'

'Out of the question! Didn't you see who I arrived with in the car?'

'He led you astray.'

'I beg your pardon, but the person who informed me.'

Usually, the parliamentary reporter intervened – a thin law graduate, who was hypocritical and caustic under a guise of feigned humility, would interject: 'That man of yours, dear sir.'

The law graduate had once tried his hand at literary criticism. He had garnered success, but had made no money out of it. He had gone into journalism. For the last three years he had barely read a book. He listened to parliamentary debates and wrote daily thirty-page summaries. His hands trembled whenever he had a late-night session. It meant he would go to bed around three. He smoked a lot and coughed. He was forever suffering from a liver complaint. He spoke slowly, spitefully, and sourly praised contemporary authors. He was virtually neurasthenic. And he no longer had the courage to leave journalism.

'A newspaper is far more dangerous than you might think. At first it takes a finger, then your hand, then your torso, and finally it comes back for your head. You go from literary polemics to polemics about political doctrine. Then, you rail against Parliament. From that day hence you are a slave to journalism.'

'I'm forty years old', said a reporter who back in the day had been the director of a newspaper, 'and I suddenly realised I'd never accomplished anything. The years passed, I wrote day after day, and what did I accomplish? I pulverised myself, squandered myself, I kept putting off my law doctorate, my history degree. And now I can read nothing but newspapers. Any book that's not pornographic or a political memoir irritates me. What sort of existence is this?'

'Don't insult journalism; it's sacred', stated Trăznea. 'The journalist is born anew every morning, indefatigable, original, he lives *in medias res*, he is the heart and brains of the nation. All of our great men have been journalists – the journalist is a hero.'

'On the condition that he write for twenty-four hours a day, and not just for a year or a month', said the Logic Professor. 'Journalists need to relinquish the stupid notion of gaining immortality through writing. An article should be ephemeral; the ideal journalist is the anonymous reporter.'

'That's right!' warmly intoned the two political reporters, dipping their pens in their ink pots.

'I see you have time for idle chatter', interrupted the secretary. 'Where is your copy?'

The buzzers resumed their jangling, cigars were lit, glasses were filled with water, fresh writing pads were placed on desks.

'Kiddo', called the fat reporter, correcting his final sentence.

'The ambassador of Switzerland is coming.'

'When?'

'Unannounced.'

'At five fifteen', specified the author of the 'investigations', without lifting his eyes from the page.

'Who's going to go?'

'I've got a parliamentary debate.'

'I've got the schools board meeting and university senate.'

'I've got the study group.'

'I'll do the story; the prefect will give me a lift back', said the red-headed reporter.

I went to do my corrections on the fourth floor of the printer's. It smelled of ink, lead, alcohol, bread, and mould. The rotors of the printing press whirred under the typesetters' boards. In the vast hall swarthy children ran back and forth with manuscripts and proofs. I waited for the damp correction sheets at a table with chairs covered in cigarette burns. The smell of the fresh shiny ink filled me with delight. I left inspired, excited, with my briefcase tucked under my arm, filled with ideas, the blood coursing through my veins.

I could not understand how newspapermen and printers could ever be tired. As for myself, I found I was more inspired and hard-working than ever. My courage grew, and I worked, far from the eyes of the world, in my attic.

Radu embarked upon the autumn more in love with Viorica than ever. She did not suspect a thing and dismissed all his declarations as jokes. Radu could not be taken seriously.

I bumped into them early one evening, on the boulevard. Viorica had just finished class, and Radu was waiting for her outside the university, smoking. I wondered what he talked to her about every night, given he had only seven years of schooling. Viorica seemed happy to see me and blushed. She answered coyly and evasively when I asked about her lectures, and courses, and romances. I had the distinct impression that Viorica was eternally in love. I was touched, because I divined she was resigned to never revealing her feelings. I was not sure if it was out of determination or shyness. Viorica kept her secret with a firmness I admired. Neither Bibi, nor Nişka knew anything. But we all knew she was in love.

I rarely saw Nonora, and then only in passing. Both of us tried to act the victor. I feigned indifference, affecting an enigmatic smile. She laughed a great deal and told me about her successes at summer balls, marriage proposals at Mehadia, and the quarrel she had provoked between a certain superior officer and his wife. She spoke to in a friendly way, with hints of gentle superiority. I was reminded of spring afternoons of sexual arousal, and grew impudent. Nonora did not mind. She read my thoughts, but did not know how far I would go; perhaps she was waiting for me to invite her up to my attic once more and was preparing some diabolical revenge. When she asked me what I did with my time, I answered that I was working, for the newspaper and for the University.

'Really?'

The astonishment hinted at in her eyes and her smile humiliated me.

'What about Nişka?'

'Nişka is taking a break after her exams and besides, I see her so rarely. I told you that I'm working.'

'That's not what everybody else is saying. At least Nişka takes care to spread the rumour that you fell in love with her at the seaside.'

'I don't believe it', I smiled..

'Nişka employs a silly metaphor. She says you are a new Pygmalion and that in the end you'll fall in love with your creation.'

'Nişka is correct up to the part about *love*', I added, embarrassed by Nonora's malicious indiscretion.

On my way back home, I promised myself to write Nişka a reproachful letter. I did not write it.

One morning I met Mr Elefterescu at the newspaper office. I was surprised to find that he was not a student, but rather a proofreader on the night shift. 'The Boss' was embarrassed by my discovery. I did not understand how he had been able to sign up to the club.

'Malec signed me up, the poor chap.'

Why did I feel so sad, thinking about the parties of the previous winter, in a attic now frozen by solitude, the parties with the chairman, Nonora, and Bibi?

'And how is Mr Gabriel?'

He told me about the discontents of Malec's wife, the fights between his wife and his sister, the exams he had missed because of his job, how Gabriel had broken down in tears one night in a beerhall, in front of everyone, how his wife had left the table and not come back, how Gabriel had searched for her like a madman the whole night. In the morning, he had not wanted to go to work. His wife had returned. His mother and sister had refused to let her in. She had tried to commit suicide; they had cried and then made up.

This tale of a mediocre and tragic life depressed me at an organic level: my head ached, I felt dizzy, I lost motor control. I was stifled to the point of suffocation by the reek of slow, inexorable ruin against slum or provincial backdrops. I did not know what to say, I did not know whether I should smile or commiserate.

Even Mr Elefterescu looked changed; he was older, more bitter. It no longer amused me when he called me 'boss.' He seemed humbled, stooped, wounded. I tried to remember the festival, the bottles we had drunk, my departure with Nişka in the middle of the night. I felt as if my soul had been torn into separate strips. I did not know how to conceal the despair and sadness that overwhelmed me. The memories seemed so out of reach, so distant. And I realised I was just as mediocre as everybody else. That the struggle was futile. I gritted my teeth. I had once more lost all awareness of what I was doing there in the newspaper office, standing next to Mr Elefterescu. He looked at me closely, unable to comprehend my agitation. It was as if our conversation had taken place in a dream, and once more I heard the depressing refrain of winter past: 'Boss, boss, look at Malec!'

I clenched my fists. 'This means I need a rest. I can no longer tell dreams and reality apart', I thought. I was smiling.

'And what brings you here, Mr Elefterescu?'

Astonishment.

'Didn't I just tell you? I'm a proof-reader on the night shift.'

'Then all of that really did just happen', I thought to myself, thankfully. The shameful feeling of agony, overwrought nerves, overflowing blockage persisted. I asked for a glass of water. The professor walked past, glanced at me, and sat down at a desk. *Who taught him to write?* I wondered. Then, I found myself tempted to move closer to see how it was his forehead did not fall with a thud on the stack of blank paper. I clenched my fists. *All because of autumn and Nişka,* I thought. 'They won't leave me in peace and now I'm forced to work in this state.' I was so weary that I sank softly onto a chair.

'Boss, you look pale.'

Mr Elefterescu was now talking right next to me. I calmed down; I wasn't dreaming. I bit my li*p to keep myself from repeating, and laughing:* Malec? Malec?

'What's wrong?'

I had forgotten how to say the word 'nothing'. I was rubbing my forehead, in bewilderment. The errand boy brought me the proofs. I gave a start. 'I wrote this.' I found a verb, and doggedly repeated it in my head: *work, work* I kept saying to myself: 'I want to work!' Mr Elefterescu gave a start. It all became clear to me, I took the proofs, and asked for an ink pencil. In front of me, at the table, the professor was writing his article. I could hear doors slamming, the distant rumble of tramcars, hurried footsteps on the stairs; I could hear the secretary taking down a press report from the provinces over the telephone: 'Louder, Louder!' I did not understand a thing. *I want to understand!* I realised that the man at the table was the professor of logic. Having taken a moment to recompose myself, I understood that I was in the newspaper office. My eyes shone with joy, and scorching blood coursed through my brain.

SEVENTEEN: MY GIRLFRIEND IN AUTUMN

Nişka has changed again. She's so nostalgic that her unwonted wistfulness had been rubbing off even on me. She has forgotten my lessons on sobriety and manly optimism. She admits that she sometimes cries at a blood red sunset. She is incomprehensible. She wants to go away, right now. But she doesn't know where or know with whom. She visits me frequently in my attic. Since we first met, she has lost the ready and superficial mordancy that used to characterise her sentences and retorts. She listens more now, attentively, but mournfully. I don't *want* to understand her, because within she stirs up a nostalgia that I had muffled to a murmur. I talk to her harshly, hotly, ransacking the cosy, mignon shelves of her soul. I take diabolical joy in demolishing her values, humbling her, trampling underfoot her all too commonplace feminine sensibilities. But I don't always succeed in conjoining her soul to mine. She wavers while still half way there. Then I scorn her; and scorn doubt myself, because I have not yet been able to create the true Nişka that my soul demands.

I need Nişka's friendship. She has so many qualities; why am I not able to complete her, perfectly?

She complains that I am too hard on her, that I don't reveal my soul to her, my friend. Naturally, Nişka expects a confession. But how could she ever understand the madness of my decision? As for her, she suspects almost everything, apart from the major decision, which nobody else knows about. She intuitively reconstructs my motivations, employing the virtues of her choice femininity and based on my suggestions. But she wants me to tell her. What? She suspects that I love her. And awaits my confession. But I can't lie to Nişka.

October afternoons with my friend in the park. She loved autumn. I hated it. Autumn and spring; nostalgia and longings that manipulated me *from without* and humiliated me. I had fallen in love with winter and summer, months of freedom, when work lasted till midnight, without melancholy or violent fits of impetuosity. I was frightened by autumn, but I faced it. The more dangerous the temptations, the more resolute was I that they should come. I knew I would prevail.

'Do you know what I'm thinking about? About going away.'

'Nişka, thinking about going away is stupid and pointless. *Going away* is the only thing that should interest you. If you want to go away, then go away.'

'I'm not sure how to explain it. I want to go away, and yet I'm anxious about it, undecided. What would become of me all on my own? When would I take my degree?'

'Well then stop thinking, and start working. In my adolescence I had similar desires. They troubled me, exhausted me, wasted my time. Now, I only want to think about what I have to do. When I'm finished, I'll go away, without thinking about it beforehand, without regrets.'

'You have the will.'

'Nişka, complaining about it doesn't entitle you not to want it too.'

'I think that too much willpower mutilates you, turns you into a machine – you become a cog, you will do away with all life's temptation, all its charm. I don't understand you; you've gone too far.'

'You talk like a schoolgirl. When you overcome temptations it doesn't mean they disappear; they increase; didn't you know that? And willpower doesn't make you mechanical, it makes possible the most intense freedom. I want to help you understand this one truth; that in gaining power over an insubordinate will, you will be able to allow yourself every experience, every vice, every voluptuous feeling, every aberration. But only after you've got to know yourself, after you've unshackled the manly consciousness.'

'But I can't do that.'

'A woman cannot, it's true, but a woman must either renounce or imitate. Your nostalgia is a hybrid. If you are not able to go away on your own, then find a companion for yourself.'

'But who?'

Her green eyes became pensive.

'Find a companion and awaken his will. You have the power to influence male souls; this is a special gift. A man, by your side, will be tortured by the obsession of excelling. Your husband will be happy, unless he is of the Paul type.'

'I'm not going to take a husband.'

'Yes, I know, you told me that last spring.'

'Paul was an accident.'

Sitting on a bench in the park, we both laughed, not at Paul, but at the seriousness with which I had been discussing women. Nişka was intrigued; what right did I have to speak about them, if I do not know them? Perhaps I was a Don Juan.

'In which case I wouldn't have known them. Don Juan had nothing but sexual conquest, a puttering, uncertain light. You can only really ever know that which you decline to master. And besides, women experience things in so many countless ways. It's really not necessary to play the role of the young lover, or to exhaust yourself in the bedroom. In a consciously male soul, the female soul can be intuited through the process of introspection. When it comes to the body, conversation is irrelevant. I never talk about the female body, because my valuation is based on other criteria; I just wouldn't be understood.'

I lived a strange life; I worked at night and in the morning, determinedly, serenely, perfecting my masterpiece: *my brain*; in the evening, I met with Nişka, shaping her soul. My two lives, however, were not mutually exclusive. I realised that my friendship with Nişka did not waste my time, but rather enriched it with experience. I cultivated and loved her like a favourite book. I wanted to make of Nişka another living masterpiece. I wanted every wellspring of elite femininity to pulse within her. I understood that no matter how perfect she might become, I would not find happiness through her. I understood my task; I had to be tempted by Nişka, by her soul, as a reflection of my will, and nothing more.

I was passionate about our friendship; as she grew lighter, I grew darker. But from thence to love was still a long road.

I had forgotten the decisions set down in *The Diary*. I was following two lines of growth: that of my personality and that of Nişka's soul. I saw them both so clearly that one could say that I was just a spectator.

EIGHTEEN: **JASSY**

The chairman had reconvened the club. New members had enrolled, and a new committee had been elected. The deputy chairman attended less and less often, and when he did, he coughed, looked pale, and smiled for long moments. Bibi was now the librarian, Gaidaroff the secretary. We met in a room with lots of chairs, on an upper storey whose windows overlooked the boulevard. Nişka, Viorica and Radu were always in attendance. Radu was still in love, and Viorica was as enigmatic as ever. What I told them about Mr Elefterescu and his friend caused a sensation. The chairman regretted that the previous committee had resigned; he would have liked to conduct an inquiry into how Mr Elefterescu had been allowed to join the club.

Măriuca seemed the most satisfied of all with my discovery. She always came, accompanied by Gaidaroff. She had even stopped being shy about it, now that everybody knew they were in love. He was in a hurry to finish his law degree; he told me, one night, that Măriuca was the wife he had been dreaming of since school. He seemed glib and spiritually empty; I found him wishing for an early marriage, a warm inviting home, a loving, faithful wife, a long, decent life, with friends, a vineyard, and trips to Italy, Vienna, and Paris. I felt great love for Gaidaroff that night. I wanted him to be happy, at Măriuca's side. I then lingered on a childish thought: It would be fun to match up the most compatible couples in our club. I smiled. The 'Florenţas' had beaten me to it; they came to meetings with their fiancés; a young history professor, and a polytechnic student. Proud of their chosen partners, they held weekly *thés dansants* and invited us. There, in two rooms, with the carpets rolled up, Radu danced with Viorica, Bibi with Andrei.

At every committee meeting or gathering, the chairman recounted the circumstances in which an old man had funded the club. He had not forgotten that the club had been created for the sole purpose of receiving the endowment. In the summer, after endless red tape, it had become a *legal entity*. Since then, several unforeseen difficulties had cropped up. The Prefect, who had an old dilapidated house, hinted to the chairman that he should persuade the old man to buy it, repair it, and turn it into a student hall of residence. He was asking five million for it. The chairman was against the idea; the benefactor wanted to build a modern house, with bathrooms, radiators and electricity. The Prefect had then wielded his clout. He rescinded the club's funding from the prefecture's budget, and redirected it to teachers' aid. A complaint filed with the minister went nowhere. The old man fell ill and asked that the forms be expedited, in order to see his endowment fulfilled. He made his last will and testament, but not how the lawyers had wanted. Two nephews were threatening court action over the inheritance. The old man added a provision to his will, disinheriting them, but the nephews made it known that after he died the will would be declared null and void; the old man was to undergo physiological tests as soon as possible. The news alarmed the committee. But the chairman kept his composure. He postponed his doctoral thesis in order to take care of the club, the endowment, and the student house. The committee was no help to him. The members only convened once a month or whenever they knew there would be a dance with a gramophone. But the chairman did not despair; he searched for solutions. He wanted a tight-knit club. But the borrowed hall was too big, too cold, and uninviting. The Prefect had promised us a proper building, he had also promised firewood, but all that was forgotten after the chairman turned down the business with the house.

Since the beginning of November we had been awaiting the decision on the dates for the Congress. That year, the Student Congress was to be held in Jassy. The chairman could not attend, occupied as he was with the endowment. There was a large group going from our club: around thirty delegates. To our surprise, and Măriuca's delight, Gaidaroff was appointed head of the delegation.

Hours of waiting in the medical student association headquarters, with students from every school, to obtain our identity cards and travel documents for the congress. Our group, in the corner with the library, admired the work and perseverance of a student organisation that had built a hall of residence for nearly twenty million lei. Other groups around us vied to crack jokes with various provincial overtones.

Nişka forced me to go apart with her, and we sat on the stairs. There we talked in secret about things that could have been revealed at anytime to anyone.

'Do you know why I'm laughing? Because everybody thinks we're in love and is gossiping about us. I'm delighted by the thought that I might be spoken of unkindly. I want to know everything they're thinking.'

'Nişka, don't forget that you are a woman, and that a compromised woman is a fallen woman.'

'I deride their words and opinions. They are all imbeciles.'

'You've stolen my word.'

'I've stolen more than that: also the ability to identify, out of a hundred, authentic imbeciles and imbeciles who are the product of snobbism – they're all insufferable! I'm not sure whether I should thank you if now they all seem to me so puffed up, such perfumed ponces, mediocrities, stereotypes. They get on my nerves.'

'I feel sorry for you, because, *no matter what you do*, you'll have to put up with them, but really, imbeciles are harmless, if you know how to isolate yourself.'

'But they're so impudent, they think they're handsome, they think they're seductive, they think they're intelligent.'

'Perhaps they are.'

'That's not true. I've begun to be able to sniff out the perfect masculine type. I've never met anyone who even comes close to it; not in school, not in the salons, not on the street.'

'Surely you exaggerate, Nişka', I smiled barely concealing my joy.

'No, no! They disgust me; I don't even know how to describe them; "clowns" isn't strong enough – they don't work, they don't suffer, they don't enjoy anything. They just pose.'

'Nişka, it would be prudent to say all of this with a calmer tone; we're in a hall full of strangers.'

'I couldn't care less!'

'Nişka, you've grasped everything I've always wanted you to learn. You're even beginning to understand the ethical conception of masculinity – only one step remains. To be silent. What's the use of annoying them by telling them they are imbeciles and clowns? If you are able, then laugh. Avoid having them affect you; that's all. Do not tell them the truth you have discovered, because you are a woman, and a woman cannot fight.'

That night I wrote in my *Diary*: Nişka is making dangerous progress. Unwittingly, she judges my sex by a criterion that is no longer feminine. She has become as exi gent as a manly soul. If Nişka does not meet with some imminent disaster, succumbing to mediocrity, if she does not forget everything I have taught her, then she will suffer greatly. The men she dreams of are rare indeed, and only to be found in books.'

It was night. In the Gara de Nord, two trains waited to depart, each with additional carriages for students travelling to the congress. The platform, buffets, waiting rooms, and corridors swarmed with students. Regular passengers were jostled, scattered, crushed. No one even attempted to form an orderly queue After finding that the first train would be departing in a few minutes, students pushed their way into all the carriages, packed into compartments, jammed the corridors, and even sat on the steps. The conductor, guard and porters were alarmed.

'Students, sirs, please get off the train. There will be another train departing at nine forty.'

Reluctantly, a few students got off the train. The train departed late, to the cheers of those who remained on board.

Every student was trying to get in with acquaintances who had an entrée to the general committee. The chairmen of the county student clubs grew exasperated, besieged as they were by the inquisitive, by parents, by bashful female students. When the train carriages arrived in the station, there was another crush. But within a quarter of an hour, things calmed down.

In our third-class compartment there was no electric light. Candles were lit, having been brought by foresighted delegates. We assembled on two wooden bench seats, the whole of our 'elite'. Nişka was jubilant.

'We're on our way, we're on our way!'

'On our way to Jassy.' I took delight in teasing her enthusiasm. 'In fact, we're not on our way, we're being taken there. Doesn't the nuance trouble you in the slightest?'

That evening, nothing could annoy Nişka. She laughed, smiled, lauded, clasped my arm, kissed Bibi and Viorica.

'I really don't know what has got into me.'

She grew sad. I pretended not to notice anything.

'Maybe you're just tired.'

If only I could depict Nişka's smile here on these pages!

We left the station. The two of us sat by the window. The night sky was unexpectedly clear for late November. We felt a breeze on the tops of our heads, and we liked it. We sat in silence. I tried to put my feelings for Nişka into words. Perhaps she was hoping for a confession. But how could I tell Nişka that what I had to confess was something entirely different, something so monstrously lofty that it would have petrified her? We sat in silence. Inside the compartment the others looked at us inquisitively.

Light-headed from the breeze, Nişka dozed off, her head resting on Bibi's arm. Whenever I saw her exhausted like that, I burst with fresh, unsuspected, savage powers. It had taken me some time to understand why I was so invigorated on realising that a female companion of mine had capitulated, was bowed in defeat.

With all the compartments having degenerated into a din of banal merriment, I was reminded of Mr Elefterescu's 'games'. To me they were always insufferable; wet kisses on strange cheeks, as malevolent, jealous, lustful eyes looked on. Why did I nominate him so boldly to so many strangers? They all accepted him, with exclamation. Next to us, there were groups of enigmatic young women and brazen young men. The young women thought they came across as emancipated if they were quick with innuendo-laden replies. The young men believed themselves intelligent if they could talk copiously, quickly, loudly, without blinking when making risqué remarks, without becoming intimidated when confronted with a clever reply, without hesitating when it was time for innuendo to lower itself to action. Naturally, not all the young men or young women in our carriage fell into this category. But at night, on our way to a congress, all differences were levelled. I felt, without the slightest embarrassment, an urge to join them. I spoke loudly and freely, laughing and addressing unfamiliar girls as if we were on first name terms. I revelled in it all.

I wavered when I ought to have kissed a blond girl of average beauty, whom her companions referred to as 'the student from Vienna'.

'Come on, mister, don't keep me waiting.'

Her encouragement irritated me. Given that I had been summoned to do so, it should not have been very hard for me to kiss an unfamiliar blonde. My group applauded me. They were ecstatic at the new game and the willingness of these girls we had only just met. Nişka had woken up and was looking at me. I looked at her and went on talking as loudly as before. I did not want her to think that I was bound to her, or that I could not seek pleasures *on my own*.

The game continued. Nişka called me over to the window. I asked her if she wanted to join in the game. She said that she was tired.

'Will you let me sleep with my head in your lap?'

Of course. She pretended to sleep; and I wound her curls around my fingers, one by one. I furtively checked to see whether anyone was looking. I was met with Viorica's smile. Did she never get tired?

How long did it take Nişka to fall asleep? She woke at dawn, pale, and with heavy eyelids. I had been looking out of the window the whole time, unseeingly, uncomprehendingly.

Wet from the rain, soot-stained, Jassy greeted our eyes as we alighted from the carriage. The train station was unrecognisable, swarming with young men and young ladies with rosettes, with flags. We were borne down a passageway by throngs of exuberant delegates. In the square, we formed a wide, endless column. I looked all around, listened to the cheering. I smiled as I walked, with my suitcase in my right hand and Nişka clinging to my left arm. For years we had both nurtured a nostalgia for Jassy, falling in love with it in lycée, when we first read Moldavian literature, a city dreamed of in solitary springtides, longed for. We could feel the spirit of the city caressing us with its silences, its soulful nooks, its melancholy. And I received this strange, poisoned spirit, in the light of my will and my cold, harsh brain. With my eyes on the streets, on the sky, on Nişka, I allowed disquiet and sadness to creep in, whereas in my attic I would have torn them out with pliers. I felt the atmosphere of the city inflame me, arouse me, weigh down on me. And I did not wish to shake it off resolutely, but rather smiled, and walked arm in arm with Nişka.

The opening ceremony of the congress at the National Theatre, packed to the seams with students wearing tricolour rosettes. I did not listen to a single speech in its entirety. I could not focus my mind. The issues were unfamiliar to me, and I was unwilling to accept the speakers' conclusions without examining every join of the sources. And besides, I was thinking about how we only had three days in Jassy, the city I had dreamed of for so many years. The autumn days were beautiful, and so I walked downhill past Copou Park. And I did not know what to see or pick first: the lanes, the houses with their verandas, the bucolic scenes, the lindens ...

Our first meal, in a restaurant with our jubilant leader and all the 'elite'. I do not remember anything about it: neither Gaidaroff's jokes, nor Bibi's silences, nor the personal toasts we each made in turn, nor the postcards for the chairman and deputy chairman we had all signed in violet ink, dated 28 November. The one thing I do remember was our first visit to Copou Park, awed by the presence of the sacred linden beneath which Eminescu once wrote. Nişka was genuinely moved. We all felt changed by the experience. I understood what was happening, but allowed myself to be carried away with the rest. A single thought: all these things would pass, but I would remain, alone once more, and then I would regain control of myself, because a soul can only be its own master in solitude.

self-imposed person

I spent the night with Gaidaroff in the room where we had been quartered in the centre of town; he talked to me of Mǎriuca, and I remained silent, gazing at the embers in the fireplace. I regretted not having brought my *Diary*. I was unable to write on any other paper. Everything that I felt at the time I have now forgotten. I have forgotten, and never will I be able to remember.

We gazed upon the hills of Jassy; they were floating in a violaceous mist. We also climbed the hill to the Cetățuie quarter. We roamed the artisans' districts. Nișka wanted to look at the fresh graves and monuments in the cemetery. I accompanied her everywhere. Naturally, in the cemetery, she cried. The sun was setting; the two-day congress had ended; we would soon be returning. Among tombs, I am always prone to deep reflection. Nothing more. Why should I weep? Does the sun not rise and set every day *for me*?

There, by Nișka's side, I felt mournful. 'I permit myself too many weaknesses', I thought. And I smiled, squeezing Nișka's arm.

The ball. The members of our club were inseparable; we entered a dance hall seething with couples, having first entered the adjacent café. Nișka had changed once more. She was no longer sad, no longer pensive. She was voluble, full of laughter.

It was impossible to dance. Groups dissolved into the crowd, fragmented into couples. What did we say to each other, so caught up in each other, as we were that whole night? I would have liked to know what the members of the 'elite' thought of us. We were, without a doubt, viewed as lovers on the eve of a secret betrothal.

In the morning, Nișka gave me an envelope, on which she had written the date; within it was a strip of her ball gown, as wide as her palm.

'Last night I wore it for the last time. It was practically in tatters.'

Nișka's eyes appeared unchanged; and so did mine.

Both of us were the invited guests of a mild-mannered, fair-haired student whom Nișka had met on the train, and who was of ancient and noble stock. The student was enamoured of her. I strove to encourage their friendship; had I been successful, I would have gone even further; I wanted them to become engaged.

I said nothing of this to Nișka; but she acted as if she had divined and shared my thoughts. She laughed a lot with the fair-haired student, curiously asking him questions about Jassy, and begging him to take us to visit the offices of the venerable *Viața Românească* magazine. Maybe the young man really liked her. He had white hands, long fingers, a straight nose, red lips, and a famous family name. He was fond of her. It made me happy.

I took pleasure in the thought that their lives would be conjoined because of me. I daydreamed about the details of their new life together.

The visit to the offices of *Viaţa Românească*, among editors who looked upon us as transient visitors from a city of factories, giving meaningful smiles and winks – it was suffocating. The situation was awkward. The girls gave strained smiles, while I feigned interest in the casual conversation about traffic on Lăpuşneanu Street in which the fair-haired student was engaged with the magazine's director, a man whose haunted eyes had dark circles and a diabolical gleam, beneath eyebrows grizzled by cigarette smoke. When he bid us: 'Good night', I sighed in relief. We ran down the stairs. I expected to hear guffaws of laughter behind us.

The final hour, spent in Copou Park, with the student enamoured of Nişka. I rejoiced in having been forgotten. I understood every recess of Nişka's soul. After all, it was I who had thus endowed it, made it more expansive, more restless, more eager: try as she might, she could never tear herself from her master's watchful eye.

The student was not sure what to think. He was afraid to hold out any hope. He thought that she and I were in love, or even engaged. We laughed. I gave him a friendly pat on the shoulder.

'We're just two unusual friends. She helps me in my studies; and I'm helping her find a companion whom she might love. I am her confessor, and she is my assistant.'

Why did she not look deeper into my eyes?

They returned together, in a compartment of the Polytechnic carriage. I was left alone with Viorica, standing in the corridor. I talked to her warmly and at length. I was ebullient. I felt strong once more. And Viorica was happy.

After my return, I was unable to work on anything at all for a number of days. I wrote in my *Diary*: Jassy was far more dangerous than I am able to conceive even now. The journey not only exhausted me, but wiped out four whole days. Never before have I felt so weak. There is simply too much to say on the topic. I understand all too well now why I should be against Moldavia.

My victory was mere appearance. I am going to try to befriend Viorica as closely as I can. I shall attempt on her the experiment I carried out with Nişka; I shall give her a soul. Nişka is no longer an enigma to me. And besides, she will now be spending her time with our host from Jassy. I understand, and perhaps she understands too.

I must resume the work I began early this autumn. Everything will pass. After a few weeks of sixteen-hour days, every trace of sentimentalism will disappear. And, in its place, more calm, and more sobriety. No one needs to know that I came back from Jassy vanquished. Nor does the struggle now commencing need to be announced with fanfare. Even the plan I solemnly set down here in the *Diary* is absurd. I am no longer an adolescent. Deeds.

And with that, reminding myself that Viorica's eyes are without compare, I shall conclude.

NINETEEN: PETRE'S NEMESIS

If there was one thing I had understood about my friend since school, it was that he was an *arriviste*, he wanted to go up in the world. He rarely confessed to the ambition that gnawed away at him and troubled his sleep. But he would give himself away: he chose his friendships, sought as many new acquaintances as possible, stayed abreast of political influences, never missed an aristocratic tea party, flirted with rich young ladies, spoke at seminars, and frequented professors who might eventually be of use to him. Everyone knew that Petre wanted to go up in the world, and they all approved of his ambition. Sometimes he would be vindictive, laugh maliciously, lash out with venomous jokes. A best friend would be declared 'worthless' when Petre found himself in company that needed to be won over. In seminars, even when on the losing side of an argument with a friend, he would never concede. He never backed down in front of strangers. He employed years' worth of pedantic syllogism and his sharp intelligence to demolish arguments if his opponent faltered for a single second or stumbled over a single word in a well-stated question or sentence. No matter what happened, he always had to win.

He worked, but he wanted his work to be publicised and remunerated. He only read books that could help him as a lawyer and political figure, or the latest novels, for the sake of high-society conversation, or works on erudite subjects simplified for the layman, from which he memorised details and quotations for seminars. I do believe he was interested in history and philosophy, but he did not have the time to study them more deeply. Every afternoon he went out: to the University, to tea parties, to friends'. He had discovered an excellent method to expand his culture: he would ask friends to summarise the latest books they had read. Naturally, he absorbed very little of the essence of such books. But enough for him and everybody else, enough for him to be able to drop the books into conversation at the university or in the salons.

He learned English, paying dearly to do so, but only because he was *un homme du monde*. English literature was not discussed in salons; and he did not read English. But before the premiere of *Sfînta Ioana*, he bought himself a copy of Shaw's play, read it, and alluded to it in conversation throughout the run of performances, referring to it by its original English title, pronouncing it impeccably: *Saint Joan*.

He helped me and worked for the university magazine; it was a good means for him to win the admiration of the professors; he himself aspired to become a university professor. The magazine interested him, naturally; he understood its purpose, and the need for it. But, if we judge it like that, there were so many other good things to be done at the University. Petre may have just complimented our work, and stopped there; if he had not understood its benefits, he would not have worked with us. He was intelligent enough to appreciate an activity and to become involved only after weighing the risks and outlay of time.

We were even better friends than before. We got on well with each other and exchanged ideas. In each of our souls remained a well-guarded secret. I discerned his, and he probably suspected mine. We knew that friendship was one thing, and ambition another. Petre was blinded by his passion. Why should I be upset if in future he should see me on the street and walk straight past? I understood him so well that I liked him all the more when he confessed that there were days when he hated me, and days when he envied me. He nurtured his feelings of revenge undiminished, without forgetting even the most insignificant slight. I was incapable of taking revenge against another person. I understood vengeance as an upsurge of hatred whose purpose was to make me surpass myself, to renew my powers of work, to spur me to create. I sought vengeance by elevating myself, rather than by lashing out. Petre lashed out, venomously and with a smile. Only those who had understood what drove him noticed his vengeance. He masked his hatred with jokes, making light of it.

My friend's ambition went unconfessed for many years. His greatest humiliation came one sultry night at the beginning of the holidays. The two of us had lingered over a meal in an outdoor restaurant, drinking a good wine. Petre's eyes were troubled. We reminisced about our school years, about our enemies and our friendships, about afternoons at The Muse dramatic society. We looked back; we had both beaten straight paths, without faltering. And then, by sharing with him the purpose of my life, he betrayed his to me. I was stunned listening to him, even though I, as well as many others, had intuited the truth for years. He told me that he ground his teeth whenever he heard any of us had enjoyed some success, that he would awake with a start in the night, from dreams that slaked his thirst for fame and political power. He told me that he never had a single day's peace, that he could never put out of his mind the ambition gnawing away at him. But now, it was too late to be cured. His only salvation would be finally to go up in the world, and no longer to seek solace in dreams.

'I admire your ambition', I said. 'It's a fierce, masculine passion, of which you should never have to be ashamed and which you should never have to conceal.'

'You forget that concealment of my ambition is demanded by my ambition itself. I want to make it politically; therefore, I must act like a political man; covertly, cautiously.'

'That is the very part of it I do not like. Your ambition is limited to the political, it is the ambition of the parvenu. You need to cultivate your passion, lend it a metaphysical aspect, develop it against a backdrop of cosmic proportions and implications. As you can see, I am using big words in an attempt to suggest to you the impression I get when I talk about ambition. I would have liked you to be Promethean; but you can't even manage to be a Rastignac.'

'I have to make it. Your metaphysical nonsense would prevent me from making real, political progress.'

'If the passion is authentic, progress is irrelevant; it will never be satisfied. Ambition, like glory, goads and torments you the higher you climb. This truth is embarrassingly banal. Any satisfaction you gain will only serve to inflame redoubled desires. I believe that only by depriving yourself of something will you ever be able to possess and enjoy it.'

'A paradox. You've started to be buffeted by the winds of mysticism. It's all the rage these days.'

'It depends what you understand by mysticism. Women and feminised societies have always required a theosophical tonic. The substitutes employed by you intellectuals and social climbers have as little to do with mysticism as Abbé Moreux's three-franc scientific pamphlets.'

'Are you being ironic?'

'No, I was making a point. My mysticism is not bookish, it is not snobbish mimicry. It is an ethical experience; soon, perhaps, it will be a religious experience. Although we are the generation destined to search for God.'

'What about those who came before us?'

'They lost Him; absurdly, stupidly, without inner torment, without crises. I believe that *God was taken from them* that they might function more comfortably in their mediocrity.'

'You're engaging in polemic.'

'No. I am criticising the fact that you, a member of a generation that roots every action and value in a transcendental plane, are bringing into the present an ambition from the past.'

'I am led by my will.'

'There is much to be said about your *will*, but however you might be, I still prefer you to the others.'

'The obsessive doctrine of manliness, right? This time you are correct. I think masculine passions preordain suffering; and let me tell you again, I suffer greatly.'

That winter, Petre had met a girl who was studying architecture. The inevitable occurred. They spent all their time together. I understood, and kept my silence. One night, Petre visited me, anxious, downcast.

'Do you know what's happening to me? I'm undergoing an adolescent crisis. I like this girl, but instead of seducing her, I've fallen in love with her. It's the most inappropriate way of getting to know her. I'm stupid, irremediably stupid. I'm afraid. I love her; it's revolting, isn't it?'

'No.'

A look, deep into my eyes.

'You're talking strangely. And what's more, you're contradicting your principles.'

'My "principles" aren't against love, but rather against annihilation, and nostalgic idiocy brought on by love.'

'Don't you remember what you said to me this autumn? That youth is a dangerous time; and that no one finds salvation but the insane.'

'You exaggerate the way I put it. I merely said that youth is tempted by sentimental and intellectual mediocrity, by the illusion of comfortable happiness; and I also said that only an insane decision, one made in the face of untold opposition, has the power to save. The crisis of youth can only be transcended by means of passion, or madness. Or that is what I thought back then.'

'You were right. I feel like I'm about to fall, that I'm about to drown, unless I smother this love.'

'Why smother it?'

'Because it's stupid, because it prevents me from going up in the world; I love her so much that I've asked her to marry me. I'm going insane. It will pass, right?'

'Everything passes. I'm obsessed with this refrain. Try to implant it in your mind, in your soul, in your viscera.'

'I love her, I love her. You're the only person I've told; I had to tell you. I know it's humiliating, I know it's stupid, I can't control myself anymore. I love her like an adolescent. Do you understand how crazy I must have been when I asked her to be my wife? I wanted to run away; but I can't, I still have exams. I'm a fool, I lack the will, I'm a slave.'

Petre lamented. How could I have helped him? I offered a consoling look. I was interested, albeit not as a friend, in the stark tension between his two desires. I was not sure if ambition or love would win. I thought that if the metaphysical meaning I had told him about were dominant, then Petre's ambition would triumph, albeit accompanied by tenfold suffering.

'If he manages to remain insane to the very end, Petre will transcend the crisis of youth. He will achieve as much as the inferior essence of passion will allow. Perhaps Petre believes in happiness; if so, he will become an unfortunate husband. A young man doesn't need to believe in happiness. His aspirations would then take on a tragic and austere sobriety. But it's so painful and difficult not to believe in happiness. For the majority, happiness comes to be the given meaning of existence. All the worse for them. Happiness can only be known, validated and mastered once you have doubted it. Not pessimism, but lucidity, calm, and heroic will, which is to say, a masculine and ascetic will.'

I wrote all of this in my *Journal*, after Petre left. His crisis was not nearing its end. I had once more grown distant from my friends. Petre did not impart anything to me. He was suffering, struggling. He foresaw his defeat.

I followed my own bitter path, far from the eyes of the world. I could sense, in my soul, signs of a bloody reckoning. But I was not afraid. Day and night, I laboured, steeling myself. 'All of this will serve as preparation', I told myself. 'The act too will have to come to pass.'

TWENTY: THE CHARACTERS JUDGE THE AUTHOR

On the third day of Christmas, we all met at Fănică's, the same as we did every year. For us, this celebration was strange and necessary. In those twelve hours we spent together, we relived our lycée years. Fănică's guests were classmates, inseparable in their final years. The afternoon, evening, and night of the Feast of Saint Stephen had the strange effect of making us forget everything the intervening years had brought and think of ourselves as classmates once more, as characters from *The Diary of the Short-Sighted Adolescent*. Our group, so tightly knit before the baccalaureate, had been scattered once we went to university. We dispersed, threw in our lot with new groups. This joining together with strangers may have made old friends sad, but it could not be undone. We each felt the call to move forward, from one stranger to another, to begin new lives with them, to be happy or to suffer, to uproot ourselves yet again, and to reposition ourselves, whether higher or lower, but elsewhere.

But the Feast of Saint Stephen was reserved for the old family. We were still too young to feel sadness for all the years that had passed and were now only memories. We called each other by our high school nicknames, and, with a smile, relived painful moments. Past fear, suffering, melancholy now amused us. Far from each other's eyes, we had all matured emotionally. The thought was reassuring: with the lapse of time, sorrows and anxieties are forgotten. But what if other sorrows and other anxieties arise, more merciless, and more bitter?

The first to arrive were Jean Victor Robert and Mihail. Jean Victor had become an actor at the city's second most important theatre. He was studying literature at university, but did not pass more than two exams a year. He had found success in the theatre, because he had the white cheeks of an adolescent, was uncultured, self-confident, and good-looking. Robert still considered himself to be a misunderstood genius, just as I had hinted to him, mischievously, all those years ago. He had created a character, and

dep, name to read the 1st book

committed himself to play it in every role, whether cast for it or not. Robert was so ignorant of himself that it bordered on the absurd. He thought everyone else envied him. Considering himself misunderstood and persecuted, he had forged for himself a disdainful mien, with an aloof gaze, a snarling mouth, and theatrical voice. Robert was incapable of uttering even the most insignificant word without theatrical gestures. When he laughed, he pursed his lips, giving a bitter stage laugh. He always spoke in a warm baritone, whereas his real voice was a thin tenor. He still complained about his inability to work because of women.

'Darling, women are my downfall.'

He sighed, smugly, with his girlish powdered cheeks and fleshy lips.

'I get a new one every week. What do you expect, darling, that's the theatre. And I would like to write a drama, but I don't have the time. Look at all these keys in my pocket. And I have a *pied-à-terre* … And I have work.'

He massaged his narrow, pale forehead, creased by eyebrows lifted interrogatively. No matter how snidely his friends might treated him, Robert never failed to show up whenever he was called. His new friends – puffed-up, backbiting students from the conservatory, blasé, drunken actors – occasionally stirred in him a nostalgia for his more down to earth old friends. Although he was climbing the heights in a milieu of corrupt mediocrity where envy alone reigned, Robert could not do without his group of friends from lycée.

Mihail had developed slowly but surely. He had no flaws, anxieties, ambitions, or notable qualities. He was tall and had the face of a cold, serious child. He had always done well at school; he read the latest books and judged them using his own brain; he revised for a month before exams; naturally, he was studying law. He came across as bourgeois, quiet, mediocre. He set out to sample a little of everything. He frequented tea parties, balls, film premieres, and the races. He was rich, but did not advertise himself as a snob, or a Don Juan, nor a sporting man. He did not smoke, he did not drink; among friends he permitted himself to lose up to one thousand lei at *chemin de fer*. He was always impeccably dressed. He read three newspapers a day, and two thick journals a month, stretched out on his couch, with a bag of caramels to hand. He harboured no jealousy toward any of his friends, but judged them with keen common sense, and a surprisingly critical spirit. And he delivered his judgements to their face. Nothing flustered him. He carried, wherever he went, the boredom of a young man with no faults or ambitions. His enthusiasm might go so far as the flat statement: 'That's very good.' But no farther. He never lost his temper, and his disapproval manifested itself in the form of a clipped, restrained expletive. What he valued in life was limited to a few friends and some woman or other. He met his mistress twice a week at the *pied-à-terre* he rented with Robert. He replied disinterestedly when a lady or young miss telephoned asking to meet him again or to invite him to a dance. He preferred the company of his friends, because they never changed. They met almost every afternoon in a room with a sofa and gramophone. They would polish off boxes of bonbons, drink coffee, comment on the latest piece by Trăznea, on Robert's latest part, on the poems of our fair-haired friend, on the vices, sins, scandals, and rumours of the fashionable set. At night, they all went to the theatre together.

I did not understand Mihail. His critical spirit balanced his soul; his handsomeness, youth and wealth guaranteed him happiness, but even so, he did not work, did not have any goals, and did not yearn for any joy. If he had died in ten days or eighty years' time, he would not have been upset, everything was indifferent to him. He sought to have a good time, albeit as commodiously as possible, and not to worry or trouble himself about anything. There was something he lacked to make him a harmonious, living organism. Perhaps that thing was the abundance that lends meaning to activity and dynamic rhythm to life.

Soon the whole gang was here: Radu, Dinu, Petre, Noschuna, my friend, and a few others. They were all excited by the revelation I had shared with them: the publication of the memoir chapter about The Muse from *The Diary of the Short-Sighted Adolescent*. They protested and commented.

'You shouldn't have used our real names', said Noschuna, outraged. It was in his house that the performances of 'The Muse' had taken place.

'Why? If I haven't created a character, if I haven't transformed him through my imagination and will, and above all, if I haven't given him a significant role, but given him only two lines before his exit, then I can keep his real name.'

'It's embarrassing for him.'

'Not at all. My book is a novel and a collection of memoirs. If not even I, the main character of an autobiographical novel, am embarrassed to confess to so many adolescent indiscretions, why should secondary characters be? It's a mere chronicle, all the chapters to do with.'

'You might still have changed the names. Would it have been so hard?'

'Very hard. Changing the names would have left the author free to bend the characters to his will. That would have harmed the book, which, above all else, is sincere and, more especially, disciplined. I in fact wanted to hold up a mirror to adolescence, as far as I was able using the means at my disposal, naturally. The names were my unconscious guide. The phenomenon is difficult to grasp. The names were my method of control; they wouldn't let my imagination augment.'

'But even so, you put into my mouth a number of words I know for a fact I never said', protested Dinu. 'You therefore gave your imagination free rein.'

'You may not have said the words, but only you could have said them. By preserving the name Dinu, I had a precise picture of you in my mind, true to what you are really like. I let you speak the way you wanted. I'm not interested in whether or not you said a specific sentence, but rather in whether I captured your inner motivation; if I have succeeded, then any sentence I let you say is one that you could and even must say in a similar situation.'

That was when the real argument began. The only person on my side was my new friend.

'All this is of little importance', he said. 'The flaws of the novel, which I have read in manuscript, lie elsewhere. I won't mention them to you now, because we would digress too much. And besides, if it ever does get published, we'll have a chance to revisit them. Personally, I'm happy he applied our names so openly. In this way, readers will be mistaken about us when the book is published. Henceforth we are characters. But there are differences between characters and reality, and lots of them. The author has fallen into the trap he laid for us. He didn't modify us, but rather selected the features of our personalities that he liked. Thus, he neither created us nor faithfully depicted us. When the book is published, he will receive a number of complaints. Readers will write: I know X, because I recognised him from the details in your book, but he's not like that in real life; you're not a good observer.'

'The reader won't be able to complain', I replied, 'because everybody has the right to see a character differently. Besides, you should recall what I said about secondary characters: I give them a line or let them move some episode forward and then discard them without informing the reader what happened to them next. So, in my defence: character X does not resemble the living person you know, because I did not depict him completely.'

'This is a fundamental gap in the novel', observed Petre.

'I don't agree. First of all, to describe every single character and give his life story would be absurd in a *Diary*: it is self-evident that the notebook is not intended for publication, and that the author, a lycée student, is collecting material for a *Diary of the Short-Sighted Adolescent* which, in any event, he will never write.'

'Too complicated. The reader needs accuracy.'

'But complete accuracy is artificial, it's a construct, and gives the impression of an anatomic chart. Above all else, a novel needs to be alive. In real life, not everything is accurate. You know yourself, and to a certain degree you know the people around you, but beyond that, there are a dozen fellows whom you meet only seldom, and whose life stories you don't know and have no interest in knowing. Why should I alter this state of affairs in a novel? Why should I give a presentation of every single character, if I don't always know them, and if I'm not always interested in them?'

'Then you should avoid such secondary characters: combine the lines they would have spoken, giving them to just one character, whom you will present and retain to the end.'

'I would regard that as a major flaw in a novel, particularly one written in the form of a confession. In life, you do something alongside a friend and ten strangers. How could I dispense with those ten strangers or slight acquaintances in the novel? How could I claim that an event involving twelve people involved only two? I therefore deceive life and allow the ten obscure characters to speak and act at will. After which, I abandon them; they no longer interest me. I continue the story with the two principal characters. If they find themselves in a situation with other secondary characters, I don't avoid them; I let them play their ephemeral parts and then forget about them.'

'It's a risky process. The novel might seem bizarre, divergent, centrifugal. Finishing the last page, the reader will be dissatisfied; he will want to know what happened to all the others.'

'But if the novel is successful', said my friend, 'the reader won't possibly have such desires. Because the other characters won't interest him.'

'Let's leave this topic aside', interrupted Robert. 'There's something else I wish to ask him.' And then to me: 'What was your conception of me?'

'Close to what you are like in reality. I didn't want to spare you. You are a perfect example of the failings of your sex. Don't smile; I'm not joking, and I'm not going to argue with a celebrity. I realised a long time ago, ever since I convinced you that you were a genius, that you belong to that fortunate species of the male *manqué*, who enjoys the admiration of the masses and of women. That's why I encouraged you to become an actor. Above all, I like you, because you are my friend. I could not tolerate you on any other level: as a representative, as a type of the male poseur. What I despise in you is not you, my friend, but the meaning of the values you proclaim and propagate. A mere Robert cannot be dangerous. But he perverts others' minds, he lets them believe that this is the male. False and stupid. You belong to the happy race of the pseudo-males: second-rate actors, sentimental poets, snobs, womanisers, Don Juans. And that's why I didn't want to change you and chose to leave you exactly as you are, in the first novel and in all subsequent novels I will write.'

'Is it a series?'

'I don't know. But a certain kind of material gathered from experience can only be used for novels. Life is long, and experience without end. Not just my experiences, but also those of my friends, enemies, professors. The character of some of them will be me, and then I can choose other principal characters: Radu, Petre, Nişka, my professor of logic.'

'Even so, you don't know me, and do me a great disservice by leaving me with the name Jean Victor Robert.'

'But your name is too beautiful. And I do know you, I intuit you, and can even predict you.'

'A soul is more complex than your formulae.'

'I'm interested in complexities only if they don't give rise to crises. I have no interest in the few latent seeds of common sense, seriousness, and lucidity that lie in your soul. Which are content to atrophy year after year.'

'How do know what takes place in my soul?'

'You tell me. You reveal the weaknesses of your soul. When you tell me, with a sigh, "Women are my downfall", or when you say, "darling", it tells me everything I need to know about your inner evolution.'

'And what if there is something more than that?'

'Anything more than that is of no interest to me. We all want to become great men. It's not necessary to say of every character: this character wants to become a great man. I limit myself to showing the crises, anxieties, defeats and victories that occur in *some* of the souls with this will … when it comes to you, I'm not interested in your yearnings for something more, but in the inferior nature of your spirituality, in your thoughts, which are those of an adorable, women-coddled pseudo …'

'A real speech!'

'No, it was an explanation aimed at you and the readers of the novel. I shall write a preface expounding some of the ideas I have arrived at.'

Then the inevitable jokes and indiscretions began. Each wanted to know how I had represented him.

'I show Dinu just like he is in real life: wherever he goes he leaves no trace. Dinu is, in his own way, a precocious failure. I don't condemn him for not reading anymore, but for no longer taking any interest in the spiritual; he no longer has any *curiosity* about any enigma, problem, investigation, solution, or experience. Dinu has become as inert as Robert, but compromises the sex in a different way. He does not even possess the merit of a Don Juan. Dinu does not seduce, but lets himself be seduced. He doesn't go on the attack unless he is sure that he is liked, desired and expected. Dinu is not in the slightest a mere sexual tool. He is indifferent, cold, almost attenuated in spirit.'

'Defend yourself, defamed character!' joked the others.

Dinu smoked, smiling.

'What I can't stand about you is your arrogance, your blasé air, that of a man who has done it all, a connoisseur of every voluptuous pleasure. Yet you have the experience of barely a few years. The young ladies find you interesting and superior, because you smoke, say little, have handsome eyes, with dark bags. This is the danger: you also compromise manliness, the very notion of the complete and vast man. Frequenting the salons, you accustom the public to seeing your world-weary mask as an expression of the resigned male.'

'My dear fellow, you sound as if you know me better than I know myself.'

'Naturally, this is your saving grace: the world doesn't know you. And you're right, but not as you might like to think. The people who admire you don't know you. The others, who have an awareness of the manly, who have experience, direction, values, aspirations, also have an intuition of an authentic and living spirit. In you, nothing is spiritually authentic. The things you drivel on about in the salons you have copied from cinematic stars; you also copy their gestures; your clothes you have copied from Parisian tailors. Nothing is your own, created by you, by your will: neither your eyes, nor your money, nor your youth. Everything has been lent to you. Your spirit, were it to live a subterranean life, would betray itself: through a sparkle in your eyes, through a question, through a read book. There is none of this in you. And yet, you are no less my dear and precious friend for all that.'

Then came the repast, with wine in abundance. The conversation once more went off on different tangents. We had held these gatherings every Christmas since our fifth year at lycée, when we gathered for the first time. We celebrated until dawn.

TWENTY-ONE: **DEATH**

At the meeting in March, the chairman announced that the donation was in danger because of the prefect, who was hell bent on having his house be purchased for the student centre. The old man was worried. The chairman was tired, sick of it all, depressed. He had been ill for several months now. The former deputy chairman had been bedridden with consumption since autumn. He was waiting for Easter, so that he could go up into the mountains. The deputy chairman of the original committee was the only one who could be of assistance in the mater of the donation.

A few days later, we read in the newspaper: the deputy chairman had died.

A warm afternoon, achingly warm. The lilacs around the yard had come into leaf. The black banners cast their pall. We gathered around the chairman, who was pale, agitated, and suppressed his trembling with difficulty. All of us wore sad smiles and were tempted to look up at the sky. The sky was near, blue, streaked with nostalgic little clouds. From the lilac bushes came a hive-like drone. The street was long, cobbled, the pavements scorching. Somewhere out of sight I could detect acacias in bloom and gardens with flowerbeds and freshly turned furrows of black earth. The hum of the city, with its parks, factories and boulevards reached the yard of our dead comrade. And a gentle breeze carried the scent of a desolate spring.

I saw him borne on shoulders, amid weeping. I saw too the wreath from the club, with a white ribbon, with a sad inscription like a summons. My friend held my right arm, Nişka my left. Both trembled.

On the way there, my friend had told me about his parting with his lady. He had tears in his eyes and a broken heart. He cried in the street, clutching a white handkerchief.

'Only God can save me. Only God can save me.'

How could I console him? I kept silent.

In the courtyard, with sad friends, I caught sight of Nişka's frightened eyes. I gave a start. Nişka came up to me and for the whole time thereafter held her arm tightly in mine. How could I have soothed Nişka's pain, when I felt it myself?

My friend took my arm again. Again he mumbled, holding his handkerchief to his mouth: 'Only God can save me. Only God can save me.'

Nişka was worried.

'Why is he crying?'

'He's thinking about his sister, his little sister.'

'Is she dead?'

The streets narrowed. The procession walked single file. In the front yards of the houses, poplars towered. At the windows I imagined curious eyes, saddened by the young age of our deceased friend.

'Is it true you're leaving for Italy?'

'Yes, Nişka; in four days.'

'For how long?'

'Till the middle of May.'

'Take me with you!'

Why did Nişka's plea cause me to shudder? Our fellow mourners looked at us in surprise. My friend was now listening.

'It's not possible, Nişka', I whispered. 'I'm not going on my own.'

She remained silent until we reached the cemetery. Nişka's silences were never reflective, but bouts of mute desperation. She never tried to rise above them. I spoke to her.

'Nişka, you swore to me you would never let yourself be vanquished. But in the face of an insurmountable obstacle you declare yourself crushed.'

She made no reply.

My friend had let go of my arm.

'I'm going away too.'

'Why are you telling me? Just do it!'

'Won't you be sad at our parting?'

'No. Even here, we are apart. And your monologue, the only thing that really interests me, you can share with me more warmly and at greater length in writing.'

'I'm going to suffer so much far away. You know very well what I will lack once I go away.'

I was tempted to think about the first choir meeting in my attic, about the deputy chairman, now dead: the memories did not make me sad; they weighed down on me, they exhausted me physically. I drove them away. A new spring, departures, work, sadness, a clear sky … I have no reason to be sad. I am warmed by the sun, the mountains await me, the railroad tracks are fresh and without end. Why should I be sad? I'm twenty years old, I have a fierce will, my neck is unbowed, I have a steely body, I have desires, and I have chains for my desires. A friend and companion of mine has died. Henceforth he is alien to us; maybe he is happy or maybe he is not. I do not know. My dead friend will live on within my soul. So why should I be sad now, in front of everyone? My sadness will take hold of me once I am alone, as is fitting for a soul that treasures death. But then again, death intrudes upon me now, when I cannot fight. I will meditate on death when I am alone; understand it, worship it. But here, at Nişka's side, should I seem sad? Should *I* be like all the others, I who have endured and gritted my teeth when despair overwhelmed my spirit and wracked my flesh?

I thought about it, and drove away my sadness. To my right, my friend was weeping over a woman. My left arm carried the weight of Nişka's disturbance.

'Nişka, you're shaking.'

'No.'

'Did you come on your own?'

'Bibi is ill.'

'What about Viorica?'

Nişka's face darkened, in disgust.

'I don't know. She's not my friend anymore. We haven't spoken since winter.'

I refused to believe it. Naturally, Nişka had offended her.

'You don't know how bad Viorica is.'

'It's stupid to be angry at a friend, Nişka.'

We walked on, a procession of the deceased's classmates and friends. The streets widened; chestnut trees began to cast shade; the sky shook off its clouds.

'Let's not talk until the cemetery.'

'You cannot lack anything in your memories. But why should you preserve the memories?'

'Because I love her!'

Nişka gave a start. She leaned toward me.

'Why did you lie to me?'

I looked straight ahead, above the others' heads, at the wreaths that accompanied our dead friend on his journey.

Twilight in the cemetery, a summons for spring. The chairman could not stand and had to be supported. Before the black outline of the grave, his fever took hold and overpowered him. The ropes lowered his friend into the ground, amid tears and cast clods. In the sunset, a handful of clouds were still fringed blood red. Along the central path, the trees grew restless in the evening wind. The gravediggers waited for their pay. Candles flickered on other graves. I glimpsed large, expensive bouquets of flowers. Winter had left a bench with two crooked legs. The gardener picked up his coat from the plinth of a tombstone of red marble.

'Do you remember the cemetery in Jassy?'

It was Nişka who spoke. But she had changed. She was nostalgic and tranquil now. She walked with her eyes on the cypresses, on the sky, waiting for the stars.

I asked her then about her friend from Jassy, with whom she had returned from the congress, with whom she had spent so many winter afternoons.

'Everyone says we're in love with each other.' She smiled at me. I masked my joy by asking, 'How so?'

On the night of my departure I heard bits of gravel hitting the attic window. In the street, Nişka peered upward with her head thrown back.

'I saw the light on. And I came to bid you farewell!'

'Thank you, Nişka.'

'You won't forget me, will you? And you'll write to me, won't you? And you'll write to me often and ...'

'Say it, Nişka.'

'Say what? If you still want me and ... good night.'

That April night, in my personal *Diary*, rather than my *Travel Journal*, I wrote:

Today, on a street with some obscure name, I saw the face of a girl. I ran, I looked for her, I saw her again. I returned to the hotel. And now here I am, writing this. I'm in love with the girl, I am in love. I can no longer defend the ramparts of my soul. I'm in love with an unknown girl. I have gazed on her face for so long in my memory that now it has started to fade. I wanted to study her every feature. I was unsettled. And now I can't precisely remember the face of the girl. But I'm in love, I'm in love.

Maybe I am insane. On my way back to the hotel, I railed against myself and my decisions. I read the first page of my *Diary*. I know that I'm not insane. But I've lost the face of the girl; I'm in love with the girl. I tell myself: I am disturbed, on the verge of insanity. But I know that all resistance is futile. I'm in love with the girl. Is it shameful? Yes, yes, It's humiliating to be in love, it's ridiculous, it's offensive. I'm suffocating. I don't believe there is any truth in what I have written. Maybe I'm just tired from the journey, or because of Rome. Rome smashed me to pieces and put me back together again. But what if I am no longer myself? I'll look for myself tomorrow in the city. Everything I now write is lies. It's only been a few hours and I'm still in love with the girl. But tomorrow, or in a year, or in ten years? I will have to remain silent for ten years. Why did I write in my *Diary*? I didn't even manage to calm myself.

How might I meet that girl? I preserve her image behind my closed eyelids. Returning to the *Corso*, alone, I was struck by somebody who looked like Nişka. I experienced the same turmoil as yesterday. But now I know: the girl resembles Nişka, she has the same eyes and hair.

'How serenely I write humiliating confessions. From time to time I leaf through the *Diary* and reread my decisions. I am fulfilling them with difficultly. I suffer, this I can feel, I suffer stupidly.

My soul is torn apart with grief and then lifted up with joy. When I remember the face of the girl, I am afflicted with a strange and dreadful feeling; I feel gripped by a strange arm. I am embarrassed to give it a name: is it love?

'My decisions flood me with desperate, never-ending sadness. I always say to myself: all things pass. But such encouragement seems foolish to me. I wonder how I could have made use of it for so long without observing its vacuity. But what if it only seems vacuous because the temptation is more powerful than I am? That's why I always say it to myself. It will pass. The sadness of my solitude at the hermitage passed, so too the nostalgias and temptations of autumn. Everything has to pass. But this temptation is powerful, new, agile.

But why did I write about temptation last night? I forgot my decision: love should be controlled rather than driven away. I can't control it; that's why it humiliates me. Love is to blame. It caresses me, like a strange claw. I love her, I love her. Who knows what's wrong with me?

I don't understand why I was afraid. Wasn't I looking for love? Didn't I want to know it and to enslave it? This is love. I *know* that this is love. Now, I have to deepen it, and master it.

It's not humiliating. I am in love with her. The words are stupid. How can I recite the words that I've learned from others? That's why I'm not in love. It is not love that has thrown my soul into turmoil. I am not in love with her. I am in love with her.'

Capri Island. 'I'm in love with Nişka!

Night, in the train, bound for Ancona: Nişka, Nişka, Nişka.

On the boat, bound for Fiume: 'Why did I suppress it for two years? I have been in love with Nişka since the night we walked back from the monastery. I was even more in love with her at the seaside, on the train, in Jassy. I'm having a difficult time understanding anything. Why try to understand? The Adriatic is blue and my soul is serene. Maybe my anxieties will disappear. Why shouldn't I be in love with Nişka?

How should I put this? I understand and I feel differently. But I won't change any of my decisions.

I'll maintain my tragic sense of existence. I remember that I want to be a hero. What act is more heroic than self-denial? But self-denial that will be neither an extirpation, nor a victory wracked with remorse, I'll let myself be in love with Nişka. Henceforth I shall not be afraid, I shall say to myself, in my solitude: I'm in love with Nişka. I'll conceal it from others. I'll stick to my path, come what may. Love must endure, and I feel that it will endure in my soul.

Anyone in love will swear their faith in love. What everybody else does in the throes of madness, I too shall do.

That's not true. My madness is not love, but heroism. And I'm not just anybody. This I can write with my head held high. My life was not handed to me; I have constructed it myself, with all its discontents, books read, rebellions. What I endured this autumn, not one of my contemporaries has endured. I fought against sleep, exhaustion, the desires of my young body, the temptation of light reading, madness.

I conquered madness, because I willed it; and I didn't retreat in the face of it.

When I say: I will preserve this love year after year, concealed and undefiled, I must believe in it. Because I am the one who said it, the only one in whom I trust.

A curious observation: whenever I think or write the word *will*, I forget everything else, including Nişka. Nişka's love is far from me now. I should close my book and look out upon the Adriatic: behold, that's what I am doing.

Will they notice the change when I return to Romania? I feel so different. Many of my thoughts have now become feelings. Intuitions have turned into experiences. I am not sure what part of me has changed. I feel a renewal; I feel more alive; I feel more certain that this is my flesh, and that this is my soul. I cannot explain anything. I feel it!

What if the change is noticeable? How will I meet with Nişka? I won't need to say anything to her. She won't be able to understand my abnegation. She would accept me, as her companion, if not husband; of that I am sure. Nişka's soul belongs to me: I divined her desires, hopes, intentions. Even so, she doesn't need to know how much I love her. I want us to remain friends. I will suffer all the more seeing how another man possesses her, there, close to me.

I am a madman, and I struggle in vain. Nişka will deny herself, just as I have denied myself. If not, she will be lost. This is easily understood. She will be lost, no matter how prolonged her agony. But Nişka will renounce choosing any other husband.

All of these predictions are pointless. I'm in love with Nişka! This is the single new reality, next to the old reality: me. Everything else is hypotheses and games. I should not be wasting my time.

They all said to me: 'You are suffering from a nostalgia for the West, because of Italy.' No one understood; not even Nişka, whom I saw rarely, under the pretext I was revising for exams. She asked me to tell her all about my trip; how could I tell her that I went to Rome, thence to Naples, and thence to Fiume via Ancona?

I followed my course with painful steps. Everything I was trying to forget grew gigantic, deafening, vivid, and barbaric in my memory. Solitude tormented me, but was still my salvation, the means to achieve my great idea.

Summer spent wandering, without forgetting, without weeping. I returned from time to time to the city under lamplight; carrying thick black notebooks. And I would leave, with a notebook and a book. I wandered the mountains, spending little, sleeping in sheepfolds, enduring cold rains. I had begun to be accustomed to my disturbance, my disquietude. I believed that my soul would suffer eternally, discontented with what I was doing. I carried the burden of my solitude along footpaths, to monasteries, to the towns on the Danube.

And I went to the hermitage. 'Why should I weep?' I said to myself revisiting my cell. And I did not weep.

At the hermitage, the solitude brought me tranquillity. But it was merely a crisis, which greatly disturbed me. I did not despair, my breast eaten away by unconfessed longing. Concentrating on the pain, rather than on love, I reminded myself: all this must pass.'

TWENTY-THREE: **MEDITATION ON TWO AUTUMNS**

The first autumn had begun with longing under the wet chestnut trees along the boulevard. The next, with the ambitions and anxieties of exhausting work, bitter in its spasm, stubborn to the point of madness. Now, serenity has descended again. But I am afraid. I glimpse storm clouds lurking in my soul. All that I have accomplished so far, the slow and painful approach of that being I like to call the hero, might be destroyed. It is of this that I am afraid; my sufferings demand to bear fruit.

Now, autumn torments me even worse, and more deeply. No one can know. Nişka accompanies me whenever I roam far from the city. The fields are growing sere; the forests are turning red. Nişka considers me the best friend a girl could ever have. She has begun to believe that any hope of *something more* is in vain. This thought has greatly saddened her. But I am closer than ever to her soul, and her soul is sprouting from the seeds of my spirit.

Besides an austere life, begun each morning with the same rigour, and completed after midnight with the determination of one who knows that rest will only truly come with death, I have lived a life known to others. I have published what is the least vivid, original and precious among all my writings. The rest have been strange, agonising, enigmatic confessions. Who would have been willing to print them?

Sensing the approach of heroism, I observed myself with irritatingly demanding care. Nişka kept the same place; my onerous reading continued with the same strictness; cultural gaps were filled by the same method. I kept watch over myself ethically, scientifically, and emotionally. I dwelled in constant brain fever. I wanted to be more than a man. All that I endured, the experiences of the past few years, the unforgiving solitude, the mystery, had hardened my face. My bones had started to align differently. My eyes had changed. The lines, the furrow of my brow, my forehead, all wore a mask. No one could see behind the mask. I had condemned myself, by the mystery that was tearing me apart, to an austere solitude, without end.

I was waiting for a decisive act. Abnegation had been fulfilled. But I was waiting for one more temptation, to confirm it. Only in supreme suffering, would the heroic soul reveal itself. The act might happen randomly or with Nişka's agreement. But if it did not happen within the next year, before I left, I would be victorious.

The things I am writing about are still so fresh in my mind. If I were to continue, I would not be writing a story, but a *diary*.

Behold, this is who I am now: a man waiting to make the final leap. Outside, in the fields, and on the streets, it is autumn. Here, in the attic, am *I*. I care little about the autumn outside so long as I am not yet complete. All my anxieties hitherto have lent me a fear of waiting. I wait in a delirious state. And I am not sure what I am waiting for, just as I was not sure of it two autumns ago.

The title of this chapter is wrong. I shall not be writing a single meditation. This page marks the end of the story of two years of experiences, of longings, and of victories over my weaknesses. I do not know how it will end. Which is to say, I do not know the details; because victory will have to be on my side. The final victory is the only thing that lends meaning and value to certain resolutions. But until such time, I am cursed by the anxiety and the waiting that wash over me day and night.

After the rain, the sky is a stormy blue. The little windows are still beaded with droplets. Soon, I will turn on my lamp. The noise from the street rises to my attic. From my table I see two ragged poplars, far away, in an unknown courtyard. Poplars that have witnessed my adolescence.

I shall not succumb to rhetorical exaltation; I shall not pen encomia to autumn or hint at nostalgias. There is already sadness in me as it is. But perhaps it is the sadness of one who understands.

With tranquil mien, with clenched fists, among books, I wait.

PART TWO

LETTER ONE

My friend, why won't you let me see you? Why do you run from me?

I don't know how to write; I've suffered greatly, and I suffer again now that I can't say anything to you. You are hiding something from me. If you leave me alone much longer, I shall fall in love with my memories of us and start to cry. You can't even imagine all that I went through with that mediocre, happy family with whom I stayed over the holidays. They all fell in love with me: mother, daughter, son, nephew. Who knows what they're scheming now? All I wanted to do was to laugh, be happy, and thank them. Why didn't we meet? Maybe then I wouldn't have cried so much. Not even I could understand why I was crying. Maybe out of frustration another year is ending. I don't know. I don't know. The only thing I do know is that I thought about you a lot, and about our time together in Jassy. But you were insufferable, because I thought about you too much, and I spoke about you, and I borrowed your thoughts and your words. Do you know that without even realizing it, I'm trying to write like you?

I don't understand why you've locked yourself in your house and won't allow your friends to see you. Radu doesn't understand either. I'm waiting for you to write me. I basically lead a solitary life. The family that held me prisoner, over the holidays, have been thrown off my tracks. I stayed with Bibi for a week. And do you know what we did rather than revise for our degrees? We talked about you. You're sickening; but no more than that. Because your competition was a fat volume of Romanian texts from the sixteenth century and the *Histoire de la Langue*. Don't be too flattered by your victory.

Are you working on anything? Maybe my visits wouldn't have been so frequent or long. I wouldn't have made you waste so much of your time. I wanted to see you, to tell you what I suspected about the intentions of the family that fell in love with me. We could have sat together, in your warm attic. It would have been so lovely. Have you forgotten about the night of Christmas Eve, about the baklava that was so sweet, about the wine that was so old, about your friend who was so very, very happy? Should I remind you about it some more?

Let me give you a single deadline: five days. You must write to me, and inform me of the day and hour when you'll receive me. Bibi might come too. It will be an atrocious entrance; caution.

Until then, greetings from Nişka.

P.S. Don't interpret this letter as some kind of declaration.

LETTER TWO

Nişka, would you like me to write you a sincere letter this time? Or do you prefer the lively 'literary' letters of this summer?

I did not want to see you, because experiences, long intimated and encouraged, threatened to upset my decisions. You probably won't understand any of this; until the night of Christmas Eve, I was able to control and restrain myself without any doubt of victory. But then a crisis arose; it endangered the fruits I have been waiting for, and slowed my steps on a path that will lead me far from here. You cannot even imagine the fruits of my heroism, and you do not know the path. No one knows it, Nişka, that is why I won't reveal it even to you. The power of the spell increases tenfold in silence.

I know you will deplore the obscurity, the metaphorical excesses, and unfriendly tone of this letter. But Nişka, I am your best friend, because I am much more to you. If I've stayed away from you for so long, I have done so in order to prepare myself for a great deed. And you love great deeds. Therefore you cannot upbraid me for it. Believe me, I have also felt your absence, albeit without the tears. But I've overcome it. Is it not right that I stay true to myself? Tell me, Nişka.

It is unjust that you remind me about the night of Christmas Eve. I have not forgotten a thing. Neither your arrival at dusk, with icy cheeks; nor my scouring bookshops to buy you presents; nor the way they looked at us inside that warm confectionary shop, thinking we were engaged, because you laughed too much and I bought you too many cakes; nor tea in the attic, followed by a bottle of old wine. You came at five, and left the next day – to me those moments meant *too much*. Do you remember, after midnight, when you were nodding off with a smile on your face, and I was talking to you about Søren Kierkegaard? You told me that you were happy but troubled. Nişka, you did not act like a friend; you let me believe many, many things.

And Radu came at around two, and we laughed awkwardly when he hinted at our supposedly having got engaged in secret. Do you understand why we laughed so much? And then the visit to the club, the room with couples, new and happy; the ailing chairman, the new committee, the girls in their first year, whom we had not met, the boys in their first year, who looked at us impertinently. How many of us had remained from the old club? The 'Florenţas' were married, Nonora had joined the medical students' society, Gaidaroff, Viorica, Măriuca, Bibi ... We were the only ones left, and another three mediocre law students. Your heart sank, and mine too, Nişka. But what if that is the way things are meant to be? They were all happy. And so were we, and so we are when we meet; but not with them. It would be stupid for us to be sad and shed tears over the past. We cannot forever be in our first year.

It is just as stupid of me nostalgically to philosophize rather than try to write you a beautiful letter. I should recount to you, just between the two of us, our walk home, near sunrise, happy we were alone again. (Did it remind you of our walk back from the monastery, down the same cold boulevards?). In the attic there was warmth, plenty of wine, and cakes. I expected we would stay up talking until morning. But that was not what happened. You fell asleep with your cheek resting on your hand, the way I used to as a child. Your short curls lent the pillow enchantment. Why don't you ask me how I have slept on the same pillow, in the same pyjamas, during all the nights since then? You slept, with your hands held in mine, you on the bed, I in the armchair.

It was authentic, pure and raw; exactly how I like friendship to be. But that morning, something happened that terrified me. If I told you that our unexpected kiss just before parting, spontaneously erupting, achingly long, has been the cause of my confinement, would you understand? We kissed, Nişka: not like two friends; not capriciously, sensuously, or temporarily. We kissed.

Forgive me, Nişka, if I'm making you blush. I write that you might understand my solitude and see what I am going through. I too have suffered, Nişka, greatly, I have suffered with flaming eyes, with clenched fists, with tensed shoulders as I sat at my desk. Everything will have to regain its old equilibrium. I have so much to write, so many books to read, and so many visions to forget.

The crisis has not yet passed. My good friend, please do not be upset if, for now, I preserve my solitude. You do want me to be great, don't you?

As you know, I receive nobody. I will gladly read everything you might write me. I am waiting. However, if you suffer nostalgias that are too depressing, tell me. I will visit you. Before I can find peace, I must ensure the peace of my friend. Your tears are childish and embarrassing. Why did you not take action against the family that held you prisoner? But then again, why cry, when you are still so young?

LETTER THREE

Friend, your letter hurt me. In it you explain nothing. Don't you know that it's hard for me to understand without you? Why won't you let me come? I think you wrote me to taunt me or mock me. I suffer a lot, alone. Before, I used to ask you for advice. But now, whom am I to ask? You lied when you said you are my friend. Unwittingly, you did me the greatest wrong: you drew me close to you, your thoughts, your values, and then you left me all alone.

And now I can't go back. I can't be who I was two years ago. And I'm so sad, and I weep, remembering things from the time when we were good friends.

Naturally, all of this will pass. Why don't you want to help me? You owe a debt to your friendship for

Nişka.

LETTER FOUR

Nişka, I have to be alone, no matter how upset it may make you. Because this is my will, which I obey, always. Do not pretend you do not understand. There are many things you suspect and even guess correctly. Do not wait for me to reveal my thoughts to you. You are my very best friend, but my soul remains my own, and I fiercely resist any stranger – all must be strangers to me – in my process of discovering it.

On my own, I do not forget you. In solitude, nothing is forgotten, but merely the perturbations are quelled. The difference is this: in solitude I can love or think about a thing calmly, serenely; whereas in the presence of others my anxieties would suffocate me, they would deject me to the point of rage. I forget only the memories that I wish to be forgotten. Our friendship remains. Even though that which determines me to no longer see you is a violation of friendship. But as for you, why do you not want to understand?

Why did I kiss you? Do you think that we can still call each other friends now, as long as the upheaval is still fresh in my mind and blood? You accept sentimental promiscuity: both friendship and kissing on the lips. I rebel against it. This is where all friendships end: they start out borrowing books, going to concerts together, prolonging visits late into the evening, bashfully holding hands, then they move on to the first tentative kiss, then passionate embraces, then engagement or cohabitation. My friendship must remain pure. I am not subject to the rigid standards of moral mediocrity, but to my will alone. I want you to remain just a friend.

Can you not understand my desperation? I too, like everyone else, I too kissed you after a night spent so originally and so heroically. Why was I unable to maintain control all the way? Are you not stifled by the mediocrity of that kiss? Austere friends that we are, who in our unique purity are condemned and misunderstood, are we to end up like any other of the thousands of student couples? I am tormented to the point of obsession by the thought that now, at the very end, we have let mediocrity vanquish us. That is why we need to separate, for a time.

I do not want you to understand our *separation* mistakenly. Nothing will be broken off, nothing will be lost, nothing will come to an end. Our final separation will take place in autumn, when I will leave for the North, and you leave for some warm country or else remain here, in a mediocre marriage and cosy happiness.

We will spend the next few months alone, I with my books, you with your new friends. We shall write to each other as often as possible. If you need any books, I will send them to you via Radu. He is the only one I will receive, on rare occasions, in the attic.

You ask whether I am working on anything. Nişka, there are so many things to know. The books are long, numerous, enticing; the nights are long. I have spent the last few years accumulating knowledge. Henceforward, who knows what I shall do. He who limits himself to books is an impotent pauper; he who ignores books is a cripple. My path must take me wherever I will it. I will not tell you where. It will only be known after five, ten, or fifty years.

But is it not true that you are bored by all of my obscure confessions? Imploring you to understand and not to take fright, *your friend* sends his greetings.

P.S. Do you know that Radu is falling more and more in love with Viorica? It is strange; it has almost been two years since he first met her and fell in love with her. Radu has never been so determined. He has changed so much. He rarely ever drinks; he reads. But he won't ever succeed at having a normal life, of that I am sure. He lacks something: an inner drive, direction, or idea.

I'm not sure. But Radu is ultimately destined to fail. That's why I am asking if you have heard anything from Viorica.

How stupid of me. I forgot that you don't want to be reconciled with your old friend. Why is that, Nişka?

why shift to epistolary?
centrifugal

LETTER FIVE

My friend, should we separate merely for the sake of that? I am so sad. I have suffered, and I don't know what to write in order to make you understand my suffering. I have been languishing day after day. I wake up in the morning, exhausted. I would like to run away, run away. I know how stupid I am to share my longings with you. You would want me to fulfil them; but what if I don't know how? One thing I do know, and I will share it with you on the condition that you take it seriously: I need you, your presence, your voice, your body. I want to feel you next to me. When you are far away, I am in torment.

I am now going through crises that I just don't understand. Let me ask you once more: why don't you want to help me? The crises will clear up, this I know, but what if they annihilate me, in that mediocrity that terrifies us both? Please help me, protect me. I'm not sure how to describe it, but I've begun to be afraid of my fate, of people. I feel weak again, and I can't even laugh like I used to, I can't pretend anymore. In the past, when I was sad, everybody thought me impetuous, flighty, reckless. Now, they all understand I really am sad. Who knows what they suspect. It's insulting, to both me and you.

Don't you think that nobody suspects that you are in love and that you suffer in solitude? I say this so that you might understand how absurd and dangerous your reclusion really is. You will succumb to overwork, and then you won't be able to write any of the books you've promised. And furthermore, you're stupid: should we separate for the sake of an innocent and long-gone kiss? But I have forgotten it, am no longer troubled even by the memory of it. If you really have all that will power, forget it. Consent for us to meet again, and we'll pass the time as two good friends.

A warm handshake, Nişka.

P.S. Please don't write me again about Viorica. I've seen Radu a few times, but didn't notice anything out of the ordinary.

irretatingly over analytical,
LETTER SIX
beyond the limits of reason)

Nişka, I read your letter on the most beautiful winter morning, in a city whiter than white. If you only knew how much you tempted me to go down into the snowy courtyard, into the sunlit streets with their trees and happy couples. Nişka, I became tormented once more, memories darkened the serenity of my bookshelves. This after I had thought myself almost at peace and was promising to meet you. I am frightened, Nişka, by the tragic rage that I feel hovering over me. No matter how tranquil I might become, a letter from you throws me into turmoil again. The fight begins, and victory is granted to me only after long hours, and once everything has faded to memories, another letter reawakens it; and the fight begins anew.

It's stupid of me to complain about the consequences of one or another decision I myself have taken. I was the one who so willed, and I must be the one who suffers. This letter, which begins with a confession, is a proof of weakness, but it would have been an even greater weakness if I did not send it to you. I erase nothing, but rather I write to you that this morning, the sky and your letter tormented me, bitterly, desperately, as drawn out as death throes. I could not read anything in that moment. Through the window, I saw two poplars covered in snow, in a white courtyard.

No, Nişka, the turmoil has not passed. I will not be able to see you as long as that final kiss insists on reproaching me. Please also try to understand my pain, in solitude here, amid winter fields, parties, ballrooms lit till dawn. I cannot debase myself before an action I expect, but do not fully comprehend.

Forget the sadness of my letter; I am still just as powerful as before, no matter how many temptations may test me. Remember that youth is a crisis; no one survives it but a few fools, driven by their passions or heroic fortitude. You know my decision. For now, so long as I am sad and tormented, I cannot be a hero. But I must become one. My life brooks no compromises: either a hero or nothing. That is why I fight, like one who knows that behind him is ethical, sentimental, or intellectual death.

I've told you too much, haven't I?

Your very same friend,

LETTER SEVEN

I came to see you, but when I read that strange note on your door I turned around and left. I came with news; but to someone buried alive what use would it be?

There is much talk around the city about your having shut yourself away. A rumour that originated at the newspaper tells of a book you're writing and which will contain a hundred *feuilletons*. But it's a rumour nobody believes. Your friends hint that you must be in love, and that as conceited as you are, you don't want to admit it. Although your prolonged isolation speaks for itself.

Another rumour is downright offensive. It is whispered, among members of the club in particular, that you are *insane*. Don't be angry; I am only repeating word for word what has reached my ears. According to them, you went insane this autumn when you published that outrageous article. You were insane even before that, because you always wrote in the first person singular and talked about yourself as some kind of Übermensch, referring to your 'flesh, blood and spirit' as if every reader were required to bow down before them. That's what members of the club are saying. Naturally, I don't believe any of the rumours. I think you want to play some kind of a practical joke and that you want to work in peace and quiet on one of your mediocre novels. You told me about them last autumn; and I don't think they'll sell.

You can receive me, can't you? I have other things to impart that may be of interest to you: about Bibi's love life, about a gentleman who's asking me to be his wife, about a handsome young man, with very attractive lips, who is your friend, etc.

Naturally, if you are ill-mannered and refuse to receive me, I won't be upset. And don't think I'm going to waste away pining after you. I just won't ever visit you again.

In any case, I can tell you that this will be the only letter you'll receive from your friend,

Nonora.

LETTER EIGHT

You've told me nothing, my hermit-like, malicious friend. I have been waiting for specific explanations, but you confuse me all the more. I'm not sure what to make of your letter or how seriously to take it. The more I read it, the more troubled I become. Am I, a *friend*, really so tempting? We spent Christmas Eve together and you said nothing of this to me. We were like two good old friends. What made you change since then? Can it have been that poor little kiss, of which I now repent? Just forget it, forget it!

You, who extolled friendship, are behaving like the very least of friends. A stupid excuse allows you to distance yourself, having forced me for two whole years to think and feel myself your companion. It is so hard to understand that I suffer from the absence of your spirituality, the way you would suffer without Grieg or without *The Commentary of Don Quixote*?

You cannot be my friend if you force me to write this kind of letter, imploring you like a love-struck girl. It's humiliating. Two years ago I wouldn't even have answered your first letter. But it's too late. I am your friend, and I need your mind and your soul. You know that I'm a woman, and still too young to evolve on my own. I can't do anything without support, or without stimulus. I can't do anything *great*. Before I met you, I was adrift and regarded myself as free. Now, I am no longer. I cannot make my own way because I wish for too much. I need the atmosphere you breathe, your thoughts and encouragement. If you want to become a hero, then I want to become an elite woman. It's difficult, isn't it? Why can't you think of me too? The books you offer to lend me are worthless, so long as I'm disturbed by the thought that you *won't receive me*. I won't find self-fulfilment through reading. University didn't give me anything. If I have changed, it is thanks to all the things you conveyed to me, through the living word, action, and encouragement. I only understand books when I am with you. And I understand them only when I'm not troubled, as I am now, because of a friend whom I'm losing.

There are so many things I might tell you, ask you. How can I write them down, when I write the way *you* do, using your expressions?

Perhaps you did me a great wrong, as I have told you before, by teaching me to examine people according to their preoccupations, their words, and the content of their thoughts. I can no longer stand boys who flirt with me or girls who are nasty and gossipy. I can no longer stand anyone but Bibi. I don't know what will become of me.

I await the coming of spring with trepidation, but I also yearn for it. I have so many memories I would like to revisit. If I knew how to write, I would tell you so many things; and if I wanted to, again I would tell you so many things.

Is it true that you won't be angry with me if I'm enigmatic too? *Your friend, Nişka.*

LETTER NINE

Nişka, every time I read your letters I grow sad. And the only way for me to drive away the sadness is by writing you. Maybe that's why the rhythm at the beginning, and the rhythm at the end of all my letters is so different.

You're not right at all. The duty of a friend is to share the suffering of the other, you say. Even though I think otherwise, let me accept your principle. But what if I am no longer your friend, but something else? Do I not then have the duty to strive to become your friend once again? I confess this to you lest you understand me incorrectly, and lest you view my isolation as a violation of friendship.

I know that you have been remade through me, and I know that the female soul is passive, waiting to be fecundated by the male spirit and values. But I do not believe your crisis is perilous enough for me to go back on my decision, for me to be close to you console you.

You have two paths to follow: the first, which is arduous and fraught with risk to the point of self-compromise, is the path of perfect freedom. You can remain pure, virginal, illuminated by spiritual values, even with the danger of appearing depraved in others' eyes. It is difficult, because women have a hard time finding the way on their own. But on this path of perfect freedom, you must walk alone. The resources of the female soul are quickly consumed, and in the absence of another soul, the soul of a friend, they cannot be replenished. If she does not attach herself to a male mind with which to commune, to give and take, any woman, no matter how superior, will perish. Mediocrity always triumphs over the single woman.

Although it pains me to give this advice, since you are my friend, you should take the second path from the very start – that of happiness through spiritual vegetation. Marriage is the most perfect of human endeavours, when it is a permanent and living embodiment of ethical happiness. And it is the most disgusting when enacted through the cowardice of one of the spouses. This is my understanding of it. But you need to see how all the others see marriage: an arbitrary association of two people who do not know each other, who end up tolerating each other and even becoming friends; cosy domestic happiness, resigned contentment, mediocre emotional involvement throughout a series of lovers or children. Notwithstanding, marriage is inevitable; the female soul tires easily, and the body worms itself in, and its urges cannot be suppressed.

Don't think of me as a misanthrope or an anarchist. I am simply a puritan and, while vices and errors freely committed do not stir me to revolt, I am depressed and frightened by the mediocrity of ineluctable adultery. I have nothing but honest contempt for the lover who picks up the leftovers (there was another before him, was there not?) and takes advantage of the sexual inexperience of the husband, the hapless office worker in a hurry to go to sleep after a single perfunctory embrace. I have the same contempt for the husband who looks for a wife so that he can have a luxurious apartment, hot food, and children. The kind of men who do not so much as flinch when they say: this is my child.

But I've gone too far, and I'm not sure how to go back.

As for you, I suggest you try both paths. Follow the one of freedom, and soon, you'll feel drained, depressed, exhausted. You will want to transfer your worries and weariness onto a husband. Since you will not have the courage to set off on your own, you will let yourself be carried along by a companion who is now a stranger to you. Since you will not have the courage to choose one husband out of a thousand men, you will let yourself be chosen. No need to feel offended. This is your lot, the fate of women. It is true that I wanted you to become a superior woman, and now you want it too. I confess that this would have brought me the greatest satisfaction in a particular area of my life. But I don't really see it as a possibility. You have all the attributes and shortcomings of an elite woman. No matter how hard I might toil, you will always be capricious, withdrawing after every defeat until annihilated. You are perfect next to me. But our paths must part for several years. You will not have the strength to live freely during these years.

You will naturally and irremediably slide into mediocrity. Perhaps you will not forget me, but, upon my return, you will certainly not understand me.

All these things are sad, are they not? I have to endure them too, and yet I obey them, because they are more powerful than I am; they speak of destiny, and of the tragic soul I descry in the world and in the mountains.

You must always remember that all the things you read in these pages were written by me; and while they make you sad, they have harrowed my dreams and bloodied my soul. My sadness is increasingly more desperate; because I am tortured by this thought: one word, and my sadness would be transformed into joy. But it is my destiny not to say that word.

LETTER TEN

Forgive me for saying it so forthrightly, but you are virtually insane. Yesterday I came over, read the note on your door and knocked for a quarter of an hour. You were home, because you said as much on the note, and besides, the door was bolted from the inside. I kept shouting: 'It's me, Petre! I've got to talk to you!' I'm sure you heard. Why didn't you open the door? Radu told me that you won't even open the door to him. Nonora is saying the most outrageous things about you around town, spreading rumours that you've gone insane, that you don't respond to letters any more, that you're just trying to be original. What happened between the two of you? I knew you were friends. Moreover, what has happened to you?

I came to tell you about an event that no one else knows anything about: my engagement. You think I'm stupid, don't you? But if you met my fiancée, you would change your mind, just as I did. I'm going to be happy; my wife will relentlessly encourage me to climb the ladder, to go up in the world. She understood my passion and was excited for me. Since then my capacity for work has increased tenfold. I do anything I can to make her happy, I push higher and higher in order to see how pleased she is with me. I even hate more fiercely, because henceforth another's accomplishment no longer upsets just me, but also my fiancée, who would have liked *me* to make that accomplishment, rather than somebody else.

I'm confiding in you because you were the only one who knew anything about my love and my ambitions. Now, the conflict between the two passions is gone, because they have both melded into one all-encompassing passion: our happiness.

And I'm also confiding in you, because everyone is saying that you are in love with Nişka. And I wanted to warn you that disaster awaits if you take her as your wife. Because Nişka is not of the same spiritual essence as my fiancée. Nişka will not be able to ignite within you work, creativity, and courage. In due course you will find a rich and intelligent wife, who will be of great help to you; not only as a helpmeet, but also as a social step up in the world; you need to seek a good family name and a fortune.

My fiancée doesn't have these, but she does have the qualities I have described to you. I hope you won't be consumed by the mediocrity that terrifies you. Otherwise, I hope we'll see each other soon.

Petre

LETTER ELEVEN

My friend, why do you frighten me for no reason? Why predict a future for me in which you yourself don't even believe? You know that I won't accept a husband, and that I won't submit to a mediocre marriage. Do you think that our friendship of two years has not taught me what I must do?

I wept once more reading your malicious words. As you wrote them, you forgot they were addressed to a friend who has not seen you since Christmas Eve, a friend who is in turmoil, in the depths of a crisis, disoriented, without succour. You can't begin to understand how much harm you've inflicted. I was just starting to enjoy the spring, to hope that a meeting was near. I wanted to give you such a surprise. Just for you, I read a great deal from the books you gave me this winter. I marked a sheet of paper with a multitude of questions regarding some of the more interesting passages. I was feeling so happy and then, all at once, your harsh and untruthful letter.

What do you want me to say? Lately, you have not demonstrated the slightest bit of kindness, friendship, or concern. On a whim, you drove me away, after you urged me, for two years, to be close to you. Would you like me to say more? Would you like me to end this letter with a lover's lament? It would be stupid and point-less. Rereading the last pages of our correspondence, I realise that nothing will convince you of your savagery, even if I told you that I love you. I admire and am jealous that you possess a soul that is so cruel and unfeeling. You lie when you tell me you suffer in sol-itude; if you were suffering too, you would not write me letters in which you admonish me to mediocrity, after two years of helping me escape from it.

I don't understand you. It is so beautiful outside, so warm, there are so many flowers. And I'm crying like an adolescent and think-ing desperate thoughts. How can you stay in your attic? I hate you; you're as stubborn as a brute! Forgive me; I know that your will harrows you, bloodies you. But I also bleed, alone, without my friend, with so many unseen gifts, in the spring, with a sadness that overwhelms me. I don't know what I'm going to do. I think about you all the time, I reread your letters, I remember our time together with Bibi at the seaside, and our summer vacation. I could weep in chagrin at my behaving in so sentimental and lovesick a way, I, your friend, Nişka.

LETTER TWELVE

In my Diary:

Reading Nişka's last letter today, I was in such despair, I felt so alone and abandoned that I wanted to go down into the street, to run, to go to her, to tell her: I love you!

I decided to send her this personal notebook, that she might understand what I have done, that she might understand my pain, and to write a few more pages of final explanation here.

I knew that Nişka would have accepted me as her lifelong companion. I also know that Nişka is the only woman I would want as a companion. Not only is she the girl with the most qualities, but also she was created by me; and I love her. I write all of this with the bitterness of one who has reached the limit of his endurance. I sense I will not be able to fight against a tormented soul and a rebellious body much longer. I feel that, if insanity doesn't lay hold over me in the next few days, the ruin of heroism will be utterly complete. I feel so ashamed speaking of heroism here, on this page that will be read by Nişka. I, who ultimately was unable to keep silent, who sent the *Diary* so that my friend might discover how much I loved her, how much she tortured and tempted me.

I love Nişka, Nişka is perfect, she is free, she is beautiful, I love her. Now, perhaps more than ever, I am tempted by the thought: why should we not be companions? In autumn I shall be going away; why not take Nişka with me, even without our being husband and wife, just as she dreamed?

But despite all this, I must renounce it. I must renounce it because thus did I will, thus did I wish. The magic of the word will work its effect. I shall utter and think 'will' for a few minutes, and then I will change.

I am sadder, but more serene. I can write so that Nişka will understand. My friend, from whom I must tear myself away forever, divining her end, enveloped in mist, in the city of endless roofs.

Nişka's companionship would be, for me, the only happiness I might hope for. You only fall in love once, and you only have a single chance to possess the soul of a woman. But I cannot believe in happiness. I am afraid of happiness, it terrifies me. I can neither conceive it nor feel it. I cannot believe in the reality of happiness. But in my soul, companionship with Nişka is inseparable from happiness. All of my experiences, all of my struggles hitherto have instilled in me a tragic sense of existence. For me, the tragedy is real; it is neither words devoid of content nor childish fear. I feel guided by destiny. Destiny that directs me through my will. Understanding that my will is bound to another will, I obey it. The last few years have revealed it to me with their personal lessons, which eluded me at the time. Meeting Nişka, at the beginning of a crisis, was tragic, the same as our friendship was tragic, having been transformed into love within me, a love that was due to and yet against my will.

I cannot believe in happiness. My life will be dark, austere, nostalgic, sober, and austere, because that is how I want it. Later on, when heroism will be more than just a goal, perhaps my soul will reflect other lights. But for now, this is the direction of my life.

And then again, for me Nişka's companionship would also be a never-ending torment and perhaps, an opportunity to annihilate her friendship and admiration. Nişka would be a torment for me, because I would want her to think unceasingly about me and me alone. I would not be able to tolerate it if she also admired a tenor, painter, or athlete. I would want her to admire me in all those guises. I would want to be the tenor, painter, and athlete.

I would have been restless, I would have thrown myself into my work, and then ended up not working on anything. I would have been with her all the time, and I would have wanted her to always be with me, by my side, I would have wanted her to tell me everything, to hold nothing back. I would have been able neither to work nor relax. Within a few years, without intellectual activity, I would never have recovered. My evolution would have been illusory. My will would have remained the same, without surpassing itself. I would not have completed any of the works promised to me and to Nişka.

But Nişka is my friend and my creation only in my inner life, which I have been able to temper, shape, rein in. Nişka admires me, because I am above her, with my values and my aspirations. But what if these aspirations are never realised? It is Nişka who will have been deceived. She will regret everything that she believed to be great, powerful, and original in me.

But then again, even if I were able to create with Nişka at my side, I would feel humiliated. Nişka would know the larva, the blind, labouring mole, his tears of frustration, his face haggard from sleepless nights, his depressing despair and defeat. Nothing of the solitary, calm, intense, detached serenity she now admires in me from afar. I would reveal myself with all the sins of the flesh, and the weaknesses of the spirit.

None of this has prevented me from loving Nişka, so very much. But love has no influence on everyday life. She will remain in my soul; I am not afraid to carry her with me, for years. Why should I be afraid of love? Why do I try to kill it, because I cannot meet its summons?

It is a sign of strength: not to let myself be carried away by love, but also, not to hate or despise it.

I want the only light from without that is permitted in my soul to be Nişka. Henceforth I shall not avoid her. She will once again be my good, my close friend. I will descend again into the world. Even though I still do not have proof of my ultimate victory.'

Nişka, I'm sending you my personal diary, whose final page I finished just now, weary and drained. I feel defeated and broken. I barely have the strength to write. I won't even reread it. I think I have included several obscure sentences. My mind grows dark. I am tired, trembling with fatigue. Nişka, believe me; I was very strong, I was exactly how you wanted me to be. I did not let anyone be higher than me. Forgive me.

Your only friend.

LETTER THIRTEEN

My friend, forgive me for everything I wrote to you. How can I describe the joy and the tears that washed over me while reading your *Diary*? I have all but learned by heart the pages from Italy. If only I could write, I would confide so much in you now. But why should I have to write well? I can say what I want to say to you sincerely and happily, the way my soul is right now.

I didn't want to believe it at first; it sounded so strange: 'I love you, Nişka!' Your actions of late have forced me to see you as a man who is incapable of being in love. I saw you as so high up, and so detached and I suffered, I who needed you, I who was unable to elevate myself.

How should I put this? I'm hesitant to write it here: 'I love you!' Because I know that it's much more than that. I'm afraid you won't believe that I'm in love. Maybe I am, but I'm also something more. A girl's love is strange and inconstant. Mine could be no different. But I do feel bound to you more deeply, more utterly. For me you are neither an ideal husband, nor a suave fiancé, nor a skilled suitor. You are what I did not want to believe existed, you are a God who created me and endowed me with a soul. I would like you to be my master, and it is no humiliation for me, because I know you are a *man*. I would like to bow down at your feet, not because I am in love with you, but because I feel your power, your greatness, and you are the creator of my lights. All that is luminous in me is thanks to you. You know how every girl falls in love each spring; but that love passes, and is forgotten, without leaving any traces. But I feel that I am yours, I feel that I cannot live unless I am by your side, because by your side I think and I feel, the way you want, and the things you want. We can no longer be apart. There is no need for us to be apart. Why torture yourself, why suffer and squander your powers? Your heroism, which fascinates and governs me, will henceforth be fruitful. You have passed the trial of the will. What you have endured has steeled you sufficiently. Abnegation does not lead to insanity.

Why should we part? You say that you love me. I would say so many things were I not so troubled and in such a hurry.

You declare that for you I am your source of tangible and authentic happiness. For me, then, why shouldn't we remain companions, for the rest of our lives? We won't meet each other's like again. Neither of us will find anyone to replace the other. You created me, you created me like this to answer the callings of your soul. Why not take me with you?

Now that I know that you are suffering even more, and also because of me, I shall not be too timid to ask for you, to give myself to you. Later, with both of us happy, you empowered, and I close to you, you will thank me. Your life will lose its direction without me. Our proximity – of body and soul – will not harm your work. When you are tired, weak and depressed, I will comfort you. Didn't you teach me this? Didn't you instil in me an appreciation of femininity?

Have no fear of being an amorphous, blind larva. I will be able to forget once your life's work shines forth in all its perfection. I, who was once so weak, am not frightened by human weaknesses. I know that you will always succeed in defeating them.

Do you see the sunlight this morning? Does spring make you restless, does it call to you, does it rend you? When do you want to meet? I too also receive my degree this summer, and then we will depart. I'm rich and I'm free. I feel sorry for those who stay behind; they'll gossip about us when they find out that we've left together without having married. We'll be married, but without witnesses and without the registrar's office. Isn't that how it should be? Isn't it original, isn't it novel, and isn't it, above all, real? We could leave tomorrow. But we'll wait until summer.

What else should I write to you? I too am tired and happy. But I could still shed so many tears, because I still feel sad. My friend, tell me why I am sad when I am so close to the happiness that previously I didn't even dare dream about? Spring, again.

I'm returning your *Diary*, as you requested. Last night, reading and rereading it, I would have liked to copy out certain pages. But there's no need for that now. The *Diary* is ours now, isn't it?

For, you can't say anything but yes now. The crisis has passed. You have no reason to set yourself against our living together. Your insanity must end here. Considering everything I've written, you cannot be forgotten, I expect either happiness or death from you. *Tertium non.*

But there will be only happiness. Happiness is calling to both of us. We've been sad and confused long enough. I have tormented you long enough, and I have suffered long enough because of your insanity. How could you say no to spring? The longing to depart will now be transformed into deed. Haven't you wanted since adolescence to walk along shores, by rivers, through mountains *with me*? Do you know that I am burning with the flames of impending departure? Let us wander, let us roam. You'll write your memoirs; and I shall listen to you, in the evening, and smile.

What can we not accomplish, together? I will help you, always. Didn't you teach me to help the companion of my choice? I have chosen you. I demand you, I want you, I love you, and you are my master. I'm not sure of anything anymore. I'm not sure of anything anymore, only that I am still sad. When are we going to see each other? I'll be so … I don't know, I don't know what to write. I've said too much. I feel embarrassed.

But you must come, to talk to me, and we'll go together. You can't leave me alone anymore.

This is what I will write you for now, drained, weeping without knowing why. My friend, I am your friend,

Nişka.

PART THREE

Today, the 8th of April, Nişka celebrated her engagement to the eldest son of the family who held her captive over the winter holidays. The son is an engineer and is in love with Nişka.

I heard the news from Radu. My friend gazed at me closely, trying to bore beneath the surface. I smiled and said to him:

'Nişka was lucky; it will be a happy marriage; they are both young, beautiful and rich.'

That evening I wrote her: 'Your friend wishes to congratulate you on etc. He is upset that you did not share your decision with him in person. Once again, congratulations and best wishes. P.S. I do hope that you and your fiancé will pay me a visit. You know how rarely I go out.

*

From the 9th to the 20th of April, I worked like a madman, desperately, tirelessly. My eyes water from reading. I am pale, enfeebled, and my hand trembles.

Today, for a while I walked the streets at night. In the garden, the lilacs flowers have faded. So many books have accumulated on the shelves that I have started to stack them on the floor. The small windows of the attic admitted a refreshing breeze.

I would like to see my friends. But they are tired of coming and not being received.

I would like to see Nişka again.

*

22 April. A visit from Viorica, fresh-faced, her bag full of notebooks and books. She is working on her degree at the Academy. She tells me that Nişka has postponed her exams until autumn, that she is no longer working, and that she spends the whole day with her fiancé.

From Bibi, she knows that Nişka is no longer sad, but laughs, jokes and lingers late at the *thés dansants*. Her fiancé is happy that she has changed.

I listened closely, serenely to Viorica's revelations. She was alarmed at my feebleness, at my trembling hands, at the dark circles around my eyes, at the piles of filled notebooks.

'You'll overwork yourself.'

'The only ones who ever overwork themselves are those who wish to rest', I smiled.

'Do you have much more work?'

'Until autumn. In autumn I'm going away.'

'Where?'

'I'm not even sure, Viorica, but I won't leave before gathering five years' worth of reserves. Because I don't even know if I'll be able to read where I'm going.'

Viorica shared her sorrows with me. She will leave university without any close friend, and she doesn't know what everyone knows. And she is appalled at the life she will lead from now on. She'll become a teacher in a provincial town. She'll barely find time to read a magazine, or one book a month. She who now scours the whole Academy. And how hard she would work if only she had support. How many hopes she nurtured over the last two years. And how quickly the years had passed, how quickly ... Of course she will end up like any other student of literature; the wife, in the best case, of a high school teacher. And she hasn't even met him yet. How nice it would be for her to fall in love with a fellow student and for them both to become teachers, right here in the city. Oh, how much she would love him. But there are still a few months left. After her degree, she will go wherever the ministry sends her. You have to make a living, don't you?

'Viorica, your rebellion is futile.'

'I am not rebelling, I realise that's the way it is, I realise that all my dreams were just dreams, but it's just so sad. You're a boy, you can go away, you can know everything, you can go anywhere. But what about me? Do you know that I'm going to cry the day I take my degree? For me, that's where it ends. I'll be done with my stupid youth, not ever having known any danger, or significant sorrow or joy.'

'Viorica, all of that is bound to happen soon enough, it's only natural.'

'I know ... But isn't it sad?'

'No. You're suffering from end-of-university melancholy, they way you suffered end-of-adolescence melancholy before that. It will pass. You're going to start a new life, with new people, and new places. You connected yourself to certain friends, you wanted certain things to happen that now will never happen. Everything is soon forgotten. Who among us still holds onto the desperate sadness of our first romance, in adolescence? It's the end of an era, and endings are always sad. Your duty is not to let yourself become overwhelmed by it, but rather to lend value to mediocrity, to find meaning in all the actions that now, in time of crisis, seem stupid, lethal, dull to you. The fight against mediocrity is won in two ways: either by escaping it through a madness of the soul, or by transfiguring it. You can live in the utmost mediocrity without becoming mediocre ... but it is difficult.'

Viorica left just as sad as before, and now I write in this notebook everything she confessed to me, and everything I said to her in reply.

I am so happy that I feel young, fresh, with a broad chest and strong shoulders, steadfast in the battle with myself, with the world, with destiny. Who could defeat me now?

*

Why did Măriuca and Gaidaroff separate? Măriuca is now taking strolls through the park with a student from the Polytechnic. Gaidaroff is in love with some unknown girl. Their love lasted two years. Long enough. Now they are both going their separate ways. Măriuca is hoping for a hasty marriage. Gaidaroff is preparing for the Bar. Maybe he is hoping for a wife with a dowry, a good family name, and political connections.

I heard some sad news about Bibi. Andrei almost made her lose her mind. And Bibi still loves him, really loves him. Everybody knows about their love, and everybody knows about Andrei's caution. I heard a rumour that Bibi made a fool of herself trying to keep him, even attempting the means of last resort. I don't know, and I do not believe it.

How did she not realize, all those years, that he did not really love her?

*

The change in Radu has me worried. He is tormented by an absurd thought: to become a monk. But he is still such a sinner. I advised him to go off on his own, to travel, to forget the urge officially to shut himself away.

I understand his thinking, but I am afraid of the consequences. Radu's mysticism, as dark as it is, is without discipline. He will be a worse sinner in the monastery than ever before. And he won't find any peace.

I encouraged him to take the last two years of lycée, which he missed when he dropped out five years ago, and then to come to a decision. He should wait a while longer, ponder further. He can still be an ascetic and solitary in the midst of others. Official, enforced asceticism is rife with temptations. It brings no tranquillity, no serenity. The cloistered life of a young man brings not relief, but torture.

*

I still haven't seen Nişka. I cannot go to her. I'm just waiting for them here, upstairs, in the attic.

*

Today, around nightfall, on the boulevard, I met Nonora. She had forgotten my impudence, the letter with no reply, the heedlessness with which I let so many months pass without seeing her.

Today, Nonora was more beautiful, warm, passionate than ever. She confessed that she was in love with a young actor, whom she is to marry. She showed me his photograph, which had a stupid and adorable dedication. She kissed her photograph on the street.

What did I feel in that moment, more strongly than my will, more strongly than my respect for Nonora's love? I whispered to her, trembling.

'Nonora, come to my place!'

'I can't anymore. I'm engaged.'

'Nonora, in the autumn, I will be going away, and once I leave, the house will be demolished. It's too old. Don't you want to see the attic one last time? Two years ago you couldn't get enough of it – don't you have any memories of my room?'

'Will you behave yourself?'

'Like a friend.'

She smiled, took my arm, and off we went.

I sensed her taut body, her vast, vast soul.

'It's starting to get hot in this attic of yours …'

'Take off your beret, take off as much as you like.'

'You've started talking oddly.'

'I just wanted to kiss you in more comfort.'

'Out of the question!'

I pressed against her lips and bent her backwards. She was unable to finish her sentence of protest.

'Nonora, it's pointless your pretending to be chaste … remember?'

'We can't! I'm engaged now.'

'All the worse for your fiancé. I like you, too.'

'I don't know you any more. Leave me be!'

My arms were too strong. Her shoulder clasps gave way. I glimpsed her breasts, brown and trembling.

'Nonora, there was a time when you used to let me kiss your breasts.'

'But then you'll want even more. It's out of the question!'

How could Nonora divine my thoughts? I was annoyed by her resistance, like that of a virginal tease. I knew I could exert mastery over her by feigning innocence, entrancing her, and then taking her by stealth, once her defences were down. I chose a different tactic. I asked her openly and honestly. She began to laugh. I could sense in her the turmoil caused by springtime, feelings, my behaviour, the unprecedentedness of the act she could divine in my eyes.

I pushed her down. With one arm I pinned her arms, with the other I parted her knees and subdued her thighs. The act took place before Nonora could even comprehend, and before I could hesitate.

We pleasured our bodies.

'Why did you do that? Why did you do that?'

In my bed, among my books, another man's fiancée was weeping.

I gazed out of the little window. And I felt unquenched turmoil, and I desired anew the body of the girl whose scent was that of lilac blossoms.

*

From the letter to Petre.

You have not been victorious; you have run away from the fight. I reread everything you shared with me at the beginning of spring. You praised your fiancée whom you now consider an obstacle to your social conquests. You took the step that must now trouble your conscience; you made promises; and you got engaged. And then, one contemplative day, after passing your exams, you realised your mistake and you ran away. Your flight is not a sign of your will, but a cowardly act. You fled after you had given your word of honour that you would remain bound. For me, that word does exist.

And now, from that distant and immense city, you write to me that your insanity has saved you. It has saved you, in a manner both mediocre and humiliating. To me you remain vanquished.

I didn't like the damning words aimed at your fiancée. She is not to blame. You were so weak that you hated the being who, in effect, demonstrated your weakness. Why despise her, and why run away? You should have stayed here, and broken off the engagement, pretending to be in love with someone else, or inventing vices that would frighten her off. This would have been the manly thing to do, rather than running away. There, in a city of temptations, you'll forget about her. It's humiliating; it will be an organic forgetfulness, that of a soul born of the flesh, rather than the true soul.

And you write that you feel strong, great, thirsty, and you suggest I do the same, should I find myself in a similar situation.

And so I shall, with one distinction; I will leave once I am victorious. My departure will not be flight, but rather the act of one who wishes to heal his wounds in solitude.

Otherwise, I do not need to leave, or to run away. My life and my will are my unvanquishable succour. I sense summertime within me, within the trees. The burning sap brings me unimagined powers. Nothing saddens me: neither the dissolution of the club, nor Nişka's engagement, nor the prospect of my going away for so many years, nor the demolition of the house where I spent my childhood, the attic with its memories of adolescence, so many memories. I am not saddened, because my soul is so vast that within itself it encompasses sorrow, happiness, defeat, nostalgia, longing, without breaking apart, without complaint.

Around me, everyone is sad because summer has come and now they must part. Why should I be sad? I know that all of this must come to pass. There are but two wills: the cosmic and the heroic. Both are tragic. The world will have to bend down and accept its fate without a murmur. Henceforth, I feel absolutely above everybody else. I can never return from whence I came, because my soul has been transfigured. I do not know if you understand my serenity, my confidence in my progress across countries and the years, the heroic purpose I elucidated after three years of trials and so many months of tribulation. My reclusion was not an escape, but a meditation, a regrouping of my means of battle. You cannot understand how much I cherish the victory, because you do not know who my enemy was.

I have every reason to be sad, and yet I am exuberant. Not a temporary or faked exuberance. Such things passed away with the final reminiscences of adolescence. This exuberance springs from my sufferings, from my latest experiences, from the meaning that *I* give to the world. The vast, and endless world; my soul is vast; my aspirations are without end and their fulfilment must needs be without end. That's what I say. I, who have endured the magic of the word 'must'.

The sun exists; so long as I feel its warmth, why be sad, why be troubled, why cry? I no longer have any longings, because my longings have transformed themselves into achievement. I will leave. Nothing will bind me to the places and the people of the past. Every hour, there are others. Ever farther, ever higher. I can think these things, because I will them to happen. I am not leaving or travelling in order to forget. I will not forget anything. The more memories accumulate, the happier I will be. Not happy in the usual sense. But happy, which is to say, myself.

I finish this too long letter reminding you of your cowardly, mediocre, craven deed. You have no right to encourage me by your example, I, who have climbed so much higher, without anyone even knowing it.

*

My friend writes to me:

Passing through Lausanne, in the university sanatorium I visited the tubercular student with whom we talked at the hermitage two summers ago. He is seriously ill, but serene. He studies mathematics in his head, without the doctors knowing. He asked me about you. He asked me whether you had found faith or whether you still persisted in your arrogant heroism. I did not know what to answer. I told him that I pray God that His grace descend upon you and that He deliver you from your turmoil.

We passed much time in conversation. He said that he is on the trail of a discovery that will surpass anything that has come to pass in this world heretofore. I am worried about our friend.

I haven't heard anything from you. We haven't seen each other and haven't written each other for such a long time – why have we forgotten each other, I wonder? Am I not your best friend still?

I have begun to be cured of the love that ended so bitterly. I am unable to express it here, nor can I tell anyone how much I have suffered. I wept, I begged her, I fell down at her feet. I was on the verge of madness, of suicide. I prayed to God night and day. I found no solace in study, but only in faith. Understanding that nothing could ever be the same, I wished to forget. And only now have I been able to forget, after one whole year, after travels on which I have spent everything I had. I shall return penurious, a Christian, and eager to work. I have gained depth. All that lingered of adolescence in my eyes, on my face, on my lips has vanished. I feel I am more bitter, sadder, and I feel I will remain this way forever. I've been defeated, trampled underfoot, drained of strength. Now, I will rise again.

What are you working on, what are you planning? Rumours have reached me of a terrifying labour, begun in autumn and completed only now. I look forward to seeing the fruits. You're lucky that you can work in silence, unaffected by the temptations of love. My friend, listen to me: never fall in love. You will suffer greatly, you will endure unnecessary humiliation and defeat. Seek tranquillity, and then guard it. It is the only thing that matters in life.

*

Today, the 21st of August, I watched the sun set beyond the plains of Dobrudja. My soul shuddered once more to the orgasm of vast urges. Every morning and every dusk I gaze at the sun. It ignites a fire within my veins without which I cannot live. I worship the sun each morning and mourn it each night. My existence is simple and austere. I reside in the same little room, in the same cottage as two years ago. But I no longer write stories in a notebook with blank pages. And in the village stretched out along the coast I no longer meet Nişka, Andrei, Bibi, Paul. I meet other people, and I smile at them. I have not been sad a single moment. I roam the plains, drink in the briny air, and lave my eyes with the sight of the sea. My thoughts are difficult to put into words. My soul is just as warm, and cherishes Nişka just as immaculately as before.

Nişka is spending her vacation in the mountains, with her fiancé. I occasionally think about her, about the erstwhile members of the club, about whom I hear little news. I'm not sad that all of this is over. All that I see ahead of me, the paths that entice me, the windswept crossroads, the sky with its temptations, the darkness and its dangers don't allow me any time to be sad. There is so much to be conquered, to discover, to taste. There are lands that beckon me, islands that await me, books that long for me, and so many reams of white paper, cold, and tempting, that incite me. Formerly, I would be saddened by each memory, by the thought of separation, by an orchard in bloom, by an autumn evening. Now, these memories make me obdurate, to the point of turgescence. I still exist, but they have passed. The thought thrills me with delight. I remain: how then could I be sad, when I have conquered death, endured the years, and remain.

I am bringing about the idea of creating myself, of illumining myself, without making my life, my mind and my soul into a masterpiece. I am bringing about all the things I promised. Work, vigils, roaming the fields and along the shore make me happy. I have loved the sun, the light, the downy stalks of the flowers. I no longer feel alone. All that was once obscure and mysterious in my soul now gains dominance. I can no longer feel alone: because the soul decanted in solitude is now the only soul, and living with it no longer stirs up the longings and anxieties of the other soul that was shackled to the world.

This notebook, begun on a tormented summer's day, will soon come to a close. Henceforth, I hesitate to set down my thoughts on pages that come after pages written in another time.

This notebook will end naturally, without shouting, without excitement, and without lamentation. Calm and restrained, just like my path will be. I will leaf through it, occasionally, at night. And I will be strengthened by that mirror of the weaknesses and tumult that were defeated because they had to be transcended.

*

October. Autumn is clear and warm. I finish my exams, with a soul reinvigorated by the autumn, tossed back and forth by the calls of lands foreign to me. I make ready for my departure.

I met Nişka. She hesitated for a few moments, and then shook my hand. We did not ask about each other. I looked at her: she was changed, beautiful, with black curls framing her pale forehead. We spoke about exams. On finding out that I was leaving, she asked me to go with her to the monastery where we first met; perhaps that day would be the last day of our friendship.

'I'll go Nişka, though the road to the monastery will not be the end of our friendship. That is how I want it, and I have the right to choose, here.'

She smiled at me. She was so shaken by the encounter, by the words I had spoken to her, by my ardent yet restrained glances, that she slipped off her engagement ring and hid it. I smiled too.

*

Every morning was beautiful. It was cloudless and sad, with lofty skies and stark fields, on the morning of our meeting. I was determined to help Nişka, to remind her and convince her that I was still her best friend.

We met in the train station; she had the same violet eyes, her oval face was sadder, her lips paler.

'Good morning, Nişka!'

I started to speak to her, to laugh, to joke. I told her about all the new things that await us on our separate paths. Mine would perhaps be a path of mountain peaks, but hers too deserved to be travelled sincerely, cheerfully, with pleasure in the delights it brought. She was even more downcast, and merely smiled, as she sat next to me, gazing through the window of the train carriage at the fields in autumn.

We arrived, I took her arm, and we set off down the path that led around the lake. Memories were painfully revived. The forest was now blood red, its paths deserted, covered in windswept leaves. The walk dizzied and frightened me. I had grown so much in three years.

'When do you leave?'

'In a few days, Nişka.'

'You'll forget, won't you?'

How could I have told her that I would never forget?

'It's stupid, my wedding's at the end of the month – and you won't be here any more.'

I stroked her hair, smiling.

'Do you know what my gift to you will be? A blank notebook, bound in leather, and at the top of the first page, a date. I want you to write down your life. When I return to find you changed, defeated by your surroundings, by mediocrity, I will try to find out all the circumstances in which the soul that came from me perished. You know, Nişka, I take a passionate interest in my own agony and the agony of my creations. It is tragic, but comforting for me.'

'Why are you telling me this?'

She started to cry, her arm trembled, and her gaze grew deeper under her tears. I watched her, I listened to my rebellious soul. I gazed fixedly at the horizon, at the sky's cold flames.

'I thought you would comfort me, help me.'

'Nişka, by predicting your happiness in mediocrity, I offer you comfort. The word makes you uneasy, I know. Say it then however you'd like: matrimony, cosy happiness, in a provincial town, with an honest husband, and beautiful children. You choose the word. I meant to say that you will begin a new life, one that will not be the life we both chose together, in the years of our friendship, but that it will make you happy, because it will stultify you spiritually.'

'What are you saying? Why are you telling me all this? Don't you know that as long as you exist I can never be happy?'

'You will forget Nişka, in my absence, you will forget, just as you forgot when you got engaged.'

I let her cry. In the forest, the wind now swayed the branches. I saw white clouds gathering. Nişka trembled ever more painfully. I would have liked to console her, to tell her I loved her, but my soul was now at peace. And the more restless the forest, the more tranquil my soul.

'Do you know what I'd like to do? To look for the log by the lake where you read my palm.'

'Nişka, a storm is coming.'

'I want to remember. It was spring then, it was so beautiful, I was so naïve. I was in my first year.'

'And now you have your degree. And it is autumn. With rain and a cold wind on the way. Let's go back to the station, Nişka.'

'No, no. I also want to see the monastery, and the church again.'

'Nişka, it is getting dark.'

'What do we care? I'm not afraid of the rain, or the forest. I want to see it one more time.'

'And I want us to go back. You live in memories, but I live in life. Why should I care about memories? Why should I care about nostalgia for that spring? They have their place in my soul, but I don't want to resurrect them now, when it looks like it is going to rain. Why should I go back three years when life stretches before me, vast and enticing? We are going to the station, Nişka!'

She no longer resisted. Her eyes filled with tears, and the tears ran down her cheeks, like in the eyes of an icon.

The forest roared, heaving back and forth amid eddies of leaves. The sky had darkened. We went out into the fields. The fields were dark, the grass ravaged by sun and hoarfrost. As we walked to the station it was through curtains of rain. *more innocent +*

It rained, and rained. We caught the scent of fields fecundated by the seed of the clouds. And the wind unleashed by the mountains *puerile* wracked the forest. Its moans flitted above the furrows. *than*

We walked through the rain, our heads bowed. Nişka softly wept. *student* I could feel my blood stirred by the cold, my muscles coiled around my bones, my tensed shoulders. I was strong, strong beside Nişka's tears. *today*

In the station, we waited in silence for the first train to the city. We watched the rain. Through the rain-lashed trees I could see sunlit lands, snowy lands, cities. I thought about the path I was to take, impassioned by everything I would find, everything I would discover, everything I would learn in the years of my youth, which had only just begun. Nişka dabbed her eyelids from time to time with a small white handkerchief.

The train approached.

'Today will be the last time we see each other.'

'Yes, Nişka.'

'From now on we'll be apart.'

'For five, ten years; and then, we'll meet again.'

'Yes.'

'Nişka, the train is coming.'

'We have to leave, don't we?'

Of course, we had to leave. We were the only people in the waiting room. Nişka, standing up, pointed to her cheek and smiled. I kissed her on the lips, a kiss as long and aching as a sigh.

We boarded the train sad, troubled. We did not speak until we reached the station in Bucharest. In the carriage, I squeezed her hand once again.

'Goodbye, Nişka!'

The sky above the city was clear and fresh after the rain. I set off on my own, down cold streets.

*

The University has been invigorated again with a wave of young students, of timid students. The corridors blaze with eyes, smiles and faces. And the halls seethe with the restless energy of first-year students. Once more, in the lecture halls, the new boys sit at the back, joking amongst themselves, the new girls, with their white hands, at the front.

The Professor of Logic arouses the same tumult. Everything is alive, fresh, new. I do not know anyone. Everyone has moved on. In the couples made to feel awkward by others' eyes, I divine bonds that the years will strengthen and then break.

*

The final day and final night.

I am leaving, and my attic will be demolished. On the site of the old house, another, tall and grey, will be built. Upon my return, I will no longer recognise my street, my childhood, my adolescence.

The burden of memories will vanish along with the attic. I feel relieved, free, svelte, excited, rested. Why should I be reminded of the past everywhere I look in that low-ceilinged little room?

My books were carried down in crates. Some of them will go with me out of the country, and the rest will await me in my grandmother's celler. The shelves are now bare. My attic looks strange, wounded, mutilated. The picture frames have been taken down, the light bulb from the lamp removed. Papers from drawers, accumulated and written over ten years, the Diaries from lycée, notebooks filled with stories and thoughts, have been crammed into a trunk. I have set aside a few envelopes, and a few papers.

In the evening, Radu came and grew sad as I rummaged through drawers and stacked books in the trunk. He was sad as he remembered how he met me in gymnasium school, how we became friends, the nights of adolescence, the timid reading of our very first writings, and the gatherings of friends, Marcu and Petre in Paris. A friend in Geneva, the other in Turin. Others scattered throughout the city, among people strange to us. He grew sad thinking about Nonora, about Christmas Eve and its joys, about carolling, about Bibi, about Viorica.

'Radu, you are such a child. Only the walls are going to be demolished.'

I leafed through a stack of papers, so that he wouldn't see my eyes. His tears were more powerful than my grimly determined will. I was in a hurry. I had to wake up at dawn.

Radu cried, smoking. Light congealed among the empty bookshelves, above the bed now without an icon.

I sighed only once; when I found a box full of forgotten mementos. I smiled as I read the words on the envelope of a greeting card; *What are you thinking about? About he who must die.* I smiled as I opened an envelope dated April, in which was some cigarette ash. In the box I also found my passport for Italy, and between the pages of the passport, in the section headed *Les personnes qui accompagnent le porteur passeport*, there were a silk ribbon and a picture of Nişka with the dedication: *Devinez, devinez toujours.* I put the box in the trunk, next to photographs from childhood, lycée, and University.

'Radu, please try to be here the day the house is demolished.'

He cried, I embraced him. It was past midnight. I felt exhausted and strange.

'Radu, I have to get up at daybreak – time to part ways.'

We kissed each other on the cheeks. I gave him the most beautiful book I could find in my open trunk. He gave me the only things he had on him: a comb and a notebook.

I accompanied him into the courtyard with the buried roses and lilac bushes. It had turned cold, cold. Lamps flickered on street corners.

'Farewell, Radu.'

Now I write this final page. I will take this notebook with me, as I roam.

I am not sad, I do not weep. I merely feel weary, weary of the fight that has gone on for too long and has been too fierce.

*

My train slices through hills and over ploughed fields. I worship the sun that has risen in the frigid sky. Autumn is serene and casts a blue light over the forests.

Upsurges of life engulf me. I want the train to go faster, to roam far and wide, to set me down in unknown stations. I hunger for the foreign city as I would for a succulent fruit. I hunger for the years I will spend in that city as I would for a body. Life calls to me, in all its vastness and diversity, frightening and alluring, with painted lashes. I am intoxicated by the journey. I leave nothing behind me; neither memories, nor tears, nor sadness. Everything is ahead of me, in a foreign city, in the new world that awaits me. All my thoughts and desires are focused on the years ahead of me, on all that I must accomplish, on all that I must learn and endure.

I am not afraid of anything. Life incites me like a perverse spring. I will not allow any of the things promised me to escape me. Every morning, I will be reborn. Every night I will bestow myself.

The sky is now blood red, serene. The sun is setting over a forest and a river. I listen as the train hurtles thirsting for the wind. A ripe field unsettles me. I cannot tear my eyes from the horizon toward which the train untiringly races.

My soul is harsh, vast, serene. I sense the others left behind me, and before me, the glimmers of destiny.

Clinceni, 1928
11–19 February
2-8 March

GAUDEAMUS. WHAT FOR?[8]
AN AFTERWORD

Written in 1928, when the author was twenty-one, *Gaudeamus* continues on from Eliade's first novel, *Diary of the Short-Sighted Adolescent* (1924-5), but is also closely connected to all the texts that Mircea Eliade wrote in the same period. The biographical therefore intersects with the literary, but also with a number of articles written weekly for the press, despite their different rules of composition. His young age notwithstanding, Mircea Eliade wrote feverishly, and probably daily. This is why today we read *Gaudeamus*, an autobiographical novel, not only as a sequel to his first novel, but also in the context of his articles for *Cuvântul* (The Word), the paper at which Eliade was invited to work by his university professor, philosopher Nae Ionescu – presented in the novel as 'the professor of Logic' – and the *Journal* that he was writing at the time, but which has since been lost. Widening the 'autobiographical context', we also find his *Memoirs*,(later published firstly in French), his correspondence, and other novels about his generation: *Return from Paradise* (1934) and *The Hooligans* (1935), which were written with the same obsessive desire to provide a documented portrayal of a generation he saw as unique in Romanian culture.

However, each of these writings have specific histories in their transition from biography to text. *Gaudeamus* frequently quotes from the *Journal*, but since the latter is no longer extant, it is hard to verify the authenticity of the immediate data. The *Memoirs* are based on his recollections, as well as on the *Journal* and his correspondence, yet a number of questions arise: What then is narrated more or less faithfully and what is fiction? What is the relationship between 'document' and personal vision? In other words, what did his various peers really think and what words does the narrator put in their mouths? Is *Gaudeamus* a self-portrait or a historical reconstruction?

---

8   Translation by Alistair Ian Blyth.

THE ORIGINAL GROUP

By the time of *Gaudeamus*, the lycée students of *Diary of the Short-Sighted Adolescent* had scattered; studying different subjects at university and living in different places. The group dynamic in this book therefore becomes more apparent than previously, no longer determined by a shared place, but rather by a shared outlook on Romanian society of the time, despite their viewing it from different positions. In his *Memoirs*, Eliade often names the members of this group, which included Dinu Sighireanu, Haig Acterian, who went on to be a theatre director and essayist, Jean-Victor Vojen, and others. Historically, apart from Eliade, Acterian and Mircea Vulcănescu, an outstanding philosopher and sociologist, few of them went on to have careers as intellectuals. Eliade refers to his best friend at the lycée as Marcu, who was Jewish, and who would soon move to France, to Eliade's deep regret. Marcu was in reality Mircea Mărculescu, but he also reminds us of Ionel Jianu, a Jewish art historian and good friend of Eliade's, who was not to emigrate until 1961; Eliade was later to write a book about Brancusi, the Romanian sculptor who lived in Paris. Other members of Eliade's generation remained less well known, or else they went on to make a name for themselves only later, as was the case with art historian Petru Comarnescu, Emil Cioran, and Eugène Ionesco. All three became leading public figures in the 1930s, when they formed the highly active *Criterion* Group and gave public lectures. The 'Eliade generation' is therefore an objective fact, but also a cultural phenomenon that came into being gradually, thanks to the unifying factor of Mircea Eliade's writings. Thus Eliade was describing a phenomenon that was coming into being, and thereby also provided the impetus for it to come into being.

A NEW GENERATION

Gaudeamus has remained little known, since it was not published as a novel at the time of its composition. However, the articles in *Cuvântul,* two or three every week, provoked numerous responses, both positive and negative. These reactions are detailed in Mircea Handoca's excellent edition of the novel, published by Humanitas in Romania.[9] Here, we are able to read not only the often ironic reactions of certain writers (Camil Petrescu) and journalists from the previous generation, but also Eliade's defence, rooted in a breadth of reading and thinking truly astonishing for a man of just twenty-one. We discover his unusual capacity to absorb and organise cultural information – although stormy at the time, politics is completely absent from his articles – precisely because Eliade contradicted prevailing public attitudes.

In 1918, all the provinces with a majority Romanian population, but which had for centuries been part of various empires – namely Transylvania, the Banat and Bukowina, formely part of the Austro-Hungarian Empire, and Bessarabia, formerly part of the Tsarist Empire – joined the 'lesser Romania' created by the Union of the Principalities of Wallachia and Moldova in 1859, in order to form Greater Romania. In the early 1920s, there was a legitimate and understandable climate of public joy in Greater Romania, which was apparent above all in the press and public political discourse, but also in various areas of the cultural discourse. The same can be said today, in the centenary year of the Great Union, although in some places the cultural discourse is reserved, while the political discourse focuses on the deficiencies of public life and, in particular, those of the political parties in power. Just as a hundred years ago, there is alarm at certain problematic social situations as well as joy at the strengthening of the Romanian State. Then as now, public achievement was criticised for its large costs, while pride in the former was overshadowed by indignation at the latter. However, while the relationship between these two attitudes was typical of the previous generation; Eliade's generation, on

9   Mircea Eliade, *Romanul adolescentului miop. Gaudeamus,* ed. Mircea Handoca, Editura Humanitas, Bucharest, 2008.

the other hand, wished to move forward, completely leaving behind any eventual reconciliation of the two. Ten years after the event, in talking about his own generation, Eliade does not lend it primary importance for establishing the general order of public discussions. For the previous generation, as well as in the official history of Romania, the Great Union was the beginning of a new road. Contrariwise, for the younger generation of 1918, both the costs of the Great War and the benefits of the Great Union that came thereafter were a closed subject, history, the past. For them, the new was only what came *after* the Great Union, which is to say, the fact that Romania had at last been recognised as part of Europe. The past was not forgotten, but blended into the background: in 1918, just as in 2018, in a free and united Europe, a new arena for new confrontations took shape: what was decisive was not the 'right' that had been won through historical suffering, but the assertion of a new cultural creativity.

Many years later, in his *Memoirs*, Eliade calmly but firmly reconstructed the post-war conviction he shared with his generation:

'The myth of infinite progress, belief in the decisive rôle of science and industry, the primacy of the rational had all been shattered on the front line … The crisis that gripped the Western world proved to me that the ideology of the war generation was no longer valid. We, the "younger generation", had to find our own meanings. But unlike our predecessors, who had been born to and lived with the ideal of national reunification, we had no readymade ideal to hand. We were free, available for "experiences" of every kind.'[10]

The searches for meaning that took place in the period described in *Gaudeamus* were experienced as dramatic and open-ended, whereas their result, described in the *Memoirs*, is viewed a posteriori, having been crystallised. They coincide conceptually, but are at odds from the viewpoint of emotional experience. Hence too, the differences in how they are reproduced textually. What we now see is precisely the way in which hazy emotion translates into concept and programme, and vice versa; the way in which Eliade employed appropriate textual structures, for example 'inventories' of 'objective' characters to serve as credible spokesmen for

---

10   *Memorii*, pp. 136-7.

various differing attitudes. In *Gaudeamus*, he moves from concepts to characters, he stages discussions as conflicts between different characters, as a 'theatre of ideas', but employing real people, his friends of the time, who half stand-out from the background, who are half-imaginary, half-real, and therefore attached to an original reality known only to him, but not to the reader. We therefore find a sort of bas-relief, like in famous sculptures the Elgin Marbles, a bas-relief which the writer partially detaches from the background in *Gaudeamus*, but which in the *Memoirs* he reintegrates into the background, revealing its real, known substratum, which as a novelist he had not publicly confessed. Hence too, the interest presented by Chapter Thirty of the novel, in which the characters judge the author. The author declares that he has kept their real names in the novel as a means of control, to prevent his imagination from adding anything. A number of characters rebel against this; Dinu accepts 'such transparent names' but notes that the author 'has picked the features of our souls that pleased him. Thus, he has neither created us nor faithfully portrayed us. After publication, he will have a whole host of unpleasant problems.' The author replies that on the contrary, every reader who meets them 'has the right to see a different kind of character.' Such an attitude on the part of the author imperils any interpretation of the text as a *roman à clef*. In any event, whereas for Eliade's old friends, the characters were indeed transparent to an extent, for todays' reader the key has long since been lost. The text has shed its initial transparency, it can no longer be read as a book of memories, but rather it becomes an ordinary novel in which only the categories of characters are recognisable, not the people on whom they were based. In a way, the chance publication of the novel after the author's death has made the text intransparent,[11] but it is this seeming lack of information that lends the text density of meaning. In losing its (one hundred per cent) autobiographical quality, the quality

---

11   I employ the term 'intransparent' in the general philosophical sense employed by Joseph Margolis, which he derives from Barthes, Rosalind Krauss and Gadamer, in *Interpretation Radical but not Unruly*, University of California Press, 1995: 'Reality is cognitively instransparent, that is, all discourse about the world is mediated by our conceptual schemes and there is no way to tell whether what we claim about the world directly 'corresponds' with what is there, in the world, independent of the conditions of inquiry' (p. 2); 'texts are in some important regard intrinsically indeterminate but determinable ... by interpretation' (p. 27).

of being a *roman à clef*, *Gaudeamus* gains the far more important quality of being a period novel, the novel of a specific period of time and way of life, and becomes historical in one way, and ahistorical in a second.

INTELLECTUALS AND POLITICIANS

Chapter Fourteen of the novel is titled 'Petre's Enemy'. In it, the reader learns of Petre's desire to 'get ahead', something typical of the time, but also very much of the present: the ambition to become an important person in society as quickly as possible, by means of intrigue and connections, but without possessing exceptional human or professional qualities. Petre himself says, 'I want to get ahead politically; I must operate as a politician, in concealment and cautiously.' The narrator, i.e. Eliade, talks to him in the first person, yet the title of the chapter places Petre's 'enemy' in the foreground, who in this context of the dialogue must also be Eliade. The construction of the dialogue is typical of the rest of the novel, where the star is not the character – the (morally) negative arriviste, comparable to the protagonists of nineteenth-century critical realism, presented by an invisible narrator – but rather he who attacks him, condemns his as mediocre, which is to say, a more than visible narrator, a true *raisonneur* of the novel. Eliade takes on the part of soloist precisely because he delivers his critique of the character of Petre so trenchantly, rather than presenting him to us more subtly, in the manner of the old critical realism. But there is also a surprise here: the criticism of Petre is not that he is an arriviste as such, but that he is a *mediocre* arriviste, a lowly conniver rather than a giant of the stature of Rastignac, the protagonist of a number of Balzac's novels, beginning with *Le père Goriot* (1835, first published in book form in 1842). In *Gaudeamus*, the narrator openly urges Petre: 'You must cultivate your passion, give it a metaphysical meaning … I would have liked you to be Promethean, but you are incapable of being a Rastignac.' (Here we are immediately reminded of Eliade's passion for reading

Balzac, which he confessed in *Diary of the Short-Sighted Adolescent*).

The petty ambition of the ordinary arriviste is something negative; ambition is positive only when elevated to the metaphysical level, which is to say, when it is pursued to the absolute, beyond any immediate advantage, and by means of the grandeur of evil, if not through the good, Eliade suggests. Grandeur resides in the explosive force of behaviour, rather than in its intrinsic morality or social application. As in the romantic period, what matters is personality, passion viewed as a memorable symbolic gesture, rather than social utility. Torn from his immediate context, a character is no longer viewed as *doing* something good or bad, but as *symbolising* something good or bad publicly. This move away from descriptive realism toward a symbolic, somehow ahistorical viewpoint is striking in the thought of the young Eliade. It is precisely here that I see the rupture he wishes to bring about in the younger generation's mode of action. As he himself explained in 1927 – and even more so in 1928, in various essays contemporaneous with *Gaudeamus* – his generation thought *differently* from the previous generation, whence the impassioned investment of thought in questions which, using a present-day term, we might call *post-political*, if we take into account that the political, particularly in the nationalist sense, such as in the writings of the great historian Nicolae Iorga, was precisely the way of perceiving the world to be found before the Great War and the Great Union. 'Our generation, those who went through the war at the end of childhood'[12] (1928, p. 271) is how Eliade situates the group historically, probably meaning that the generation in question lived through the disaster of war, but did not share in the euphoria of its outcome for Romania. Such a definition differentiates Eliade's generation from that of historian Nicolae Iorga (born in 1872), or novelist Liviu Rebreanu (born in 1885), or even the slightly earlier generation of novelist Camil Petrescu (born in 1894): the first was obviously nationalistic in his numerous books and public actions, while the other two were authors of dramatic but balanced novels

---

12 Mircea Eliade, *Virilitate și asceză, Scrieri din tinerețe* (Manliness and Ascesis), 1928, ed. Mircea Handoca, Humanitas Publishing House, Bucharest, 2008, p.271. Further references to this work are indicated by the year 1928 and the page number.

about the war and its aftermath. A distance of one or two decades makes Eliade view his own generation as a *victim* of the squalors of war, but without the compensation of the ideology it gave rise to, namely the joy of national achievements. The war is over, Eliade seems to say, what now? For Eliade, the question did not demand the political and national answers accepted by the others and, precisely by this refusal, lent outline to a new generation, for which the meaning of the present had to be different. Eliade's new generation therefore brought with it a new, strictly cultural paradigm, not adjoined to but against the political paradigm of the preceding generations:

'Was the war a crisis? It is pointless for us to dwell on it. The existence of our nation hung in the balance ... [But] could the meaning of the previous generation remain our meaning? What did they want? Some wanted national unification, others the cultural progress of the people, others still a national rather than a political literature, a rich wife and a few handsome children. We can no longer want the same thing. Purely spiritual values, which find in ethnic potential only a vehicle, are the only values that rule us' (1928, p. 175).

But he also asks: 'What is a generation? It is a plurality of personalities' (1928, p. 174). And he gives the final caveat: 'The meaning given to the world is the bridge uniting me and the world. But meaning signifies *valorisation*. I do not know what the world is, or if I do, I am not interested in what it is. I am interested only in the world that prevents me from committing suicide ... [i.e.] the philosophy of meaning ... the spiritual creation of the world' (1928, p. 214).

A NEW CULTURAL PARADIGM

I have given the foregoing quotations in order to highlight the break in the cultural paradigm that occurred in Romania in the 1920s between the old and the new generation. Completely de-politicised, the new generation turned away from its own traditions and toward Europe, but here too there were specific choices sooner linked to philosophy, religion and individual salvation than social politics or public actions. Also interesting is the fact that Eliade admits he speaks on behalf of a group, although he seemingly does so on behalf of the entire generation, while knowing that that generation was not homogenous. To speak on its behalf was sooner an appeal to share in one's own particular choice than a statement of its homogeneity, as proven by the case of Petre. Nor is it very clear what the term 'spirituality' means. Obviously, it is opposed to the material and, given it is an individual experience, the interests of the group. And further? In 1928, Eliade quotes and comments on countless European and Asian philosophical texts, literary texts (Papini, Gide, Gentile, Kierkegaard, Menendez y Pelayo), and religious and magical texts. He does not put forward any of them as an example or personal choice. He talks about Orthodoxy as the religion of the Romanian majority, but without granting it any priority and without declaring himself as an Orthodox Christian believer. Announcing his essay 'Apologia for Manliness', due to appear in *Gândirea* (Thought) magazine, Eliade argues, 'Our generation – or the elite of our generation – cannot live and create without a spiritual sense of man and existence' (1928, p. 162). This meaning had thitherto been borrowed from the dogmas of the West, but the latest generation was the only one to have created major figures in this spiritual sense, thanks to Orthodoxy: 'And I believe that the majority of those from the latest generation will decide upon Orthodoxy' (1928, p. 163). But it is significant that Eliade claims only that he *believes* this, rather than that he himself shares in the same religious faith. He was to maintain this attitude throughout his life, at least in the writings that have been preserved and published up to now. Even the great Professor of the History of Religion in Chicago was always to remain a theorist of other people's faiths. We also note that even humanity is no longer experienced in the traditional Romanian way[13]: 'Our *humanity* is an *agony*' and therefore differs from the humanity about which Iorga and Sadoveanu wrote such unforgettable works (1928, p. 128).

Many details of the novel beg further discussion; one important episode being the students' repudiation of the anti-Semite Malec (Chapter Three) which is accompanied by a strange conversation that the narrator has with three other young people: Marcu, his close Jewish friend from the previous novel, a communist, an anti-Semitic student; and the latter's Jewish girlfriend who claims to be neither a nationalist nor an internationalist. The narrator refuses to get involved in their argument and merely evinces his deep sadness that Marcu is going abroad and that he may never see him again (Chapter Twelve). Attacked by the anti-Semite for his lack of courage, he replies: 'I have more courage than you might suspect … My duty is to balance and illumine my awareness.' Marcu is amused, for they are not fools, they merely love one another.

I think this reaction is worth analysis. The narrator is in fact shocked at the way the anti-Semite talks, as much as everybody else in his group, but he does not want to express it as such and tries simultaneously to save face. This attitude was once analysed by Barthes in a lecture given at the Collège de France, in which he made explicit the virtue of 'the Neuter', an attitude which politely refuses to support either side in a disagreement and thus avoids peremptory attitudes that can lead only to ideological and even physical aggression.[14] In so doing, he also shifts the object of discussion from the lower, political to the higher, intellectual level, as he always endeavours to do in the novel.

---

13 The Romanian word *omenie* is very difficult to translate. It means kindheartedness, tolerance , gentleness etc. and in traditional Romanian culture, which would certainly include Iorga and Sadoveanu, it sounds like a typical quality of Romanians. Eliade does not disagree with them, but sees 'his generation' (also) feels it in a different way. I think the English word 'humanity' might cover all these nuances (S:A).

14 Roland Barthes: *Le Neutre*, cours au Collège de France, 1977-1978, Paris, Seuil, 2002, p.87, 116 etc. This attitude sums up what he had earlier praised in *L'obvie et l'obtus*, Seuil, 1982, namely *l'obtus*, as meaning not unwillingness to understand something but rather rejection of any extreme attitude pro or contra a (political, military, philosophical) position in order to look for safer nuances.

HOW DOES THE AUTHOR FIGURE HIS CHARACTERS?

How might we explain more exactly the manner in which the young Mircea Eliade writes in relation to the reality from which he sets out? Recent discussions, particularly in French, but also in Romanian,[15] on the concept of the *figure* seem to me pertinent here. They commence from philologist Erich Auerbach's concept of figure as opposed to allegory. In his study *Figura*, which dates from 1938 but gained international currency after publication of an English translation in 1984, he distinguishes between allegory, as a representation of virtues or institutions, and figure, as a concrete, datable event, but which also prefigures a subsequent event (from the viewpoint of the writer, who comes after both events as such). A typical case is the Beatrice of the *Vita Nuova* and *Divine Comedy*, who was the historically real Beatrice Fortinari of thirteenth-century Florence, but who also had a spiritual, mystic meaning for Dante. Auerbach argues that Beatrice 'is an incarnation of divine revelation and not a revelation pure and simply.' To generalise, we might say that something concrete is both real in the present and a prefiguration of something in the future, as Auerbach shows.[16]

In the same way, Mircea Eliade's various lycée and university friends are for him as a writer *figures* of more general meanings, which is why he turns them into characters in *Gaudeamus*, just as he had done in *Diary of a Short-Sighted Adolescent*, but without losing sight of their concrete presence. It may also be said that Eliade *trans-figures* such concretely biographical memories of people, scenes, places, and above all the famous attic of his adolescence in the family house on Strada Melodiei, (now called Strada Radu

---

15 'The figure designates reality as grasped by perception; we give appearance a figure in order to recognise and understand it ...[the figure] takes us from the perceived reality to the representation thereof.' Ralph Dekonininck, Agnes Guideroni, 'Thinking through figures: regimes of figurability in the Early Modern Period', in *Usages de la figure, régimes de figuration*, ed. Laura Marin and Anca Diaconu, Editura Universității, Bucharest, 2017, p.20.

16 Erich Auerbach, *Figura*, in *Scenes from the Drama of European Literature*, University of Minnesota Press, Minneapolis, 1984, pp. 74-75.

Christian), in Bucharest. While the same phenomenon probably applies to all of us, and certainly to most writers and artists, what is striking in Eliade is the fact that he *suspends* in this intermediate phase a process which in other writers is strictly personal and does not reveal itself as such in the form of a novel. Eliade arrests movement at this intermediate phase precisely because he himself occurs as one of the characters, as the narrator writing in the first person. The self-declared 'short-sighted adolescent' of the previous novel now takes a step toward the abstract and becomes merely a verbal presence, the speaking 'I' of the text. In other words, he moves farther toward textual autonomy than in the previous novel, but without inventing characters and situations that are completely new, and non-biographical. The trans-figuration of events and characters remains partial compared with the great objective novels, for example those of Balzac, which Eliade admired so greatly throughout his life. Eliade continues to talk about himself, but at the same time claims to provide an X-ray of the new generation. I think that here, in this procedure of figuration, resides the complete image of the 'new generation': on the one hand, it is historically real, demographic, as it were, and on the other, it is Eliade's own creation. The book remains largely his own 'invention', in the press and literary world in general (whence the question that an older writer, E. Bucuţa, asks Eliade, as recounted in his *Memoirs* (p. 138): 'how is your generation doing, Mr Eliade?'). If we accept this principle of figuration in the sense of a dual truth – concrete presence and symbolic value – we will be able to explain not only the relationship between his life and work, but also the relationship between a number of novels, from the earlier *Diary of a Short-Sighted Adolescent* to the later *Hooligans* (1935). Thus the novel is a *figural narrativisation* of a number of the author's own experiences, including the erotic. Chapter Eight, 'The Way Back from the Monastery', tells of the walk back to Bucharest from a monastery near the city in the company of Nişka, with whom he then falls in love. This narrative level will continue for the rest of the novel, and is complicated by his strong sexual attraction to Nonora, another girl from the original group of students.

It is curious that during the long nocturnal walk, which is neither romantic nor erotic, Eliade, as first-person narrator/character, talks to the young woman Nişka, among other things, about the books he is reading. One of these books is Jack London's novel *Martin Eden*, which he discusses in the same terms as he had used in an article for *Universul literar* (The Literary World) on 17 April 1927 (1927, pp. 145-9). Here we find an amusing intersection of discourses as a new form of figuration; now within a discourse in which a speaker addresses a listener actually present, but also, in accordance with the model of an entirely different discourse, addresses her in the way a writer does a faceless reading public: the first figuration follows the model of the second one. *Abstract intellectual discourses take thus precedence*: Eliade sees himself as Martin Eden who through the intensity of his intellectual pursuits wishes to win over a budding young woman such as Nişka, trying to do so in the same way as Martin Eden does when making impression on Ruth Morse in the afore-mentioned novel. To put it more broadly, the *concrete* behaviour of the young Eliade often seems to be a calque of intellectual models from various books he has read, although he himself regards it as being motivated by the inner structure of his generation, a structure which, precisely for this reason, he wishes to make public as a new mode of behaviour for the younger generation. Eliade himself was afraid of being compared to Papini – an objective similarity, so he believed – but a comparison of his first novels with Papini's autobiographical *Un uomo finite* (1912) sooner points to the differences between them. Papini's violent language, his grandiloquence, his individualism[17] are not to be found in Eliade, who is sooner interested in the construction of new ethical attitudes, in truth, in collective activity.

---

17 Giovani Papini, *Un om sfârşit*, trans. Ştefan Augustin Doinaş, Polirom, Jassy, 2011, p. 192. Despite a certain shared spiritual quest, against bourgeois philistinism, which Papini expressed in sometimes anti-Catholic, sometimes pro-Catholic terms, Eliade remained far from Orthodox Christianity and did not move toward a negation of European values – quite the contrary. Eliade was also far from other attitudes expressed by Papini, such as, 'I do not look for a man, I do not look for Man, I want myself, only myself' (p. 192), 'woman appeared to me neither as a Beatrice … nor as a Circe' (p. 115), and so on

LOVE OR MISOGYNY?

It may be surprising for modern readers to be confronted to what might be called Eliade's misogyny. From what we know, Eliade's misogyny was also shared by the young Cioran, and the Eros seldom occurs in the writings of their group as a whole. Granted, to resist 'temptation' in order to preserve one's energy for intellectual purposes is something that sounds strange today, but I think it should be read as a fear of self-dispersal rather than a rejection of woman. In his conversations with others, Eliade declares: 'you can only genuinely know that thing whose possession you renounce' (*Gaudeamus*, Chapter Seventeen), ultimately employing this statement in order to know Nişka better by renouncing her. It is true that erotic relationships are viewed by most men as possession of a woman, not only as partnership, but Eliade's statement ultimately signifies a refusal to play this game and the wish to set her free. But then again, his strange magnanimity toward Nişka runs parallel to a violent Eros in his relationship with Nonora. In other words, we find here a theme that was to accompany Eliade as narrator and/or main character in all his subsequent novels, as well as in his *Memoirs*, where the real names of the female characters are given. The symbolic binary of Eros and affect seems to have pursued the author of the novel for a long time, in the life of the writer as much as in that of the narrator. It is therefore important to ponder the question whether the effort to break with one of the two, more exactly with Nişka in *Gaudeamus*, is not merely a fear of sexual obsession, which is already explosive in the case of Nonora. Is then the obstinate misogyny merely a mask, or do we find here too a figure, that of the fear of sex, precisely in an author who did not flinch to describe violent erotic scenes in other novels, just as in this one? 'Vanquished temptations do not vanish, but grow', the narrator confesses to Nişka in the same chapter.

TRAGIC ANTICIPATION

The solitude of the novel's ending is dramatic: it is not by chance, I think, that the separation from Nişka is accompanied by a vision of the demolition of the house of the author's birth, of the 'world of the attic', in other words, the world in which he lived up until his departure for India. 'I am leaving, and my attic will fall into ruin. On the site of the old house, a new house, tall and grey, will be built. When I return, I will no longer recognise my street, my childhood, my adolescence.' In the novel, these sentences are dated February-March 1928, just after the separation from Nişka. It might be said that this passage forms the logical conclusion to a novel whose preceding pages have been taken up with the exchange of letters between Nişka and the narrator. But they also sound very strange if we look at the text from the autobiographical viewpoint with which Eliade provides us. How could he know that the house would be demolished and that a tall, grey block of flats would be built on the site, which is really that what happened, but only after Eliade's departure to India? Once again, we must ask: How much is fiction and how much is autobiography in the novel? Interestingly enough, Eliade returns to this point in his *Memoirs*, written much later, and recognises the fact that, moved by his striving for a permanent break with his past in order to withstand the present – meaning, probably, his departure to India – he 'anticipated' this demolition, which, as a matter of fact, occurred only in 1935.[18] No other explanation is added, not even to account for the amazing detail that 'a tall, grey block of flats would be built on the site'!

The *Diary of the Short-Sighted Adolescent* staged the *imaginaire of characters* who were often ironized for their attitudes, rather ridiculous, but understandable given their age. Here, in *Gaudeamus*, what appears is the *reality of the author*, which is intended to be something else entirely, namely the portrait of a real generation, albeit a portrait constructed by the author. Both novels overlay the imaginary on

---

18 Memorii, p.145-146.

the real, but the two never coincide. What the characters in the first novel figured, with each proceeding from his or her own obsessions, in order to conceal them, the narrator now figures, in order to release himself from them and make them figure a generational portrait posited as historically real.

Gaudeamus, the song we unthinkingly sing at various celebrations, without being aware of the tragic meaning of its words, is given as the title to the novel, but without any commentary on Mircea Eliade's part. The vigorous first part of the book perhaps includes a *Vivant professors*, although not a *Vivat Academia*, and perhaps also the summons of *Gaudeamus igitur, Juvenes dum sumus* (Let us therefore rejoice, While we are young), but the sadness of the last part appears only in the quasi-visionary final passage. *Venit mors velociter, Death comes quickly*, seems, in the immediate context, to be the death of the first flush of youth on parting with the beloved. The final evocation of the death of youth abruptly widens the vision from a few individuals to a whole world. In fact, the world he constructed during the whole of his youth in Romania ended with his departure to India. And here, I think, is where *Gaudeamus* becomes a tragedy.

Vita nostra brevis est,	Our life is brief,
Brevi finietur;	It will shortly end;
Venit mors velociter,	Death comes quickly,
Rapit nos atrociter;	Cruelly snatches us;
Nemini parcetur.	No-one is spared.

Sorin Alexandrescu, Bucharest, March 2018.

Sorin Alexandrescu teaches cultural and visual studies at the University of Bucharest after having taught semiotics and Romanian at the University of Amsterdam. In the eighties he publicly protested the regime of Ceaușescu in Romania. He is a Romanian born Dutch citizen living in Romania. He has published many books and essays on modern literature (Faulkner, Mircea Eliade), semiotics (Greimas), narratology, history (the Romanian paradox), philosophy (Richard Rorty), as well as political comments and essays on modernity, painting, photography, and art theory in Romanian, French, English, and Dutch. He is currently running the Center of Excellence in Image Studies at the University of Bucharest.

Lightning Source UK Ltd.
Milton Keynes UK
UKHW02f2033170418
321217UK00005B/153/P

9 781908 236340